JACK OF ALL TRADES

BY

JOSEPH WHITE

ACKNOWLEDGEMENTS

Writing this book has been a 6-year battle between unearned confidence and crushing, all-consuming self-doubt. Without the support and encouragement of everyone around me, there's little chance the confidence would have won out.

Thank you to all of my friends and family, who didn't dismiss this idea as quickly as they probably should have. Specifically, thank you to: my wife, for helping me find the time to do the work; Matt, my first editor; Dad, my last editor; Cammy, for helping me find ways to keep creating; Krista, Gorman, Kathryn, and others, for reading; and Jeff, my chief editor, who spent countless hours helping shape this story, and to whom I will always be in debt.

I have spent a fifth of my life writing this novel I needed to write. I couldn't have done it without all of you.

Thank you.

For anyone like me

Chapter 1

When I was young, I used to love sitting in the surf. My family would spend summer vacations in Cape Cod and while others built sandcastles and perfected their tans, I spent the hours lying in the water, giving myself to the ocean's power. In and out it would toss me, lifting my body onto its shoulders with each cresting wave, carrying me to the brink of a cliff in its rush toward the beach, and throwing me over as it broke, letting me spin weightlessly in freefall before grabbing hold and pulling me back out to sea as it marshaled its resources for another assault on the shoreline. I was just another piece of artillery in an endless attack – the same as the rocks and pebbles that surrounded me, or the very water set in motion by whatever powers control such things. I was powerless against life's greater forces, and more than ready to let them wash over me.

And about two years ago, not much had changed. I was 27 then, but there still wasn't much rooting me to the ground. I was still just floating by while unseen forces pushed me in one direction, changed their minds, and threw me into another. The only difference was that at 27, it terrified me. Because at 27, there was something wrong.

You're not supposed to be adrift near 30. You shouldn't be letting anything wash over you. You should be grabbing the bull by the horns or making life your bitch, or whichever cliché you'd prefer. You should have a career and a salary, maybe even a house and wedding plans. I didn't have any of that, and I didn't really feel anywhere close to it. And I didn't have a clue what to do about it.

I'd been lucky enough to grow up with all the benefits of an upper middle-class life, but I hadn't done anything with them. Instead, I looked at the options I was being handed on a silver platter, and instead of picking something to eat, I complained about my choices – before scolding myself for daring to complain about anything.

The night this began, all of this was racing through my mind at dangerous, breakneck speed, when my concentration was broken by a sexy, well-practiced voice.

"You want a lap dance, baby?" The line was delivered somewhere just above my head, but I was having trouble locating the source, seeing no further than the exposed breasts dangling inches from my face. Apparently, deep in depression and self-loathing, I hadn't even noticed Candy, or Raven, or whatever her name was, stride over to me in her absurdly high stiletto heels – though you'll forgive me if my focus wasn't on the shoes.

"Uhh, no thanks, I'm good." I stammered, standing up slowly, taking precaution so as to not make contact. "That guy over there might be interested, though," I said, handing her a few crumpled-up dollar bills and pointing only to a section of the room that wasn't the one I was in.

"Suit yourself," she playfully responded, and bounced away, everything that should jiggle doing so perfectly, and everything that shouldn't remaining firm and motionless.

I've never been comfortable with strippers. Movements like theirs shouldn't be shared with a dozen other guys. It doesn't matter how low you turn the lights, I know what each posture adjustment is trying to hide. Still, as I watched Krystal – that was her name, Krystal – strut her way across the room, I couldn't help but find myself feeling a little envious of her. As I saw it, for whatever you wanted to say

5

about her, somewhere along the way, she'd thrown herself into this. She'd invested money into those heels, and into the body glitter, and into the lotion that left a cloud of lilac in her wake. She'd built a name for herself as must-hire bachelor party entertainment. She had roots. And in that sense, she had more than I did. And it was because of that sad realization, and not that I'd been staring at her for too long, that I looked away to scan the room.

The hotel suite we'd rented for the occasion was more expensive than any of us could really afford, but for a New York City bachelor party, we decided to go big. It was decorated almost entirely in white, with modern-looking couches and chairs forming a ring around what must have been a 60-inch flat screen TV. Hallways and doors led deeper into the suite's other rooms, but the main attraction was an expansive wall of windows, providing the should-be posh occupants a direct view at the Chrysler and Empire State buildings.

Obscuring the view that night was Krystal and the gaggle of frat boys she'd made her way toward. None of us wanted them there, but the groom's fiancée insisted he get to know her sorority sisters' boyfriends. I didn't know many of their names, and, to be honest, I wasn't all that interested in learning. What little experience I had with them told me as much. They drink; they brawl; they date rape – I assume. The strippers were their idea. So was the cocaine they weren't hiding nearly as well as they thought they were.

The rest of the crowd read like a study in varying shades of discomfort. Mike, for example, the only already-married man among us, was standing alone in a corner, using his wedding ringed hand to beat out the rhythm of the blaring techno music, as though the gold band created some kind of force field the dancers were powerless against. Brady, the bachelor, was accepting every dance thrown his way, but doing so with a white-knuckled grip on the arms of his chair,

6

leaning so far back that he threatened to topple over a few times, and finally did when Candy – or was it Sugar? – tried to flip herself up onto his shoulders. The two tumbled backward spectacularly, Candy – definitely Candy – thrown a few feet over the top of the chair, Brady landing hard on his back and rolling once or twice, coming to rest on top of the stunned, g-stringed professional.

The frat guys howled with laughter while the rest of us – including our high school friends Noah and Will, who'd been using strength in numbers to ward off any scantily clad advance – rushed to Brady's aide, pulling him up to his feet and handing out the requisite apology and tip.

"You alright?'" one of us asked.

"I don't like to be touched," Brady sighed, trying to pull his disheveled self back in order.

"A trait that usually pairs well with strippers," another quipped.

"Well, *they* wanted them," Brady explained, nodding toward the others, who'd collected near the windows. "They didn't think I could have a bachelor party without them."

"And how's that working out now?" Will asked.

"...I don't like to be touched," Brady repeated sternly, continuing with the joke but clearly at his end.

"Then let's leave," I interjected, having seen and heard enough. "You're not having a good time, Mike looks terrified, none of us do coke. Let's leave them with the strippers and do something else."

"Like what?"

"I don't know. *Anything*? It's New York, I'm sure we can find something." And with no more convincing, there was silent consensus, a testimony to how uncomfortable we'd been.

"But how do we tell them?" Will asked, pointing toward the jocks, who had welcomed both dancers into their midst.

"Hey!" I shouted, picking up a full beer can and tossing it toward them. Eyes fixed on the ladies, they barely even flinched when it landed a few feet to their left and rolled past them. "I think we're good; let's get out of here." And we all made for the door.

Chapter 2

"You really think you could make it a month?" Mike asked once we'd hit the street and started making our way south, headed nowhere in particular. It was a warm late August night and the city was alive. Brady wasn't getting married for months, but we thought a summer night in the city would be fun. It was approaching midnight, but the streets were crowded and the bars and restaurants were overflowing onto the sidewalks.

"At least," I said. The conversation was a leftover from one we'd started hours earlier, during a game of what we call "Questions." We'd started playing it in high school, desperate for something to do in my parents' screen house or around the backyard fire pit. Essentially, it was a conversation starter. Someone threw out a random question, someone answered, and, if necessary, defended that answer. We played for hours back then – the questions devolving more and more into the ridiculous as the night dragged on. That night's query came from Brady, who wondered how long we thought we could evade police capture with a two-hour head start.

"You're full of shit, you know that, Connor?" laughed the ever-gruff Will, who we should have considered an authority on the subject – at least more of one than the rest of us. After joining the Army ROTC in college, Will took a civilian job at the Pentagon and began serving his time in the reserve. Or so we thought. We still don't really know much about what Will does. He isn't allowed to tell us and we aren't really allowed to ask, though the latter doesn't stop us from doing so, and his refusal to tell us because of the former just drives our imaginations into hyper drive. "There's no way you'd last more than a day," he finished.

"You keep saying that, but I don't see how it's true," I fought back, the warm breeze blowing back my hair. "Two-hour head start? That's an eon. Change my clothes, clear my bank account, buy one of those untraceable, pre-paid phones and head toward NYC – probably in one of your cars."

"One of our cars? Don't you think the police would figure that out pretty quickly?" Brady asked as we came upon and, without speaking, passed over a collection of bars – each complete with a group of smokers talking, shouting, and shoving outside their doors.

"You're missing the point," I said. "I'm not trying to make it cross-country in *that* car. It's not about *that* car. It's about getting south. I've got two hours before they *start* looking. By the time those two hours go by and they figure out what car they're looking for, I'll be in the city. Look around, guys," I said, swinging my arms wildly. "It's 11:30 at night and the place is buzzing. You don't think I can blend in?" I asked as we continued our walk. It was Broadway we were on, then, surrounded by thousands of swanky partygoers calling it an early night ahead of their Sunday morning brunches.

"A slice costs $3.14. I guarantee it." Noah interjected, pointing toward a bakery called Slice of Pi. He does that. It's the way he's built. Noah is effortlessly brilliant, and his mind works differently than everyone else you know. He bounces from thought to thought, moving on from whatever you're talking about to whatever pops into his head, then returning back to you later if his mind calms enough to let him. He's shorter than the rest of us and thinly built, and sometimes, he blends in and you can almost forget that he's there – until he interrupts your fugitive conversation with something about pie. If you don't know him, he seems flighty, but in reality, he's just a genius. A real genius, not just a collector of useless information like the rest of us. He'd sailed through high school and Princeton undergrad high on whatever recreational drug eased the noise most. He'd given those up, though, when he started med school in D.C. – unwilling to hold another man's life in his hand with a dispensary's worth of weed coursing through him. "And where are we going?"

"Ask Connor," Brady responded. "This is his safe house, after all. I'm sure he knows all the nooks and crannies."

"You guys suck," I countered, turning right to follow the cheers of a large crowd. Ahead, we saw a group of thirty or so gathered outside a vertical sign that read 'The Bridge Troll'.

"Dunk him! Dunk him!" the crowd chanted before erupting into raucous applause a moment later.

"*That* is where we are going, Noah," I said.

"The Bridge Troll? You know it?"

"Sure don't," I responded. "But it seems like a fun place to hide out."

Chapter 3

The Bridge Troll was a large, wide space, with a trio of open garage doors at its front to allow the breeze in and the crowd out. It had a stone bar on either side of the room and dozens of wooden tables crammed in throughout the rest of the open floor plan. Round, single-tiered steel chandeliers hung from the ceiling, giving the room a medieval feel – like something you'd expect to see in a Camelot movie.

Stepping through one of the garage doors we all fell in behind Will, who used his wide, barrel chest to push through the crowd and pull us toward the bar's center, as a loud chorus of boos erupted from the back.

"Way to go, asshole!" someone yelled.

"I got a napkin if you need to dry off!" taunted another as we finally spotted the focus of their jeers. A thin, red-haired man was stomping toward us from the back of the bar, fully clothed but dripping wet, as if he'd just fallen into a pool.

"Fuck this place!" he grumbled, grabbing his jacket off the table next to us and storming off without stopping for his friends, who waited until he'd gotten a few steps away before bursting into laughter and collecting their effects, following him out the door. Greedily, we dove into their seats, grateful to have lucked into an easy table on a crowded Saturday night.

"Oh, I get it. That's hilarious," Noah laughed as we were just sitting down.

"What? What do you get?" I asked.

"The Bridge Troll," he chuckled, pointing. And then we all got it. Fenced off against the back wall was a half circle-shaped pool, with a five-foot-high stone bridge arching across it and connecting small pathways around the water on the room's sides. And just as we all finished putting the pieces together, a booming voice erupted across the loudspeakers.

"Who will be next to challenge the bridge troll?" it asked. "The fire-haired man did not fare so well; his flames were extinguished. Perhaps you can do better. The rules remain the same. Answer the troll's three questions correctly? Win two thousand dollars. Miss one? Swim." And it manically laughed itself off the mic.

But before its echo had even stopped ringing, someone seated up near the makeshift pool stumbled to his feet and slurred something about a challenge. The bar erupted into applause as he grabbed hold of the railing and used it for support – shuffling along the water's perimeter and to the base of the of the bridge. Bending over, he used his hands to help scale the incline to where it leveled off at the top. He was a short, stocky kid with a backward hat and the look of someone drinking for the first time. As he finally balanced himself atop the bridge, the laughing returned and an inflatable troll slowly rose directly across from him. Three spotlights clicked on as the rest of the lights in the bar dimmed. The first on the kid – with his dumb, goofy smile broken by the tongue that was hanging out of his mouth – the second on the troll, and the third on a stone box on the bridge's far side.

"Who dares try to cross?!" the troll's voice roared.

"Uh, Timmy," the kid chuckled, and the laugh returned, this time with the audience chiming in, none of us impressed with a grown man going by "Timmy."

"Where are you from…Timmy?"

"Boston," he responded, arms raised in triumph, prompting a round of angry boos from the New York crowd.

"Well...*Timmy*...I trust you know the rules. You want to pass? You want the cash in that box? You must first answer me these questions three. Question the first, what is the chemical abbreviation for potassium?"

A murmur spread through the bar as we all quietly answered the question, but as our eyes turned to Timmy, we saw only a blank stare on his face, and as the seconds clicked by with no answer, the truth became clear.

"He's got nothing!" someone screamed.

"Timmy! We hardly knew you!" shouted someone else behind us as the rest of the bar added their own mocks and boos.

Panic spread slowly across Timmy's face as he stepped up to the mic that hung from the ceiling, his eyes frantically searching the bar for an answer. When nothing came, he leaned forward and said quietly, "um, P-T?"

Throwing my head back, I nearly missed the floor swing out from underneath him, but I looked back up just in time, and heard the mocking cheers double as I watched his body hit the water with a dramatic splash.

"Timmy, Timmy, Timmy. Poor, silly Timmy," the troll laughed again. "May the next challenger be more worthy!" he cried before signing off.

We stood for a second, watching the others at Timmy's table engulf him in a barrage of slaps and shoves as he returned to his seat, shaking back and forth like a dog before slumping back into his seat and attending to the fresh beer his friends had bought him for his efforts.

"Well, as New York City theme bars go," Will said as we all collapsed back into our own seats, "this one works."

"It's definitely better than that carnie-games place we went to for your 21ˢᵗ," a quieter-than-normal Mike responded. "Though maybe that has more to do with your performance at the air rifle range," he finished, referring to the ROTC man's failure to hit any of the five targets, and the $100 bet we'd lost to a group of guys we'd met earlier in the night.

"I can't believe they let you kill people with that kind of marksmanship," Brady said in his trademark deadpan.

"For the last time, that wasn't my fault. I shoot actual rifles. Not those airsoft junks," Will defended, ignoring Brady's implication.

"So, the actual rifles are the ones you use to kill world leaders. How's that going, by the way?" I asked, essentially asking him how work is.

"I'm going to say it one more time," Will fought back. "I don't kill people," he concluded sternly, and a touch too loudly as a mix of alarm and confusion spread across the surrounding tables. "My normal, desk job is good. The red tape's been a pain in the ass lately, but they're asking me to do more, which is good."

"So that *next* coup d'état will be yours, then, right?" Brady chirped.

"I hate all of you," Will sighed, dropping his head in exasperation and joining in on the laughter the rest of us were already enjoying.

And so the night went on. Five old friends finally around the same table again, remembering what it was like when they saw each other every day rather than every few months. We joked and laughed for hours. We talked about fiancées and girlfriends and wives and jobs and hobbies and more. Round after round with the world outside our small table nothing but a dull buzzing beneath the roar of our new stories told and old stories re-told.

Brady used to call us 'jacks of all trades and masters of none', because we could talk all night about everything and nothing at the same time, bouncing from one thing to the next with ease. That night was proof enough. Noah told us about his ongoing neurology rotation – how he'd watched his professor drill through a woman's skull earlier that week, and how he'd been asked to assist on the same procedure on Monday. And somehow that reminded us of the chemistry teacher we shared in high school, and the mad-scientist vibe he gave off. That, of course, reminded us of Shelly Linderman, who sat in the front row of that class smelling of sweet pea and wearing outrageously short skirts.

Those skirts reminded Mike, a high school music teacher, of a weird new fashion trend his students had started, which led him to tell us about the new rock choir he wanted to start in the fall. That reminded Brady, a designer at a digital media company, of the new music site he'd been asked to design, which led the group to turn my way and ask a question I hadn't thought about since before Krystal put her breasts in my face and broke my anxious concentration: "how's things?"

A loaded question.

"Things are great!" I wanted to exclaim. Because they were. Truthfully, in the grand scheme of things, they were. I had a job writing columns for our hometown's biggest newspaper, I had a girlfriend who loved me, and I had a great group of friends willing to bail on perfectly constructed strippers for a dark ages theme bar. I had it made, and only an asshole wouldn't admit that – wouldn't stand up on the table and shout it out for the entire room.

But I'm an asshole. Because I never got my brain to stop there. Instead, I thought about everything else. I thought about the differences between my girlfriend and me, and about how those columns I'd written weren't published under my name. With newspapers struggling to survive, the *Albany Tribune*'s once-thriving opinion section wasn't ginning up the same community involvement, and they hired me to help. I supplied the community involvement. I was writing the columns, but under names like Pablo Garcia or Ken in Colonie. But I wasn't about to say all that. I didn't want to. Not on that night. Not on Brady's weekend.

"It's good," I said. I knew they didn't believe me, but I also knew what would happen next. Will would colorfully tell me I was lying, Mike would comment on how great it was that my words were getting published, Brady would say something sarcastic, and then Noah would jump in with something wildly off topic, maybe about the asbestos in the walls, and we would all forget what we were talking about.

So, before that could all get under way, I watched the still-quiet Mike shift nervously in his seat and threw him under the bus.

"Anyone have any idea what's going on with flop sweat over here?" I asked, pointing his direction. We all looked at Mike and he straightened up nervously in his seat, self-consciously wiping is brow.

"Well," he started with a deep, heavy sigh. "I've been looking for the right moment to tell you all this." He paused and took a long drink of his beer before placing it back on the table and bowing his head. He sat there like that for a second while the rest of us exchanged sideways glances. Finally, he looked up, made eye contact with each of us, and exhaled. "Sarah's pregnant," he smiled.

"Holy shit!" we all exclaimed at once, erupting into celebration, stumbling over each other to embrace him. We asked all the questions you're supposed to, and found out that Sarah was in perfect health, that she was due in December, that they didn't know the sex, and that they'd likely conceived on their kitchen counter – all the things guys would ask about. And when those questions were all answered, before we'd returned to our seats, buzzing with excitement as we were, I yelled out toward a passing waitress.

"Garcon! Tonight is a night of celebration, we require your largest, finest bottle of champagne!"

"That's $1,000," she replied snidely.

"Well then, I guess we will also require some cash," I squawked confidently and began climbing up onto my chair. Standing high, then, looking over the assembled crowd, and with my friends looking up confused, I turned toward the back of the bar and, like Babe Ruth calling his shot, pointed toward the stone bridge. "I CHALLENGE THE BRIDGE TROLL!" I screamed in as deep a baritone as I could manage, just before the lights dimmed and that laugh cracked the microphone.

Chapter 4

The spotlights were brighter than I anticipated. I had to shield my eyes from their sting as I assumed my position atop the trap door that had betrayed Timmy only a few hours before. Soon, though, they adjusted, and I was able to the see whole bar, jammed wall-to-wall with what must have been two hundred people – all of whom were turned in my direction, eyes fixed, waiting to erupt when I plunged.

"Who dares challenge the bridge troll?" the voice bellowed again as a microphone descended from the ceiling to hang in front of me.

"It is I, Connor Hall!" I exclaimed into the mic dangling in front of me, hamming up my confidence for the crowd who laughed their appreciation.

"Where are you from, Connor?"

"I have come to your land from the north," I said with a coy smile, "but I will soon be taking up residence on the other side of this bridge. Do your worst, troll!" I finished with a bit of flare, the audience throwing up a few whoops of approval.

"A cocky competitor, I see," the disembodied voice replied. "I should warn you, we don't take too kindly to hubris. And as they say, pride cometh before the fall..."

"What fall?" I said, hopping up and down a few times on the platform. "It seems pretty sturdy to me." The maniacal laugh of the troll returned at that line, nearly drowning out the supportive ones from the crowd assembled before me.

"We shall see," it said. "An arrogant fellow like you knows the rules, I'm sure. You want to cross this bridge and claim the cash? You must first answer me these questions three. Question the first, who is the Greek God of agriculture?"

"You tricky son of a bitch," I laughed. "Demeter is the God-ESS of agriculture," I said, not trying to contain the smile spreading across my face, the bar's patrons not trying to contain their pleasant surprise.

"Well, well, well," the voice answered. "You may well be worthy. Question the second, The Beatles had how many number one hits in the United States?" The troll had barely finished the question when my smile went from sly, to full. I took a long, expansive inhale and confidently began:

"*I Want to Hold Your Hand; She Loves You; Can't Buy Me Love; Love Me Do; A Hard Day's Night; I Feel Fine; Eight Days a Week; Ticket to Ride; Help!; Yesterday; We Can Work It Out; Paperback Writer; Penny Lane; All You Need Is Love; Hello, Goodbye; Hey Jude; Come Together; Let It Be; The Long and Winding Road; Get Back;*" I paused and inhaled again, just so I could so firmly exclaim what came next. "Twenty." And I added in a smug sniff and shrug for good measure.

A choir of "Oh's" shot up from the impressed crowd, who applauded the rain-man act as I turned to face the inflatable troll to my left, arms out, with as much cockiness as I could muster.

"You pompous bastard." The voice boomed, feigning anger. "Question the third, for the money. Let's see how you fare with this one: who was the United Nations' first Secretary General?" Silence spread across the crowd, anxiously awaiting my answer. I reveled in that silence a minute. Drew it out and drank it in, already knowing what no one else did.

"The original Secretary General of the United Nations," I started calmly, "was the United Kingdom's Gladwyn Jebb. Later Knighted, so known to you now as *Sir* Gladywn Jebb," I continued, ramping up the excitement, grabbing the microphone. "Now let me pass and claim the prize that is rightfully mine!" I finished, yelling into the mic before detaching it from its cord and dropping it onto the bridge from my extended, shoulder-level hand.

"Are you not entertained?!" I yelled, turning back to the crowd with my hands high above my head before striding over to the slowly deflating troll and standing chest-to-chest with it, arms still out as it withered. When it finally had, I stepped over it and toward the small chest waiting at the bridge's end, while the crowd roared in applause. Opening it, I found a small wad of cash, $2,000 in hundred dollar bills, and holding it in a fist raised in triumph, I headed back up through the bar, through a swarm of back-pats and high-fives.

When I got back to the table, my friends were still sitting, looking like they'd barely moved. As I held up the money, they looked up at me shaking their heads with smug, knowing smiles. I shrugged and retook my seat just as the waitress arrived with our bottle of champagne. Licking my fingers, I made a large show of counting out the ten bills and handed them to her, accepting the bottle and popping its cork with great ceremony. We each took a glass and filled them to their tops.

Raising mine in the air, I looked at both Brady and Mike and paused,
suddenly overcome by nostalgia. Growing up, Brady, Mike and I had always been together – joking and laughing through stupid fights and late-night philosophy sessions. Later on, we brought in Noah, Will, and our other friend Z, but from grade school to middle school and high school to college, there was always Brady, Mike, and me. We

were three suburban kids growing up together, until one night we went to a bar in Manhattan and discovered that only two of them actually had.

"To new lives," I said finally with a sincere smile, overcome by how happy I was for them both. "To Brady and Mike, and to the best for you both." We drank down our glasses with greed and drank down the bottle soon after. We chased away the champagne with other, harder liquor, and soon enough the night spun away from us. We slowly stumbled our way home, stopping at every bar and pub along the way, spending the rest of my winnings. We pressured some local college's a cappella group into doing a set in one bar, and threw darts with a Central Park softball team at a second. We joined a house band on stage to cover James Brown in a third, and helped direct traffic outside a fourth.

At least that's what I think happened. The only thing I remember with certainty is the laughter, the laughter that can only be shared by old friends. The laughter that reminded us all what it was like to be young, and spend similar nights in the screen house talking about the meaning of life and Shelly Linderman's short skirts. The laughter that was about nothing at all, but somehow meant the world.

It's the laughter I remember, because the laughter is what I've always remembered. And because in the waning hours of that alcohol-fueled night, I felt again like the breezy, cocksure kid I once was, at the dawn of his days with his whole life in front of him. And as we stumbled up 7th avenue and turned east, we were greeted by the pink and purple streaks of the rising sun, painting the sky with the hope and promise of a new day. We walked toward that new beginning and I found myself thinking about our own – about Mike's and Brady's, and about where mine was waiting for me on the horizon.

Chapter 5

Brady was my first friend. I wasn't his, he's always had his then-fiancée, but I've known him almost as long as she has. We both have older siblings and our parents were in the PTA together. They used to get together to work on fundraisers when we were still in diapers, and quickly enough, playmates turned to friends and friends turned more into twins than anything else – Brady and I growing into one another like two trees twisting their branches together as they reached for the sun.

Just before we started first grade, the Andersons, Mike included, moved to town, and though he was quiet, we liked him instantly, and his branches found their way into ours. When my mother started an after-school day care in our house, Brady and Mike were two of the kids she watched, and so the three of us spent all day together, and pulled our families along with us.

We used to have big family barbeques in our backyard, and more than once, we all went on vacation together. We were close back then, and grew closer still after Mike's dad died during our last year of grade school. He was in a car accident on his way to lunch one day.

I can still remember it like I'm there now. A phone call my mom took to the other room after the first few words; the redness in Mrs. Anderson's eyes when she finally came to pick Mike up; the brilliant, mocking sunshine a few days later at the funeral, and all the confusion that came with it.

Mike had panic attacks for weeks after, always getting worse at night. We all tried to help as best we could, but what can you really do but be there and hope you're making a difference, even if it's unseen?

Brady and I started sleeping over a lot after that, and I even spent a few weeks at their house, living with them, sleeping next to Mike's bed so someone was there when he woke up screaming. Things got better after a while, but he's never quite been the same. Every now and then, he still calls me late at night after waking himself up – it's why I always sleep with my phone on and the ringtone at full blast – and every year, on the anniversary of his dad's death, we take the day off and go to the cemetery.

When we went to middle school, our trio expanded with Noah, Will, and Z – who couldn't make it to the bachelor party because of work – and there was always the six of us after that, growing up together.

When you grow up in the suburbs, you grow up bored. You shouldn't, but you do, and every second of your day is spent trying to fill the void you're certain you feel, and you'll use any means necessary: movies, music, video games, girls, the Internet, politics – even if you have no clue what you were talking about. For us, it was all of the above. We listened to and played as much music as we could. We saw every movie we could spend our parents' money on. We obsessed over TV. We watched sports, we played video games. We even watched and read the news. And it shaped each of us in our own way.

Mike's love of music was born back in those days when he discovered a Velvet Underground album in an old record store. He spent the next few weeks learning how to play its songs and lecturing us on its historical importance.

Z became engrossed in movies, infatuated by the visual poetry a director could make with a camera and a bit of lighting. The rest of us would go to the mall to see some raunchy comedy and emerge reciting a few jokes and commenting on the size of the leading lady's chest. Not Z. Asking for his input on whether they were C's or D's would always return something about fill lights and rack focus – not the type of rack we'd asked about. It was no surprise to anyone when he left for film school.

When Brady started sketching his favorite cartoon characters, the art world opened up to him. As Noah asked questions he didn't have answers to, medicine became the way he could get them, and as we let Will pull us more and more into long debates on the week's news stories, he fell for politics. While I fell for it all.

We spent plenty of nights at Brady's house watching movies in his parents' home theater, and plenty others playing music at Mike's – every word to every song and every scene in every movie memorized and parsed for meaning – but most times, our nights were spent playing Questions in my parents' screen house. Those were my favorite, when we'd stay up long past midnight jabbering on about whatever came to mind. All of or none of the above. It didn't matter. All we needed was a topic and an opinion. And regardless of either, I was in. I was always ready – even on the morning after the bachelor party as Brady and Mike staggered through the parking garage toward my father's Cadillac, which fared better on long trips than my old Jeep.

"I hate everything," Brady said, pushing the passenger seat back to fit his tall, lanky body, and adjusting the sunglasses he wore despite the dark conditions of the garage.

"Little hung-over, there, Brady?" I asked from behind the wheel, with a bit of manufactured sprite to twist the knife.

"You're not?"

"I was about six cups of coffee ago."

"Your talking bothers me."

"Good." I said. "Now get in the car."

"You're gonna drive slow, right?" Mike asked in a low, haggard bass as he hurled his then-heavy frame into the Cadillac. "No sudden movements? I've thrown up four times."

"Well, now you know what morning sickness is like. You're welcome," I joked as I put the car in gear and gingerly stepped on the gas.

It was almost six when we finally made it back to our empty hotel room. The strippers and the frat guys had both left, and we dove into whatever bed we could. Sleep came as quickly as you'd expect, but didn't stay long for me – it hadn't for a while. I woke up after only a few hours, finished off the continental breakfast's final pot of coffee, and cleaned up the remnants of the party – the beer cans and the glitter and the vomit.

When the others woke up, we had brunch delivered to the room and they nursed their hangovers while we talked through the night. Quickly, though, Noah and Will's train came calling, and we said our goodbyes, unsure when we'd all be back together again.

The ride home was quiet for a while, the alcohol's lingering effect still having its way with Brady and Mike as we traveled north. Eventually, though, after an hour spent with faces pressed against the cold glass of the car's passenger windows, they began to stir.

"I'm never drinking again," Mike finally said from the back seat.

"Ditto," Brady agreed, the color returning to their faces.

"No, I mean it," Mike said sternly. "When this baby comes, that's it. No more booze." It sounded like he wanted to say something else, but he didn't, and he didn't need to. We knew what was running through his head as he looked out the window, eyes fixed on the rapidly passing foliage along I-87, a heavy weight settling on the car.

When Mike got married, our lives changed, but not in any significant way. He wasn't around as much, he and Sarah merged their bank accounts, and they each picked up an extra piece of jewelry. That was about it. But this was different. This wasn't that. This was the *real* plunge.

Mike was about to take on a responsibility none of us could imagine, and was about to destroy any misguided notion that we were still more like teenagers than adults.

"I know I said it last night, at least I think I did," I joked, "but I just want to say how happy I am for you both. And Mike, I'd be scared, too. But you'll be fine. I know it," I finished, my own gaze never moving from the road in front of me.

The car was quiet for another few minutes after that, the three of us pondering the life about to come until Brady broke the silence.

"A little Questions for the rest of the ride?" he asked, Mike and I agreeing immediately. "What is the worst state in the union?" he posed, clearly a question he'd prepared before the weekend.

"New Hampshire," I said immediately, prompting an eruption of incredulity from my passengers.

"New Hampshire?!" Brady said shocked. "What?!"

"Defend that." Mike demanded.

"'Live Free or Die' is a ridiculous motto." I responded. "There's about a million shades of gray completely ignored by the entire state. You can't trust people like that," I finished, as laughter broke out from both Brady and Mike. After, Brady stumped for Florida while Mike made his case for Texas. And then I asked which wild animal you'd least like to fight, prompting a long debate over sharks and hippos – which ended with no agreement, but more questions and more answers as the miles clicked away, and as thoughts of the coming future gave way to one more happy moment in the ever-dying present.

Chapter 6

Deep in a picturesque corner of a picturesque town's most picturesque neighborhood, sits my parents' picturesque house. At the end of a cul-de-sac in the prestigious Meadowbrook Estates, it's a large, brick colonial adrift in an expansive sea of dark green – with a plush lawn around it and thick ivy crawling up its face. Tall, strong maple trees pepper the property, while perfectly tapered pines line its borders – shielding it from much of the normal suburban bustle. It's a monument to old money, one of 400 in the development my father helped build.

He was 22 then, married and expecting his first child, and desperate for a way to survive in this world. He'd put himself through school and took the first job offered to him when he graduated. It was an entry-level gig with a residential construction firm, and he spent the first two years erecting one of the biggest neighborhoods in Saratoga Springs.

I imagine my father back then, leaving his wife and son in their small, cramped apartment to walk to the construction site and spend his hours building the gaudy visions of pampered, entitled jerks – or so the other guys on the job would grouse. I doubt my father was ever so bitter; it's not in his nature. Still, a few years later, I'm sure he sported a wry grin when he took the money he'd made starting his own construction firm and bought the biggest house he'd helped build.

My parents raised four kids in that house. I'm the third of those four. Growing up, it was perfect. There was grass to run on, leaves to jump in, and a pool to swim in. Behind our house, there was a quarter mile of thick woods to explore, with trees to climb, streams to dam, and, eventually, a lake to boat on. It was an adolescent paradise, and it's filled with rich, thick memories that all come flowing back when I drive through the maze of trees that lead to 28 Cobbler's Court – like the night Brady and I spent three joints exploring the woods and rearranging the Jansen's' Christmas decorations.

Or the one my sister Maggie was reciting when I parked the Cadillac among the other cars gathered for Sunday dinner, and walked through the front door.

"So, we came hobbling out of the woods and up to the backdoor," she said. "Ed's bleeding from the leg, I've got a black eye, and Connor's spitting blood. And we get up to the door and Dad's just standing there. And he looks at us and just sighs and says— "

"I'm raising idiots!" I jumped in, quoting my father while stepping out of the large foyer and into the kitchen, where my family stood nibbling on snacks around the island. My mother was at one end arranging the steaks they'd just grilled, while my sister stood opposite her, beside her husband. They're doctors, the two of them. Pediatricians at a private practice who'd met while Maggie was in med school. Next to them was our older brother, Ed, whose own wife was wrestling with Maggie's two kids in the living room.

"God, he was so confused," Maggie said as some of the laughing died down. The story is one of our old favorites. Deep in the woods behind our house, there's a narrow, winding dear path down the hill that leads to the lake. On snowy days, we'd hike back to that hill and sled for hours. On this particular day, Ed, Maggie, and I left our younger brother and headed out. After a few hours, we started looking for new ways to conquer the hill and decided, like the idiots our father said we were, to form a chain and slide down together – with the youngest in front. The run went horribly array when we hit the jump we'd built at the bottom. The chain broke apart in midair and we landed in a tangled heap of bent and bruised limbs. In the flailing chaos, I punched my sister in the face, leaving her with the black eye, and she landed on top of me, driving my face into the dirt and shattering the retainer in my mouth. Ed bounced a few times and landed in a bush, slicing his leg on its thorns. We staggered back to the house after that, leaving a trail of blood behind us and meeting our confused father at the back door – who took us into the bathroom and tenderly cleaned our wounds after letting us know what he thought of our grand idea.

"So, we couldn't figure one out earlier," Ed said after I'd told everyone about the bachelor party. "Spencer Tracy." He was asking me to connect the actor to Kevin Bacon in less than six steps – it's a game we like to play together, testing our movie knowledge for hours on end around our dinner table.

"Amateurs," I smiled. "Spencer Tracy was in *Judgement at Nuremberg* with Max Schell, who was in *Telling Lies in America* with Kevin Bacon."

"I told you he'd get it," my mother gloated as the others sighed as if the answer had been on the tip of their tongue the whole time.

"Hey, where's Aaron?" I asked, just realizing that our little brother wasn't in the room.

"He's out in the garage fiddling with the battery," Maggie answered before stepping into the living room to ask her 4-year-old to stop hitting his younger sister with a plastic hammer.

"Go check on him, will you?" my mother asked. "I get worried about him out there."

I turned and headed out through the door off the kitchen. Aaron was sitting in the back of the garage at the workbench my father had built him when he was 12. Even then, he loved tinkering, and I think my dad built him that station to keep him from doing it in the house. When he was six, he borrowed one of our father's screwdrivers and took apart the VCR. Our parents came home from a banquet and found him sitting on the living room floor amidst its thousands of pieces. Ed was never allowed to babysit again.

For his birthday a few months later, they bought him a K'Nex set and he never looked back. From then on, he was building anything he could imagine. At 10, he rebuilt the lawnmower's busted engine, and at 11, he gave my father a homemade, electric tie rack. A few months later, he built a food processor to help our mother chop vegetables before parties. She still uses it today. At 12, just before the workbench was built, he tried to reinvent the T-shirt cannon. Unfortunately, the project was shut down after he shot Maggie's favorite dress through the kitchen. Not the window, the wall.

With a truckload of science fair awards to his name, he cruised into the mechanical engineering college in town, and was entering his senior year its star student – designing and trying to build the world's first self-sustaining battery, though I'm sure he'd like me to point out that I'm simplifying that.

"Hey there, baby bro," I said.

"How was the bachelor party?" he asked without turning from his work.

"It was good," I said. "The parts of it I remember, anyway. How's the battery?"

"I'm close," he answered, still not breaking away from the soldering he was doing on the bench. "I had to break everything down and rebuild it, but I've strengthened all the connections and rerouted a few things and I'm this close," he finished, not even bothering to throw up a hand and show me how close together his fingers were.

"How's he doing out here," our father asked as he stepped out through the kitchen door and into the garage, crossing to the fridge to grab a beer.

"He may be on the verge of a revolution," I said with a smile as he popped the top of his long neck with the opener he keeps on his smaller work bench and looked at Aaron with a proud smile.

"No felonies this weekend, I trust?" he asked, turning back to me.

"Just a few misdemeanors," I said.

"Done." Aaron said suddenly, with much less gusto than you'd expect from a guy about to solve the world's energy crisis. "Time to test it," he said, standing up and grabbing a flashlight he'd retrofitted to accept the new battery. My father stuck his head inside the door and bellowed for the rest of the family to come out and witness the reveal. As the crowd gathered, Aaron took the battery – a long, thin cylinder of silver metal – and carefully inserted it into the flashlight. He took a deep breath and paused in nervous anticipation. Then, with an exhale, he flipped the switch and a brilliant bit of light burst forth, illuminating the back half of the garage and prompting the celebratory release of a family's worth of held breaths.

"That's incredible," Ed laughed, as our father embraced Aaron in a congratulatory hug and my mother ran inside to grab her camera. "So, what happens next?" he asked after the rest of us had added in our accolades.

"Well," Aaron started as our mother bursted back into the garage and began choreographing the pictures that would soon be framed on our wall. "The idea is that the battery will keep recharging

33

itself. So, I'll leave it on the work bench with a camera on it and let it go for a while, and see how long it lasts," he said while our mother demanded that Ed, Maggie, and I pose next to him, then handed me the camera so she and our father could step in.

When our mother had gotten all the pictures she'd wanted, Aaron handed me the flashlight and crossed back to his seat to call his girlfriend – another engineer at his school. I looked down at it in my hand, marveling at what my younger brother had built from scratch. He'd built a battery. Built. With his bare hands. Hands not so dissimilar to my own, which, I realized after a second, were starting to burn.

"Aaron," I said, shifting the flashlight from hand to hand to keep one from getting too hot. "Is it supposed to be getting this warm?"

"It shouldn't be getting warm at all," he answered, stepping back toward me and taking it from my hand. "Crap," he muttered after a long pause, unscrewing the cap and removing the now smoking battery. "Everyone stay in the garage," he said, calmer than I would have expected, but with a definite sense of urgency. He ran out into the driveway, threw the battery into the yard and dove behind his silver Toyota.

Nothing happened for a second. Aaron just sat behind the car with his hands over his head, while the rest of us exchanged confused glances. But just as I started to step toward him, a flash of green and orange light shot across the driveway, followed by a thumping boom you almost felt more than you heard, sending the lot of us diving to the ground with shrieks and yells. We stayed there for a second, waiting to make sure the coast was clear before slowly standing up and pulling ourselves back in order, as bits of plastic and metal rained down over the front lawn. Aaron was standing too, looking out toward where his battery had just exploded.

"Well. I think that's dinner," our father announced, leading the family back inside – but not before nudging me toward my dumbfounded brother. I stepped up and stood next to him for a second, neither one of us looking at each other, just staring straight ahead in silence.

"Can I help you pick anything up?" I asked finally.

"Not sure there is anything to pick up," he responded without taking his gaze off the black patch of grass where he'd tossed his invention. "I don't…I don't understand."

"You'll figure it out," I said, patting his back. "Come on. Let's eat." Slowly and reluctantly, he followed me back inside and into the dining room, where our family had just finished up collecting small pieces of battery that had made it through the open windows. We settled into our normal, familiar seats and our normal, familiar routine, telling and re-telling stories – tame and inappropriate, alike – until, sometime later, as Ed finished a story about the time we saw under our dad's robe, my phone buzzed.

'Hi,' was it all it read, which is what Mack sends when she's annoyed – though she'd hate that I just called her Mack. McKenzie Winter is her full name, the girlfriend I mentioned earlier. She's also Brady's fiancée's best friend, and while we were having his bachelor party, she was at the bachelorette. We'd agreed no cell phones over the weekend, but I was supposed to have let her know when I was back in town.

"McKenzie?" Maggie asked as I muttered under my breath.

"Yeah. I was supposed to text her three hours ago."

"Tell her she's welcome here," my mother called from the kitchen – she'd gotten up to serve the pie she'd made earlier that day.

"Nah, I better get home," I said. "I think she came straight back to my apartment; I should go see her." I stood up to collect my things and kiss my niece and nephew before heading for the door.

"Fine," mom said. "But you're taking some pie home with you."

Chapter 7

McKenzie and I started dating toward the end of college – but most people we know were surprised it took so long. We've known each other since we were little, and she was in most of my classrooms between then and our college graduation. We were a lot alike growing up: smart, opinionated, and political – more so than most our age. In school, we were each other's favorite sparring partners. We took over entire classes debating the topic of the day, driving our teachers nuts. Our friends thought it was some weird flirtation – and maybe it was – but we never got together like they expected. At least not for a while.

It's hard to find the right words to accurately describe Mack. She grew up the daughter of a wealthy law firm owner and has the finely-honed sense of sophistication that comes with it. She's the type of woman who wears pearls at a barbeque – who cares about making sure her sweatpants match. She is, in a word, uptight. But she's also smart and driven, and gorgeous enough to keep you from caring – with jet-black hair and sharp, angular features to match her personality.

Her car was waiting for me when I pulled my beat-up Jeep into the parking lot of my apartment complex. It's a dozen or so brick buildings a few towns south of my parents' house, set off away from the rush of suburbia in a thicket of dense woods. I loved my apartment. It was a small, two-bedroom place, but as scenic as anything you'll find in the area. It sat on a small pond, and during the day there was sun and trees and water and birds, and at night, you could trace the moon's arc across the sky as it shined bright on the water's surface. Sometimes, I'd sit out on my deck and watch its reflection dance across the water, the way I do at my family's place out on The Cape.

Mack and I didn't live there together, but she spent enough nights that she had a key, so I knew she was already inside as I Doug and I parked our cars at the same time. That's not his actual name; it was just the one I gave him over time. We'd never spoken, but we saw each other coming and going around the complex. He was an older, heavyset man who walked with scrunched shoulders and a slight lean forward – like it was always raining and he was trying to keep the droplets from getting inside his coat. I couldn't help but feel a harsh hit of sadness when I saw him, thinking about the lonely life of a mid-50's man in a suburban apartment complex teeming with 20-somethings and a few "just-marrieds." I always wondered about his story – who he really was and how he got there – but I never had the courage to ask.

We exchanged our customary nods as I headed up the stairs and to my third-floor apartment, where Mack was sitting on the couch.

"Hey," she said, standing up and walking over to greet me at the door. "Nice to hear from you."

"Yeah," I answered, dropping my suitcase and giving her quick hug. "Sorry about that. Lost track of everything at my parents' place."

"How was New York?"

"It was good. Fun." I said, expanding from there but being careful to leave out any mention of the money we won and blew – she wouldn't overlook or excuse our irresponsibility, and, quite frankly, I didn't want to have the conversation. "How was the bachelorette party?"

She let out a dissatisfied groan as she dropped back down into the couch. "It was a nightmare," she said, and I readied myself for a story. Kaitlyn, Brady's fiancée, chose a group of vineyards for a weekend of upscale wine tastings, and Mack had been responsible for the planning. "I booked two adjoining rooms at the bed and breakfast," she went on, "but when we got there, they had screwed up and the rooms were down the hall from each other."

"Well, that sucks," I said.

"Yeah. So, I had to go make a whole stink with the front desk to move the people who had been given our room, and—"

"Wait," I interrupted, against better judgment. "You guys made people switch rooms?" I asked. Surprised, but really, not surprised at all.

"Of course," she answered, as if she had no other choice. "We had booked adjoining rooms. We wanted adjoining rooms. We were supposed to be given adjoining rooms."

"Why couldn't you just hang out in one room?" I asked, knowing it was a mistake even as the words were coming out of my mouth. We debated the point for a few minutes before I decided to drop it and move on to other stories from the weekend, like Mike and Sarah's pregnancy, and Aaron's battery explosion.

"I bought those tickets for next month," she said a while later as we got ready for bed – throwing one long leg after the other onto the counter to rub it down with expensive lotion.

It was concert tickets she'd bought, and not for a show I'd enjoy. We were going to see a pop diva I hated, but she was a fan and I was happy to tag along for her – because I loved the way we could go 12 rounds debating the merit of some news story, and I loved those long legs, and the way she always hugged me just before we went to bed, and, maybe most of all, that my bed was always warm when I climbed in.

Chapter 8

I've mentioned it already, but at the *Albany Tribune*, I was not Connor Hall. Instead, I was John Doe or Pablo Garcia or, my personal favorite, Esther Weeblehowzer, an elderly widow struggling with what's become of what was a nice, quiet neighborhood when she and her husband moved in during the 60's.

The *Tribune's* office is an old, boxy brick building – the type they built before they cared what offices looked like. The walls are all made of cinderblocks and everything was painted a stark, clean white to try and keep you from noticing. The floors were laid out like a maze, so I had to walk through almost every department to make it up to the newsroom – which was buried in the back corner above the printing press and next to the sales office.

The bullpen was as you might expect it to be: an open space crammed with desks assembled in groups of four. There were no dividers in the room, which I used to think was by design – built to allow reporters to yell to each other in moments of breaking news, the way they do in the movies. In reality, though, the paper was probably just too cheap to install them.

The three other desks in my quartet were occupied by a trio of junior editors. Sitting next to me was Rick Gordon, a man who'd never had a disagreeable thought in his life. Rick had worked the local politics beat his first two years out of school before getting bumped up to editor because he was one of the few our boss liked. Across from us sat a lifestyle editor who thinks food is art and an all-business business editor. Neither thought I was as funny as they should have, and neither looked thrilled to see me when I walked in that Monday after the bachelor party.

"Morning everyone," I said. "What have we today?" I often asked that question as I slumped into my tired, worn-out chair – once Navy Blue but more of an earthy brown color by then. The other two hardly ever answered, and didn't that day either. But Rick did, and we quietly talked about our weekends and exchanged a few ideas before I picked up the paper to highlight those familiar articles I could do something with – like the coming school board election or the highway construction or the controversial mall expansion. Some days were easier than others. Some days the governor mentioned gun control and the op-eds wrote themselves. Others, though, the Saratoga Fair's chili cook-off made the front page and I was a painter without paint.

There's very little I remember about those next few weeks, which makes me think the chili cook-off was on the front page a lot, and most of my work hours were spent inventing a persona that cared about things like swing set regulations at a local park. One late September week, though, I do remember. I remember getting a strongly worded email from our assistant editor about a joke I'd snuck into one of my columns, and I remember assuming it was why I'd been summoned to the chief editor's office first thing the next morning.

Harold McArthur was the big boss in every sense of the word. The paper's chief editor, he was the personification of every newspaper cliché you've ever heard – strong and imposing, but weathered, the aggravation of all these young, idealistic kids trying to tell him about news showing on his face. It had become difficult to walk into his office without picturing Lois Lane or Peter Parker slamming their hands on the desk yelling, 'Dammit, Harry! You can't do that!' while the son of a bitch just grinned through his cigar and plucked his suspenders.

I love that man.

"You believe this shit?" he asked as I stepped through his open office door and into the sea of papers that had amassed on every hard surface in the room.

"Well good morning to you," I replied, my eyes doing what they always did in his office, surveying the shrine to journalism's golden age hung on the walls. Before he lost taste for the relentless aggression with which he practiced the profession, old Harold McArthur had been a legendary journalist – the kind who'd move the earth for a story, and could changed its course after he'd gotten it. Framed and hung throughout the room were his two Pulitzer's, a photograph of the Marine unit he was embedded with during the war in Iraq, and the cover story he wrote toppling a corrupt governor – along with an original copy of the famous "Dewey Defeats Truman" *Chicago Tribune* front page. He used it to remind himself of the hard work that helped him never become the "lazy shit responsible for that massive fuck up."

"I sent her to the council meeting for 200 words on whether they voted yes or no. She comes back with 600 on some eminent domain sob story. What the hell am I supposed to do with that?" he asked.

"Public shame her?" I deadpanned, hoping my joke would land. Harry and I had a great relationship, but I was always a little uneasy when I walked into his office. It was Pavlovian, probably. The first time I met Harry, he told me the television blog I'd been writing for the paper's website was 'childish crap'. I don't know how he'd stumbled across it, or what he saw in it given how he talked, but at the end of a lecture on all the ways my writing could improve, he offered me the job he'd just invented – the ghost-columnist job. For the next year, I had weekly meetings with him that were mostly longer lectures on all the ways my writing *hadn't* improved, so even though we'd both grown to like one another, I was always a little gun shy when I stepped through his door.

"Maybe," he said with one, singular laugh. "But I'll probably just not run it," and he tossed the papers on top of his desk, neither of us saying what we both knew: he'd publish every single word of that 'sob story.' His irritation was real, but he loved that she'd found a deeper, more significant story. He'd bite her head off, but he'd proudly run it the next day.

"Look, I don't have a ton of time, so let me cut through the shit," he started, heaving himself forward, his elbows resting on his desk. "Tom quit yesterday," he finished, mentioning one of the paper's columnists.

"Damn," I replied instinctively. "Where's he going?"

"I don't know. He said something about a job in Cleveland? Who cares?" he growled, with all the sentimentality of a shark that just ate its young. "Here's the bottom line, I've got a columnist job to fill, and I'm going to recommend you to fill it."

I rocked back in my seat; my head cocked sideways wondering if I could have heard that correctly. I could feel the painfully quizzical look on my face, but there was little I could do about it. I was quiet for a while, staring at Harry, unsure what to say next.

"Oh, cut the shit," he said finally. "What?"

"Nothing!" I croaked. "I'm just surprised, that's all."

"Well, I like what you're writing is becoming, and more than that, I like that you're always in the trenches of a fight, not the middle ground. That's the way it has to be. Stupidity exists in this world because too many people assume it will just go away if you leave it alone. You can't leave it alone, you've got to snuff it the hell out. That's what we need in a columnist."

"Thank you," I said, unable to muster anything else.

"Don't thank me yet," he responded, leaning closer. "I'd love to give you a shot, and I'll push for it, but I need you to understand how big a long-shot it is."

"I do, and I appreciate you even trying," I said, sitting up and leaning closer as well, a wave of grateful emotion and excitement overtaking me as I considered something I hadn't before.

"The board will want some fancy name with some recognizable title and stature in the community," he said. "And that ain't you. You want it? *Make* 'em say yes. Work like hell, and don't let them say no."

"I will," I said.

"I'll do my best," he said, "but my best isn't quite what it was," and he slumped back into his chair and leaned back, eyes toward the ceiling.

"Thank you, Harry," I said, rising to my feet and making for the door.

"Now go stir the pot," he said without moving.

I turned left out of Harry's office and walked down a dark hallway shared by the paper's highest-ranking editors and columnists. I staggered into the bullpen for the first time that day still in a daze, not certain what had just happened. I bypassed my customary greeting and slid into my chair, as Rick turned to me smiling.

"Today is a good day," he said, handing me a paper he'd already highlighted. He was right. On the front page were two headlines ripe with potential. "City Council to Weigh Casino," said the first. "Local Assemblyman Denies Climate Change," said the other.

"Thank God for today," I laughed, reaching for a pen to begin making my notes. The casino story was easy. The proposed location sat just a block or two from Esther Weeblehowzer's fictional house. None too pleased with this latest corruption of her community, she would certainly write the paper in staunch opposition. The climate change story, though, was a little trickier. So much of me wanted to make a joke out of it and a write a piece listing some other scientific consensuses the politician likely denied – gravity, a round earth, George Clooney disappointing as Batman, stuff like that. But I knew that reaction would come in abundance from the public. So, instead, I chose both. For the former, I wrote as Pablo, who I used when I wanted to write as myself. For the latter, I defended him with Ken from Saratoga – a conservative talk radio fan who thought he was smarter than he was.

And then I turned on my computer and dove in, thinking the whole time about what Harry said.

"Make 'em say yes."

Chapter 9

I hadn't even called her yet, but when I pulled up to my apartment building, Mack was already standing outside, waiting for me to arrive. She was dressed in her tightest black jeans, with a tight black tank top and red stiletto heels. It's not a look you see often, but it's one that always leaves dropped jaws in its wake. She smiled wide as I pulled my Jeep up to the curb, then excitedly jumped inside and embraced me in a long hug and kiss before I pulled away for the concert.

We stopped at a drive-thru for something quick to eat on our way as I rambled on about my meeting with Harry and what it might mean for the future.

"Harry made it pretty clear that the job is a long shot, but he's in my corner, and I think if I write well over the next few weeks, who knows?"

"But he said it was a long shot, yes?" she said eventually, doing far less to hide her skepticism than I did to hide how much it annoyed me.

"Well, yeah," I said after pausing to swallow my irritation.

"Have you ever thought about coming back to law?" she asked quickly, as though the question was cued up for the split-second I answered. There was quiet in the car for a moment – partly to make it clear that I wasn't thrilled with her question, and partly because I wasn't sure how to answer. Of course, I'd thought about it. I had been only a few months away from my pre-law degree when I decided I wanted no part of it.

"I...I don't know," I eventually sighed, quietly.

"Well, you should," Mack countered, springing into a long-winded explanation of something to do with her work – no doubt waiting for me to jump in and begin the discussion in earnest.

My rebuttal never came, though. Instead, I was saved by the teller at the parking garage and a quiet walk to the venue.

We weren't the oldest members of the crowd, but we were close, and we were certainly dressed that way. Even Mack's sexy-casual look, with the $200 heels and expensive jewelry, oozed a blue-blood sophistication that didn't fit the assembled crowd – particularly while complimented by the khakis and button up I'd worn to work that day. Thank God, I'd had the good sense to lose the blazer. Everyone else around us was in their teens, and dressed as though we'd stumbled into an all-night rave. Furry boots and booty shorts weren't uncommon, and neither were spiky pink dye jobs and feather boas. We played a game with the outfits while we waited for the show to begin, trying to pick out the most outrageous one. I settled on a college-age girl in an all-white ensemble of fishnets and a fur cardigan. Mack chose another dressed in black leather pants, red boots, a green tank top, and an orange boa – mostly because she hadn't even bothered to color match.

We laughed and talked for a while in our seats, and just as I thought I'd found a new contender, the house lights dimmed and a minute later, the darkness was filled by an elaborate, strobing light show that danced its way across the crowd. Soon after, the dozen frenetic lights settled on one corner of the arena, where a pop star wearing only a leather leotard sat suspended above the audience. To the roar of the crowd, she flew through the air like a trapeze artist, and landed on stage just as the drumbeat swelled and her latest hit began.

The music wasn't any good. It was a bad mix of pop and techno, the type you'd expect teenage girls to love and Mack to hate. If you knew her, you'd bet money that Mack listened only to Beethoven or Mozart, but she belted out every note to every song that night. It's almost like she knows how much older than her age she acts, and reaches out to cling to whatever bit of youth she can. So, while I did my best to pretend I was at a Grateful Dead or Springsteen concert, Mack danced and screamed like she was in her own pair of booty shorts, showing all of the reckless abandon she rarely ever lets loose.

I loved her like that. I got flashes of it every now and then when she lost track of her guard – when the music was up and the wine was low. It was beautiful. It was spontaneous and passionate. It was life with a brilliant, fun, carefree woman. She danced and sang with everyone around her, never stopping, while I found myself standing still, drinking in Mack's energy and reveling in it, and looking around at the rest of the crowd.

Every few weeks, Harry used to burst into the newsroom with a message. "Everything is a story!" he would say. "Wherever you are, whatever you're doing, you're looking at a story. You just have to know how to write it." Somewhere along the way it must have sunk in, because as the thumping bass pounded in my chest, I began building a story.

I'd be a 50-something dad who took his daughter and her friends to the show and came away appalled at what passes for music now-a-days – an opinion I happened to share. Thinking of the story, I barely heard those final few songs while I composed a draft in my head. It was an energetic, animated article I'd be excited to see printed, and I'd almost finished the entire thing when the show ended and a giddy Mack pulled me from the venue recounting her favorite moments.

She paused only once on the way home, when she pushed me up against the car and kissed me as deeply as she ever had, with the full length of her body pressed firm against mine. She kissed me like that again when we reached my front door, and our passions took hold and carried us toward my bed. After, as we laid there in our tangled sheets, I recapped the night in my head. I thought about Mack dancing and singing with such careless disregard, and I thought about her tongue, and the way it so fully desired mine, and I thought about her energy and excitement, and I thought about my own, about how I couldn't wait for morning, when I could attack that article.

And I thought about how I wanted to always feel like that. And I thought about how soon enough, maybe I could.

Chapter 10

I woke up that next morning exactly how I'd gone to bed – full of life and energy. I raced out the door to grab my edition of the *Tribune*, which every paper employee received three days a week so the company could inflate their circulation. Mack stumbled out of bed and toward the kitchen wearing the same nothing she'd fallen asleep in the night before, and as she made a pot of coffee, I sat down to read through my paper and make the same notes Rick had made for me the day before. There wasn't much that day – just a few follow up articles on the reports I'd already written about and would see published some day that week.

Still, I kept studying the paper through Mack's shower, and as she stepped out of the bathroom, I came across an article that poured gasoline on the fire burning within me. "Eff F Words" was the title, and as I read it, I found myself both enthralled and enraged. In my focus, I guess I'd missed Mack dropping her towel and standing in front of me for a second before strutting down the hall to get dressed.

The column was written by Claire Boudreaux. I'd met her a few times and she was every bit as pretentious as her fake name suggested – though not nearly as pretentious as her article, which called for an immediate ban on all cursing in movies and on television, citing their corruption of our language and our rapidly degrading society.

"Year after year, on screens both big and small, we are forced to see salacious, bawdy bits of what they call film, but what the sophisticated call trash," she wrote. *"Gone are the days of James Stewart and Frank Capra.*

Replaced, they have been, by a crowd of smut peddlers far too eager and willing to wade into an acid-filled cesspool eroding the bedrock of our morality one four letter word at a time." She finished by proclaiming that if you wanted to, you could find her not at a movie theater, but in our city's art museum, where she wouldn't have to worry about such vulgarity.

Mack entered the room just as I finished the final line.

"What's wrong?" she asked. Apparently, I'd started pacing about halfway through.

"I don't even understand," I stammered, shaking the paper in my hands. I'd grown up on movies. We all had. They weren't just escapes, they were vessels for ideas – with each line and each shot carefully constructed so as to best portray an intended meaning. To suggest otherwise was blasphemous.

And Harry knew it.

When he first hired me, we'd spent hours talking about movies and TV, and so for a second, I thought that maybe this was a set up – a gift from the editor in my corner.

"This is garbage," I said to Mack, as a grin broke out across my face. I threw the paper back onto the table and gave her a kiss on the cheek as I ran out of the room and down the hall to start getting ready for work. "And I can't wait to tear into it!" I yelled.

Chapter 11

"Harry's looking for you," Rick said as I charged into and through bullpen.

"Well, I'm looking for him," I replied aggressively, throwing my bag onto my desk.

"Why?"

"He knows," I smiled.

"Hall!" Harry yelled on cue, striding into the newsroom carrying a copy of an editorial I'd written the week before. "What the hell?"

"What's the problem?" I asked.

"'The winds of change are odorous ones,'" he read, quoting a Weeblehowzer column I'd written about a burlesque bar that was hoping to open in her neighborhood. "'As though broken by the backside of someone who'd enjoyed Mexican dining the night before.' Is that a fart joke?"

"Fart joke. Potent metaphor. It's a little bit of both," I said.

"From Weeblewhizzer?"

"Isn't she the 80-year-old widow?" Rick asked.

"That fart joke is a piece of perfectly crafted art," I defended, trying to contain the humor I was starting to find in all this.

"Maybe, but we can't print that. And you know it."

"You're right," I said, disappointed. "But you should know that it comes back later in the piece."

"Where?!" he asked, searching the sections he'd clearly not read yet.

"Graph nine," I said. "'This change will not be silent but deadly, it will be raucous and rumbling.'" I quoted. "'And graph twelve, 'we must keep this sphincter shut, and not let this measure pass.'"

"Oh, for Christ's sake!" Harry roared, trying to contain a smile, I think, while the rest of the bullpen looked on either laughing to themselves or rolling their eyes.

"It became a motif!" I shouted back while Harry blinked an exasperated, wide-eyed blink and turned back toward his office.

"Harry!" I said, stopping him. "We printed this?" I asked, holding up Ms. Boudreaux's column.

"Don't you have other stories to work on?" he asked.

"No. Because you don't just let stupidity exist. You snuff it the hell out," I replied, drawing a small smile across the old man's mouth.

"I look forward to reading what you give me," he said, disappearing down the hallway.

"Fart jokes?" Rick asked as I faced him again.

"They were really, really funny," and we both laughed as I slid into my seat.

On the car ride in, I'd started my reply, "Eff Effing F-Words You Effing Eff" – which would likely be cleaned up. Unwilling to filter my rhetoric through some random character, I chose Pablo Garcia for the column, and on that day, he wrote ferociously and without reservation – furiously pounding on his keyboard, barely stopping to read the notes he'd scribbled hastily across the print copy. It wasn't until an hour and about 1,200 words later that I was stirred from my trance by a haughty voice.

"Do you have a problem with Claire's article, Connor?"

The voice was Andrea Lecure's, the lifestyle editor who sat across from me. No doubt, she had been the one to review and approve the column I was now ripping to shreds. She hadn't been there when Harry and I aired our grievances – she was probably out reviewing a new coffee joint whose organic, imported beans were about to make them *the* spot for the kind of people I hope you hate – but she'd arrived just in time to go twelve rounds with me before I handed in my finished draft.

"Well, Andrea," I started, leaning back in my chair, carefully choosing my words to keep from offending her. "I do. I disagree wholeheartedly with almost every single word written in it," I finished, not quite doing the job I'd hoped I would.

"Why am I not surprised?" she replied snidely. "Of course you're on the side of vulgarity."

"Well, that's not fair," I answered; surprised things had escalated quite this quickly.

"I mean, you did write a column with three fart jokes from an 80-year-old," Rick chimed in happily without looking up.

"Dick!" I laughed, turning to share a smile with my neighbor.

"See?" Andrea interjected. "Vulgarity. The swearing, the nudity, the violence. It's awful, and it's corrosive, and it serves no purpose other than drawing in the simple minded."

"A couple things. First: I'm sorry for calling Rick a 'dick' in your presence. Second: simple minded is harsh. And third: 'serves no purpose?' It serves great purpose!" I exclaimed, rising to my feet. "Yeah, there are a lot of "fucks" in mob movies, but they're not just dropped in. It's character development! They're mobsters; you're not supposed to like them. You're supposed to think they're dirty and lowbrow and reprehensible."

"So, Hollywood should just do whatever it wants for the sake of character development?"

"Yes. Because I don't think you should limit how they make their points. And you know what? Neither do you. At the end of this column, Claire tells us we can find her in a museum," I said, holding up the paper copy. "She doesn't seem to have any problem with the nude scenes Picasso painted. Why are his still-picture nude scenes so much better than the moving ones?"

"That's different, Picasso was an artist," Andrea said sternly, pointing her finger toward my chest.

"So are filmmakers!" I roared back excitedly, enjoying the debate. "You think if Picasso or da Vinci or Monet were alive today they'd be painters? They'd be directors! Modern art isn't just that woman you wrote about last week who set all her belongings on fire. It's film! Film is art – with morals and meanings implied by the creator to be inferred differently by each audience member! And in the same way cubed breasts were a tool Picasso had, curse words are a tool Scorsese has." There was a pause after that line, as we all, I'm sure, thought about cubed breasts.

"Well...I...I have a meeting," Andrea finally huffed, grabbing her things and hustling out of the newsroom as I returned to my seat to add that rant to the end of my article.

"I'd say you won that," Rick said quietly after the dust had settled.

"Yeah? What happened? I blacked out," I laughed.

"I don't think she knew what she was getting into."

"Yeah. I feel bad about that."

"Well, she came at you first." Rick said. "Plus, that article's a load of fucking, fuck-fuck shit," he finished, and we both broke up laughing.

I didn't have much work left to do on my column. I finished it quickly and took some time to cool down before starting in on the one

I'd mostly written the night before. I spent some time helping fact check a business article, and then did some research on an old building a few blocks from the office. Workers had discovered a hidden grotto in its basement, and the history of it was a passion project of Andrea's. She worked on it in her spare time and I felt like extending an olive branch. I used to do that every now and then when I had writer's block or needed a quick break. I'd help out whoever wanted it. It gave me some more experience and helped me feel a little better about dissecting their stories on a regular basis.

After a while that day, I settled back in at my desk to write the music column. I chose a new persona for this one: Jude Lennon – subtle as I am – a 55-year-old musician with a teenage daughter whose taste in music he struggled to understand. "All art forms evolve, certainly," he wrote. "But this latest one, I just cannot accept. What was so wrong with the Beatles?" That last line felt good to write. It was so rife with possibility, so sure to enrage, and so inviting to counter.

The next Monday, I took on the role of Amber, a 22-year-old living in this trendy, up-and-coming neighborhood, and responded to Jude with a defense of new-age music, though plenty of real people had already done the same online. The day after, Jude returned, and so did dozens of angry writers from around the area. Online, the back-and-forth spawned thousands of comments and set new engagement records. It even prompted another columnist to write a lengthy examination in Sunday's lifestyle section, which would have been a career first had Pablo's spirited defense of cinema not done the same.

Leaving the office that Friday, I was exhausted but excited, with a smile on my face that only grew bigger when a slick-haired man in a dark pinstripe suit stopped me. I knew who he was, but I would have bet every dollar I had that he didn't know me. His name was Mr. Carver, a member of the paper's founding family and the chair of its board.

"You're Connor Hall, yes?" he asked. "You're the one writing those editorials. They're terrific. Keep up the good work," he finished – never having waited for my response.

"Thank you very much," I managed while he walked away from me. Awestruck, I turned back around to see Harry standing in his doorway at the end of the hall. He didn't say anything; he just looked at me for a second and smiled ever so slightly before turning into his office.

Chapter 12

Mike never wanted to be a music teacher. He loved writing and playing, and he wanted to build a career writing and playing. In college, he'd started a band called The Lizards and they were good enough that there was talk of going out to L.A. to try and hit it big. But after graduation, with a fiancée, a bunch of student debt, and a mother I don't think he wanted to leave, he decided that using the fallback education degree was the safer option

He took a job at our old school and managed to keep most of the band together. They played gigs on weekends and became one of the area's premier bar and party bands. They built a pretty legitimate following playing a few concerts a month, and we do our best to make as many as we can. That Friday night, just a few weeks after Brady's bachelor party, The Lizards had a show in downtown Saratoga and I was meeting Brady for happy hour at a nearby bar before they took the stage a few hours later.

Still excited about work, I practically jumped into the empty stool next to him and filled him in on what had happened that afternoon with Mr. Carver.

"That's great, man," he said when I had finished. "Columnist Connor Hall. That'd be awesome."

We toasted to that thought before Brady started in with his updates. Kaitlyn was great, the wedding plans were coming together, and work was going well, though he was afraid that was about to change. Brady is a graphic design manager at GNS Media – a publishing company specializing in news and pop culture websites.

They have dozens of sites spread out across anything and everything that's popular. When a new TV show becomes a hit, they go out to find some blogger who'd jumped in early on, sign him to a deal, and build him a bigger, better page. Brady is in charge of each site's look. A team of editors and producers come to him with an idea and he brings it to visual life. He sketches it first, and then paints it, and then, after the advertisers tweak it, he hands it off to the web team to build.

One of GNS' recent projects, a pop culture site he'd designed with a flashy, bold look, wasn't catching on the way they'd hoped. He expected the coming week would be a series of long, tedious meetings breaking down focus group data trying to pinpoint whether it was his look or the writer's words that was the problem.

I sat and listened while he talked at length about the aggravating week to come and about the silver lining that would come after. Either way, whether redesigning this site or building a new one, he'd soon end up with the brush back in his hand. When he'd finished, we spent a few rounds brainstorming. We thought about ways to fix that broken site first, but spent more time talking about new sites we would build if we could, like a debate page we'd talked about when we were young – a website with no boundaries. It wasn't an original idea anymore, but we'd thought about it for years – never figuring out exactly how to do it. We tried hard that day, but hadn't made any real progress when the familiar tap of stiletto heels announced Mack's arrival.

"You're not drunk already, right?" she joked. At least I think she did.

"Not quite," Brady said, stepping up to hug Mack while his fiancée came through the door. The four of us hadn't been together in a while, so after the hugs and kisses were handed out, we stood around catching up, until one of us brought up the bachelor party and Kaitlyn asked a question I was hoping she wouldn't.

"So, I have to know, what does thousand-dollar champagne taste like?" she asked innocently, laughing as she did, oblivious to the fact that she'd just lobbed a live grenade into the middle of my relationship. "I mean, it had to be incredible, yeah?" she continued when she hadn't gotten the result she'd expected.

"From what I remember, it was pretty great," I said calmly, staring directly into Brady's eyes, which disappeared to the floor.

"Thousand-dollar champagne? How did you afford that?" Mack asked pointedly, learning then that I hadn't given her the full story. She looked right at me without breaking her gaze. My hand forced, I did what I hadn't the day I'd come back from the city. I told her about the Bridge Troll and the $2,000 prize and how we blew every cent of it in a matter of hours. "You spent $2,000 on champagne?!" she said when my story had ended.

"Well, a thousand on champagne. I haven't a clue what we spent the other thousand on."

"I can't believe you," she answered after my bit of slick wit had finished landing like a lead balloon. Mack comes from money. Lots of it. But at some point, she developed a rather exact sense of value, and her adherence to it is almost religious. She'll make exceptions for shoes or jewelry or clothing, because of the impact she says they have on the way people see you, but no such liberties could ever be taken on something as trivial as bachelor party champagne. We didn't have to drink the cheap stuff, but a thousand dollars was a waste.

She told us much of this in detail over the next few minutes while Brady mouthed his apologies behind her back and worked hard to contain his laughter. When she'd reached the end of her rant, she let out a sigh and announced that her and Kaitlyn would be going next door to eat because the food at the bar was far too greasy.

"I guess I shouldn't tell her how much the suite cost that night," Brady ribbed when the tap of Mack's two-hundred-dollar heels faded away.

"Yeah, please don't," I laughed before the two of us ordered the greasiest burgers on the menu and went back to trying to perfect that website we never quite figured out.

Chapter 13

In middle school, Mike and I had a band. For a few hours. We covered Simon and Garfunkel tunes with Mike on guitar and me on piano – the only time I put to use the years of lessons my parents bought me. Our only gig was a homecoming dance in seventh grade, and a mix CD replaced us halfway through. We wanted to try again, but before another show was booked, I had already moved on to the next thing.

Still, Mike and I never stopped playing together. In high school, he taught me to play guitar and we started getting high and improvising over our favorite covers, and eventually, we got high and wrote our own stuff, too– and some of it, honestly, wasn't half bad. In fact, if you look closely at the fine print on The Lizards' first two albums, I'm credited as the writer on a few of their tunes.

I'm not anywhere in Mike's league now, but back then, there wasn't much separating us. Looking back, sometimes I wish I'd stuck it out, and every now and then, when he's had too much to drink, Mike will ask me why I didn't. And I'm still trying to give him a straight answer. I loved playing with him, but where Mike had the patience to practice five hours a day, I could never be bothered. There was always some sitcom marathon, or a game of wiffle ball, or some news article pulling me away from the piano, and I was always too quick to let it.

That Friday night, like most nights at a Lizards show, I watched Mike on stage and couldn't help but wonder what it would be like to be up there with him. Brady and I had made it just in time to meet Mack and Kaitlyn and catch up a bit with Sarah before the band took the stage. The large square room was packed full with the familiar fans that tended to turn up at most shows. We looked on from a round table in the back shouting our appreciation and watching our friend as we rarely saw him. Mike has always been the quietest of us – the most reserved of a boisterous group of fools – but on stage, he's something different. He's outgoing. He's a showman. It's hard to watch him and not think about that chubby little kid who lectured us about the Velvet Underground, but on stage, he's a rock star.

When that night's raucous first set ended, Mike practically ran to our table.

"Damn, that was good!" he cried after kissing his wife and rubbing her baby bump. "You guys like it?" We all nodded and cheered, but Mike had already moved on, cutting us off to gesture toward the middle-aged man standing alone at the back corner of the room. Apparently, he was the owner of a local production company Mike had been trying to meet with for months. He told us that most of the other local acts were clients of his and skipped off to go talk with him.

The rest of us sat for a second and exchanged smiles at the sight of his exuberance before I stood up to buy the next round. Two beers, two cosmos, and a water later, I was walking slowly back to the table, doing my best not to spill a drop, when I was body slammed by a sprinting Mike. He'd just left his short talk with the label exec and was running back to kiss Sarah before getting back on stage for the second set. Instead, he sent me flying and we both ended up on our asses with a pile of broken glass between us.

"Oh damn! I'm so sorry, Connor!" Mike said as we pulled each other up. "I didn't even see you. Ben – that's the guy's name," he continued excitedly, "he said they're definitely interested and wants to set up a time to talk in a few weeks!"

"That's great, man!" I replied, ignoring the glass crunching beneath my feet. "He picked a hell of a show to come see."

"I know, right?! We're playing so well." He gave me a gentle shove after that and bounded up toward the stage to begin the second set, and I stood there for a while with a smile. His joy was infectious, and I found myself thinking about it all weekend – through cleaning up the mess we'd made on the bar floor, through the rest of the show, through a lazy Saturday with Mack leafing through the Internet looking for stories, through a Sunday dinner at my parents' that included Aaron describing how he'd stripped the battery back down to nothing, and into the only important week of work I'd ever had.

Chapter 14

Before Aaron was born, our mother was the chair of a local college's English department. She scaled back to only one class a week when she opened the day care, but she didn't miss much classroom time. We just became her students.

Every morning, all four of us had to come to breakfast with three facts we'd learned the day before. She was trying to broaden our horizons, and though it got weird sometimes – with an awkward question every now and then about a particularly racy Internet video the parental controls failed to catch – for the most part, it worked. We whined about it more than we should have, but it's how I learned about Chinese New Year before we did it in Social Studies, how I got turned onto Fitzgerald two years before we read *The Great Gatsby*, and to a less academic extent, how I discovered exactly how good The Talking Heads and Bo Jackson were.

So, on Monday morning, when I walked into work and Rick told me that a debate over education funding was back in the news, I grabbed the paper he handed me while he told me about a state senator's town hall the following week.

I hadn't been reading a minute yet when Harry's broad frame stepped through the bullpen door and started lumbering its way toward his office. He walked like he wrote – with purpose. His meaty arms swung powerfully, and he lowered his head like a battering ram, as if prepared to run straight through anyone who dared get in his way. I don't know why, but I always admired it. I didn't care for how much he labored with each step, but I envied what was behind it.

"Harry!" I called out, surprising myself as I jogged toward him. Two years before, when the same senator was pushing similar budget cuts, I wrote a scathing op-ed remembering our mother's lectures about the importance of a diverse education. Too harsh for the paper, Harry made me re-write it twice before he published it, and even then, I found myself on the receiving end of a scolding from a few members of the paper's board. "I'm sure you've heard about that town hall next week. I was wondering if I could cover it for the paper," I said. I'd asked Harry the question before, and he always gave me the response I figured he'd give then.

"Can't do it," he responded simply, sounding exactly as he always sounded. "I've got a room full of experienced reporters, here. One of them will handle it. But I'm sure whatever Pablo writes will be solid." With that, he patted me hard on the back and continued on toward his office.

I didn't park on the exchange long. Instead, I quickly retook my seat and went to work. I stayed late that night. I wrote something for Wednesday or Thursday's paper on the budget debate and powered out a few other editorials about nothing of consequence, then hung around with Rick researching and working on a much longer, more in-depth education article that Pablo would eventually 'send in'.

The next morning, I grabbed breakfast for Rick on the way in as a thank you for the work he'd helped me with the night before. We stood at our desks for a while, eating our bagels and drinking our coffee and talking about the date he'd been on over the weekend. They'd gone to some Italian place for dinner, and he was nice enough, but Rick wasn't exactly sure what to make of him – though I never found out why.

Contrary to what you may think, newsrooms aren't exciting places. In fact, they're pretty damn boring. You'd expect collaboration and commotion, but for the most part, you just get quiet. Rick and I talked to each other, but hardly anyone else said a word. They sat, instead, with their eyes fixed on their computers and their ears stuffed with buds piping in their music of choice. It was a cold, sterile place, save for the splashes of color and pattern in our desk chairs, which human resources had made us start buying ourselves. They were the only real bits of personality in the room.

So, when a junior reporter leapt from her polka-dotted chair and sprinted down the hall toward Harry's office, Rick stopped telling his story so we could watch her go and wonder what was going on. And when a second reporter sitting behind the police scanners jumped out of his chair of cheap, green leather and took off down the hall behind her, we exchanged troubled glances. And when we heard a chorus of "oh, no's" rise up from those seated in their chairs, we jumped into our own to open our computers and discover what everyone else seemed to already know – but Harry beat us to it, charging into the newsroom as stern as ever.

"Listen up!" he commanded, the gravity of the unknown situation clear in his tone. "There's been a shooting at St. Francis High. We don't know anything more than that, but we better in fifteen minutes. Jim, Leslie, Jake, get to the school and find out what you can. Frank, you're with the police. Get to the station, get inside, get whatever they know on my desk." He was decisive and resolute, with power behind every word. "This is the story now, people. I want every department working on it. If you didn't get an assignment, your job is to support the ones who did." He paused for a moment, looking across the entire newsroom as if to make eye contact with each and every one of us before dropping his head and continuing solemnly. "Look, this is about as sensitive a story as we get. As you do your work, know that. Be reporters, but be human beings, too. Now go to it."

And with that, the newsroom exploded into action. The handful of reporters Harry mentioned sprinted out of the room while the rest of us dove for our computers and phones. We called whomever we knew, and ran down or researched whatever fact we thought may be prudent. When we had something, we shouted it out across the bullpen in the general direction of the reporter who needed it. Somewhere along the way, someone cleared off the large wipe board that hung on one side of the room and started writing down what we had confirmed, and an hour or so in I caught myself just staring at it all from my little corner of the room, awed by the flurry of activity – the running and the yelling and the hand signals and the way it all seemed to work despite the hysteria, like a beautiful little symphony of chaos.

Every few minutes, Harry came in to hand out another assignment, turning me down, at one point, when I told him I could handle one if he needed me to.

"You can't help us out there," he said, stepping close and putting a hand on each shoulder, as he's never done before. "But you can in here. Write me some poetry, will you?" As he turned to leave, I could see why he got into this business; I could see the humanity in him, which he hides so often behind the leathery roughness of a jaded professional.

It wasn't until mid-afternoon that the chaos finally calmed. Together, we confirmed that a student had pulled out a gun during homeroom and gotten three shots off before his teacher tackled him to the ground. A few hours later we learned that none of those shots connected, but a few students were taken to the hospital in shock. A couple hours after that, we had those students' names and Rick was on the phone with the hospital checking on their conditions.

I wrote five op-eds that day, after all the research was done and the reporters had started in on their official stories. The first four were short position papers from random community members pushing some agenda – gun control, mental health awareness, anti-gun control, whatever. The last one, though, was different. For the last one, I thought about the whole of the day – the innocent way it started and the rollercoaster of the next few hours. I thought about myself in high school and what could have driven someone to such a dark place. I thought about how I might have reacted. I thought about that teacher and the other students. And I wrote it all down. And this time, I didn't think about a character or change my grammar to fit the profile of James in Guilderland rather than Connor in Saratoga. For the last one, I just wrote.

When I finished, I looked up to find the newsroom dark and mostly empty. Night had fallen at some point, and most of my stable mates had headed home, while my phone chirped with Mack's irritation. I had warned her I would be late, but apparently 10 PM on a Tuesday night crossed some kind of line. I picked it up to respond but set it down a second later. I was out of words.

The next day, I begged Harry to run the story with my name on it, but I was told it would run on Thursday under Pablo's. I was disappointed, but after Mr. Carver stopped by my desk to tell me much he'd liked what Pablo had written on that Tuesday evening, my frustration waned, and when Harry called me into his office on Thursday to assign me a follow up for Sunday's paper, it faded a little more. And on Friday, when Mr. Carver mentioned that he had reviewed my application for the columnist position and liked my work, it ebbed even further. And when I thought back on not just that week, but the music and the movie columns, too, and when I read over the work and realized just how much I liked all, it disappeared entirely.

Chapter 15

If my feet hit the ground leaving the building on Friday, I'd be surprised. It felt like I was floating to my car, though I'm sure I was sprinting. When I got there, I drove straight to Mack's work to surprise her. She works at Winter and Wall just a few miles from the paper's headquarters, in a large brick building with meticulously groomed gardens and lawns, and sharp, angular hedgerows cut at precise, 90-degree angles. Together, they almost scream 'don't worry, we understand money; we have it.'

The plush leather chairs in the lobby would yell it too, if they weren't all muffled by the asses of future clients enjoying them like it was just another day at the cigar club – rather than the start of a legal battle over of a deal they made in that club, or the woman they met at the strip joint they visited next.

Mack worked on the third floor with the other junior associates, but in a hard-wall office because, as the CEO's daughter who'd worked there since high school, she was not just another junior associate. I ran the three flights that day, but slowed once I hit her floor. Winter and Wall is not a place you run through. Those halls are reserved for either the brisk power walks of a go-getter with an ass to kick in the court room, or the slow, shell-shocked wander of someone who'd spent the day reading an 800-page brief.

There weren't many power walks on the third floor.

I don't know what I was really expecting the first time I walked through the office doors, but successful as they are, I think I was expecting more. I thought there'd be life and energy in the building, with passionate closing arguments rehearsed in large, crowded boardrooms. Instead, the whole place – save, of course, for the lobby – made you feel like you'd walked into the world's saddest library. It was quiet and sullen, and full of quiet, sullen books, read by quiet, sullen people.

My steps broke the odd silence as I practically tiptoed between cubicles toward Mack's office. Their heads buried in briefs, hardly anyone looked up as I passed. Even Mack didn't notice me at first, as I stood in her doorway for a second watching her work. She had three books spread out in front of her and was jumping between each to mark different passages with one of four highlighters – color-coded to correspond with different cases or rulings, I'm sure.

After a minute or two admiring the way her librarian glasses clung to the tip of her nose as she worked, I cleared my throat and she looked up startled, though any sign of it quickly faded as she smiled.

"What are you doing here?" she asked, straightening up and adjusting her pencil skirt as she came around her desk to give me a hug.

"I had a great day today," I said, my arms wrapped around her, keeping her close. "I figured I'd take you to dinner to celebrate." That hadn't been my plan when I'd left work. To be honest, I hadn't had a plan when I left work. I just wanted to see someone and tell them what had happened.

"That sounds great," she said, stepping back. "Give me five minutes to finish this and I'll be ready."

"What are you working on?" I asked, peering over her desk at which books she had opened, remembering all three from college.

"Well, you remember the Hiddelston case?" she asked, and went on to explain something about asset division and split income, but I only made it a few words in before my mind wandered off. I turned my head as she worked and looked out at the others in her office – highlighting their own passages in their own books – and wondered if they all went home and watched law dramas on TV and thought about how full of shit they are, curious if some Hollywood exec would ever produce a realistic one called *Books and Highlighters*. I was still thinking about it when Mack appeared at my side ready to go.

For dinner, we went to this boutique restaurant Mack loves in downtown Saratoga. It's a cramped space, with as many tables as they could fit shoehorned into the dining area. Mack likes it because it reminds her of the elegant dinners she had the summer her family spent in Europe during high school – which is something I probably should have mentioned when I was talking about how pretentious Mack can be. One long bench lines the left side of the restaurant and a row of small tables is pulled up to it, each table only a few inches apart.

We were seated at one of those tables – as we are every night we eat there –because while you wouldn't want to sit next to anyone who asks the stewardess for a seatbelt extender, you can't help but feel like you're nestled in a cocoon of romance. The lighting is turned down low and there's a tightly wound whir buzzing about the room. To hear your date, you have to focus hard to keep the other noises out, and eventually they all melt away and just the two of you are left.

"So, you think you have a real chance at this?" she asked after we'd been seated. I'd started recounting the previous two weeks in the car ride over.

"I do," I said through a smile, leaning in as if my excitement needed to be kept a secret. She giggled when I said it.

"I don't know if I've ever seen you like this about work," she said, the giggle disappearing from her face.

"I know," I said. "I don't know what it is, but the last few weeks, it's just-" and I paused, looking for the right word. "Fun," I settled on.

Her head tilted to the side and an almost sad smile spread across her face when I uttered the word. She was happy for me. I could see it. But I could see what else she was, too. Mack had a plan, and this wasn't part of it. She'd adjust it if needed, but she always hoped I'd come back to the career I'd left and join her at Winter and Wall, where we'd climb the ranks together, a power couple sharing our work and our love.

She'd swallowed hard and accepted it when I started working at the paper, but there was only so much she could do to repress it. So, we left it alone and talked about everything else we could think of through our three courses, but eventually, we ran out of topics, and she could no longer keep it in.

"Connor," she started. "If it doesn't work out, would you ever consider-"and I cut her off.

"Mack."

"McKenzie." She jabbed sharply.

"Sorry," I said, waiting a second before going on. "I just don't think I can," I said. I stopped there, uncertain where to go next. Mack had no idea either, so we sat in silence for a minute, making eye contact for a few seconds at a time before looking away, each of us thinking about what to say next. You could see that she didn't understand, but she was trying to, and I loved her for it. She was trying – even as I held her down. Mack already had a bright present and a brighter future. She was well on her way to becoming a successful lawyer at a prestigious law firm; I was her 27-year-old boyfriend hoping to land a real job for the first time in his life.

We sat for a few more seconds in the dense cloud of something complex and confusing, still searching for how to move on, when the table next to us stepped up and did it for us. We'd been talking all night and we'd barely even acknowledged those around us. But with our silence finally settling in, the rest of the world broke through. On my left, a young couple talked about the wedding they were planning, and the time off they'd both have to arrange for their honeymoon. On my right, a middle-aged couple discussed the merits of a great op-ed they'd read that week.

Mine.

Well, Pablo's, really, but still.

"It was great," the woman said.

"I know," the man replied, and went on to offer some kind of praise I missed as the thumping in my chest started drowning everything else out.

My eyes met Mack's and I found her staring at me with a wide smile. She was happy for me, and what's more, she was proud of me. And there was nothing else behind it. I could have stayed like that for hours – enjoying that moment and all the contentment wrapped in it. But want as you might, you can't shut the world out forever, so, finally, Mack brought it back in.

"We should go," she said, and I reluctantly agreed.

We had a lazy Saturday. I'm not even sure we left the house that day. Even on weekends, it's a rare day that Mack isn't up at six to do Pilates or head to spin class, but that day was one of those rare ones. We woke up late and made a big, hearty breakfast. Mack made eggs and bacon while I made hash browns, and we spent the rest of the day on the couch together, paralyzed by grease.

Sunday, we came out of the food coma and headed to my parents' for dinner. It was one of those warm days you get as the colder part of fall approaches – with summer sun but a strong autumn wind, a warning of what's to come. As we walked in, we found the garage door open, and I could see Aaron tinkering at its back.

"Battery?" I asked, with no other greeting.

"Yep," Aaron replied simply.

"How's it coming?"

"Well, it hasn't exploded yet. So that's an improvement."

Aaron's quiet and reserved, but if you're listening for it, there's a sharp, quick-witted sense of humor buried in his simple speech. "Be careful. It's cardboard crusade day," he said as we stepped past him and into the house, and as we walked through the door into what is normally the neat, polished kitchen, we saw only boxes – stacked chest level and labeled with orange duct tape.

Cardboard crusade days come regularly in our family. They happen at least twice a year when we open and close the family house on Cape Cod, and when we were younger, they came more frequently than that – coming every few months when our father got tired of the clutter in our rooms. With little warning, he'd get the boxes out of the basement and collect whatever he didn't think we needed anymore.

"Be careful of the boxes!" my mother called out from behind one of the familiar stacks. This was the first kind. It was just before our annual Columbus Day trip when the whole family heads out to the Cape to close it down. My mother spends the week before packing up everything she may need to help winterize the house, preparing the containers she uses to bring back what she doesn't want to leave out there all winter. "You guys are all ready for next weekend, right?" she asked as she stepped out from behind the pile she'd just labeled.

"He's not, but I am," Mack said playfully. She and my mother always got along, but I often wondered how much of their relationship was a well-acted stage show my mother put on for my benefit.

"I've got a week; I'll be fine," I defended when given a disapproving glance. I gave my mother a kiss and stepped over to the island, looking over the fruits of her labor. I looked down after a second and there, already cut out and ready to be framed, was Pablo Garcia's first Sunday column. I stared at it for a second. Our paper had never come that morning, so this was the first I'd seen it. It set me back a bit, forcing me to take a deep breath as I stood perfectly still. Silent. My words had been on these pages before, but never quite like this.

After a second, I realized that both my parents had stepped up on either side of me.

"That's a hell of a thing," my dad said.

It was.

Chapter 16

Remember earlier when I mentioned the only important week of work I'd ever had? It was. Until this one.

It started the way the last one had ended, with an encouraging word from Mr. Carver, and a few others in the newsroom, too. Even Andrea offered begrudging praise for Pablo's Sunday column, and like the one before it, the week had energy and excitement like I hadn't felt in a while. I wrote a dozen columns the first few days of that week – far too many under Pablo's byline. Some of them were crap – school board meetings and water main breaks – but others weren't, like a critique of a local homeowners' association that wouldn't let a little girl hang up the Halloween decorations she'd made at school.

Between articles, I worked on the longer piece on the town hall – my own little passion project, like Andrea and her grotto. I was exhausted when I left that night, and I remember the parking lot was covered in a blanket of thick, dark fog. I stopped to admire it for a minute before stepping beneath it, certain it would lift.

When Harry called me into his office on Thursday near lunchtime, my heart leapt into my throat – as it had every time he'd called me since he brought up the columnist job. I walked to his office in what felt like slow motion, with entire seconds clicking by between steps, wondering as I passed the closed doors of the paper's top columnists and editors, if that was the day I'd get an answer.

When I stepped through Harry's door and saw Mr. Carver standing behind him, I knew it was.

"We're hiring Wallace Williams," Harry blurted out, not wasting a single word to try and soften the blow. "From WAVC."

I don't know what it feels like when a ghost passes through you, but if I had to guess, I'd say it feels close to what I felt in that moment. The air left my lungs at the same time my blood ran cold. My heart sunk deep into my chest as I struggled, for a second, to catch my breath. I looked up at Mr. Carver, whose expression registered no emotion at all. He stood off Harry's shoulder in a midnight blue pinstripe suit, the slicked-back $400 haircut playing well with his $4,000 wrist watch – each set against the tan of a mid-40's man who spends his weekends at the lake house he'd inherited the same day he took over the newspaper.

"Son," he said, filling the void I noticed only then. 'He's far too young to call a 20-something son,' I thought, surprising myself with snark in such a moment. "We think you're a great writer. Harry showed me that column you wrote about the homeowner's association. It was great, and it's just what we want. A real conversation starter. But the thing is, we need a name, and you're not it." There was silence again as my eyes left Mr. Carver and found Harry, whose gaze never so much as flinched.

"Of course," I stammered finally. "Absolutely." I said. "Yes." I was rambling and I knew it, but there wasn't much I could do about it. At some point, Mr. Carver extended his Rolexed hand, a sign that I was overstaying my welcome. I shook it as firmly as I could manage – which probably wasn't all that firmly at all– and thanked him for the opportunity. I turned toward the door, but stopped short of walking through it.

"Mr. Carver," I said, turning back around, not entirely sure what I was saying or where I was going with it. "I know I'm not a name; I understand that. But I wonder if we could change that? Maybe, with your permission, of course, I can publish some columns under my own name instead of Pablo's? Is that something that could be possible?" I looked at Harry when I finished, who stared back at me, before looking up at Mr. Carver.

"Thing is, son," Mr. Carver said, erasing all doubt; he's far too young to call me 'son.' "Pablo has a brand. I think for the time being we should just let that continue."

"I understand," I smiled. The irony of that statement not quite hitting me then. "Thanks again," I said, turning to leave.

When I got back to my desk, I had an email from Harry.

'Take the rest of the day off,' was all it read, and I didn't argue. Instead, I grabbed my bag and made for the door, snatching up my phone and dialing Mack's number on the way.

"I'm sorry Connor," she said from the other end after I'd filled her in. "But I don't know what you want me to do. I can't just leave work." Honestly, I'm not sure what I wanted from her, either. Of course, she couldn't leave, and I told her that before we exchanged 'I love yous' and I hung up to call Brady.

Who told me to meet him at Paddy Murphy's in 20 minutes.

Chapter 17

Our high school prides itself on building well-rounded adults. It's in their mission statement, which is something I never realized high schools have. Every year, as a part of that effort, they bring in a nationally renowned motivational speaker to help the juniors get ready for the college search.

Our year, she came in for week and made our entire grade write essays about where we see ourselves in ten years. The school took it as seriously as my father didn't. They gave us an entire weekend to write them and no other teachers were allowed to give us homework. He decided it would be a good weekend to take my friends and me to the Cape.

It was spring and my parents had just bought the house, and he was doing everything he could to get out there and do some work on it before summer began. He had the money to pay for the work to be done, but I think the idea of another man working on his home bothered him. So, he loaded Brady, Mike, Noah, Will, Z, and I into the car and took us to the beach.

He spent most of the weekend fixing floorboards and painting trim while the six of us sat under the sun with the sand between our toes. We swam and threw the Frisbee and played music, but even if we pretended like we were on vacation, we all must have been thinking about that essay, because it kept coming up.

"When you think about it, it's a stupid question," Noah said apropos of nothing at the time. "There's an infinite number of possibilities. How are we supposed to guess where we'll be in a decade, especially when there's so much that could happen between now and then?" Not surprisingly, he was out-thinking the rest of us, so Z just ignored him.

"Tahiti," he said. "I'll be on a movie set in Tahiti or Brazil, working as a production assistant. And five years later, I'll be back for the sequel, but this time as a director."

"The Fillmore," Mike chimed in, as we all paused to think about Z's Hollywood fairytale. "Performing my own songs."

"Drawing something somewhere." Brady offered as we continued around the circle. And that ended up being all he wrote. The others rambled on for the recommended two pages, but he just stopped with that one line – which, in fairness, was an improvement on "somewhere," which he tried to write first.

It was my turn, next, and while I know I said something, as I drove to meet Brady and waited for him at the bar, I couldn't remember what. I couldn't remember what I said to them on the beach, and I couldn't remember what I eventually turned in. All I remembered was getting up and wading into the surf while the conversation continued. The water was still cold with the chill of winter, but I dove in and floated on my back, enjoying the chill against the heat of the sun while the ocean ebbed and flowed around me. In the background, I remember hearing Noah interject.

"Think we'll be visited by aliens in our lifetime?"

I remember assuming 'mass alien extinction' was one of the 'infinite number of possibilities' he'd been considering while the rest of us gave our answers.

I was sitting on a stool when Brady arrived, sipping a scotch you shouldn't be ordering that early.

"Do you remember the essay they made us write in high school?" I asked, not waiting for him to even slump into his seat. "The one about where we saw ourselves in 10 years?

"Vaguely," he said, motioning toward the bartender and asking for a beer. Paddy Murphy's is a quiet little spot in an old brick building on Saratoga's main drag. The inside looks like its light by shadows, with spotlights shinning on the mirror behind the bar, throwing ambient light and shade back across anyone who's pulled up a stool.

Past the bar area, the space opens up into a larger back room and balcony, with tables on both levels and a backyard area canopied by thick trees and bordered by well-kept gardens.

It's a cozy but comfortable spot – always crowded enough to keep you company, but never so crowded that the company is on your lap. It quickly became our favorite spot when we turned 21.

"Do you remember what I wrote?" I asked.

"Well, I only barely remember that we wrote anything at all, but yeah, I think I can quote yours," he joked. Brady never dropped that trademark sarcasm, just adjusted it to fit company. With me, it's in its full, uncut glory. "What does it matter?"

"I was thinking of it the whole way over here," I said, looking up at the 'Pickle Back Shots' sign hanging above the bar. "I remember what each of you wrote, but I don't have the first damn clue what I put down."

"Ok. But, again, what does it matter?"

"I don't know," I admitted, not taking my eyes off the sign. "Maybe it doesn't matter. I just really wish I could remember." Finally, I turned to look at Brady, who'd taken up the stool on my right.

"I'm sorry about the job," he said, and offered plenty of encouragement, but I wasn't in the mood to be praised. Instead, I was ready for what he said next. "What do you say? Three pickle backs a piece?"

"Please." A true pro, the bartender didn't let the judgment show on his face when he poured out six shots. We drank them quickly, and then drank down a few more after that. At some point, we ordered food and moved out to the backyard, talking about my day at the *Tribune*, and Brady's at GNS, and our website idea, too. We talked about Brady's idea that we pose questions and let our readers answer them, and my suggestion to we let users vote on the best answers. Eventually, we decided that neither would work, or figured that they already were working, and Brady brought the conversation full circle.

"Out of curiosity," he said, standing up to leave as home beckoned for us both, our early afternoon having turned into night. "What did I write?" I stared at him for a moment, confused. "On that 'ten years from now' thing," he clarified.

"'Drawing something somewhere,'" I quoted.

He grunted. "I guess I got that right."

Chapter 18

It was late when I pulled into my apartment complex, after sitting in the backyard long enough to make sure I'd sobered up. When I got back, I had every intention of heading in, but instead, I turned the car off and sat in the dark, staring out the windshield. I knew I should go meet Mack and talk to her about everything that had happened that day, but I didn't. Not for a while, at least. Instead, I absently traced the lines of the stacked brick, pausing every few seconds to peak in through the windows of the brightly lit apartments.

It's creepy, I know, but there's something I find oddly romantic about lit up homes, and sneaking a peak through the curtains while I walk or drive past – seeing one photograph on a wall or catching a glimpse of a floral pattern on a couch and imagining a whole life based only on that snapshot.

At one point that night, I remember my eyes found Doug's basement apartment, the windows peaking above ground and giving a look inside. I could see the top of his head sitting on the couch, and I remember imagining a TV dinner slowly getting cold on the fold-up tray in front of him. On the walls around him hung a number of paintings, but one in particular caught my eye. It was a large painting of a heavy-set man in a button up shirt, with a kaleidoscope of pinks and purples swung together in a misting, almost tie-die pattern, like a dream sequence in a 90's TV show. I lingered on it for longer than I should, wondering what it meant before deciding it was time to head inside to my own walls.

When I first moved into my apartment, I didn't have much money to spend on decorations, so I hung pictures I'd taken with my camera. I had the opportunity to buy real art over the years, but I grew to like that the only pictures in my apartment were pictures I took, in places I'd been. There was the lake in Central Park where Mack and I took a nap while visiting the city one spring, the sunset I snapped through the woods behind my parents' house, and the cresting waves at the Cape Cod beach my family went to before we bought the house. It's a typical tourist beach with a snack stand and so many people you can barely see the sand, but when the crowd thins, you start to notice the dunes and the marsh and the booming soundtrack of the ocean, with waves coming right up to a lifeguard tower we would jump off in the evening, the one with a hole worn through the wood – the one that almost looked haunted as we would leave at night, lit only by the moon.

Mack didn't hear me when I walked in, and instead, stumbled on me standing in the hallway, looking at that picture of the beach.

"Oh, hey," she said. We hadn't spoken since our phone call earlier that afternoon, so that was as good a place to start as any, I guess.

"Hey, I'm sorry about earlier," I said.

"It's OK," she offered, shifting her feet and smiling. She didn't ask where I'd

been or who I was with. Maybe she'd talked to Kaitlyn and already knew, or maybe she knew I wouldn't want to talk about it. Either way, I was grateful to let it go. A larger talk would come at some point, certainly, but it didn't happen then. Instead, she told me that she'd have to work that weekend and couldn't make it to Cape Cod, and we sat on the couch watching TV and making small talk until she fell asleep on my lap and I leaned my head back to stare a hole through the ceiling.

Chapter 19

I'm not sure what I expected when I walked into the office the next day, but I was surprised to learn nothing had changed. I guess I thought something might be different; I thought there'd be some outward acknowledgement of the seismic shift I'd experienced the day before – some kind of minor collateral damage, like what you see in a state next to the one that just got rocked by an earthquake. But of course, there wasn't any of that. And, really, in the grand scheme of things, why would there be? In the end, I was the only thing that changed.

I was late for the first time ever that day, and on the way to my desk I didn't stop to talk with anyone. I exchanged a few passing nods and grunts, collapsed into my chair, threw on some headphones and started working – never bothering to put music on. I wanted to write a few articles and get to the Cape as early as I could, with as little interaction as I could manage.

I spent the bulk of my morning finishing the column I'd been writing on that town hall, and just as I was wrapping it up, I got a tap on my shoulder from Rick, who wordlessly handed me that morning's sports section with a headline circled.

"Coach's Controversy," it read. Beneath it was an article about a local high school football coach who threw a player off the team because he was also doing the school play. He hadn't missed any practices, but the coach, whose mustache told you everything you needed to know about him, wanted players who were "committed to the team." I turned to a new page in my notebook to start making notes, but before I could, my email dinged with a new message from Harry.

"Come see me."

When I walked into Harry's office, he was standing in the corner, wrestling with one of the large piles of paper on his file cabinet. He turned to face me without saying anything, and without that same, familiar sternness in his look.

"Connor," he said, one of the few times he ever used my first name. "I'm sorry about yesterday." He motioned for me to sit as he walked back behind his desk. I shook off his apology as I did. There was nothing to apologize for. "There's something I need to show you."

He reached behind him and grabbed a copy of the *Tribune*. Handing it to me, I saw it was a mockup of Sunday's opinion section, with Wallace William's picture on the front.

"Williams' column will debut this weekend," Harry said in a low monotone. "It's on that town hall you've been working on. And I know you wanted to be writing on that..." He kept talking but I didn't hear anything after that. I'd already started reading.

By Wallace Williams

People like school funding. Of course they do. But they shouldn't. Because it's not working.

As a news anchor, I read lots of stories about schools and teachers, and only a couple are positive. School funding isn't working well enough.

So, what can we do? We can spend more, or we could cut bate. Now I'm no fisherman, but I think the answer is clear.

Let's not ask people to fork up their paychecks. Instead, let's let them keep their money so they can spend it.

He'd written more, but I tapped out there. When I looked up, Harry was still looking at me, like he'd been watching my reaction as I read.

"Harry," I started.

"I know," he said, and there was a pause as I decided what to say next, scanning his legendary career as it hung as decoration on his office walls.

"This is garbage."

"I know," he agreed, his stare staying locked on mine.

"Harry, if we got this from a reader we wouldn't run it. I doubt we'd even finish it."

"I know," he said nodding. "But we didn't get it from a reader, we got it from our columnist. So, we'll massage it a bit and get it ready. Look, I just didn't want you- "

"So we're going to ghost write everything he submits?" I interrupted, forgetting myself. Harry looked away and sighed.

"We couldn't hire you, Connor," he said, and we both sighed together.

"I know," I said, the truth of this whole, absurd situation no longer clouded by my deluded hope.

"We can't sell you," he continued, slapping his desk as he leaned back, as if he hadn't heard me. "This is a business, dammit." I started to respond but he just powered on. "We're a major newspaper, Hall. I was fooling myself to think it could work and I'm sorry about that. But what would we tell our readers? Our advertisers? That we're handing over our feature opinion column to a 27-year-old kid who knows a little about a lot?"

That last line hit me like a punch in the gut – the kind that drops you to your knees and sucks the air straight out of your lungs –

and questions and confirmations shot through my mind at breakneck speed in the instant that followed. *Is he right? Of course he's right. What does he know about it? Everything, he knows everything about it.* There was a heavy, dense weight filling the room as I tried to find the strength to stand and clear my mind enough to send my legs the message to do it.

"I don't know," I said, and I dropped the paper on Harry's desk as I turned and walked out of his office.

When I'd stepped out view I stopped and leaned against the wall, my back and head resting against it, eyes toward the ceiling. My breathing was quick and shallow and my hands were in my hair. I wanted to scream and cry at the same time, but more than that, I wanted to come up with the kind of response I wish I had. I stood there for too long trying to think of one, but nothing came. No scream. No cry. No response.

Because he was right. And we both knew it. And should have known it long before we did.

So instead, the replay of my conversation with Harry was gradually replaced by something different. Something deeper, something more reflective, something looking back and projecting forward with a bitterness and anger I didn't deserve to carry. And soon, I was back at my desk, face to face with that football coach and his Trooper Tough Guy mustache, no closer to any real answers. But as I sat there at my computer, everything came bubbling up from inside and poured out furiously through my fingers.

When I'd finished the column, I printed what I'd written and handed the pages to Rick.

"Give these to Harry?" I asked, more sternly than I should have. "I'm leaving," I said, grabbing my bag and heading for the door.

"Hey!" He called out. "You didn't put a name on this. Who wrote it?"

"I did." I said without breaking stride.

"Yeah, but what name do we put on it? Pablo?"

"No. Connor Hall." And I stepped out into the wind.

Chapter 20

*When my friends and I were young, our parents and teachers told us that we could be anything and everything we wanted to be. And really, it wasn't even so much that our parents and teachers **told us**. They **preached** it to us. It wasn't just something they said, it was something they sermonized. It wasn't a saying. It was a mantra. It was a religion. To them, if we worked hard, if we were dedicated, if we committed ourselves, there was nothing we couldn't do – and there was nothing we **shouldn't** do.*

It's why one of my friends wrote both music and poetry. It's why another made movies while another went to med school. It's why another studied politics and another made art. It's why I'm a writer. And it's why each of us dabbled in all of it.

It's why we all acted in plays while playing sports – and why I felt compelled to write in after reading about the young boy kicked off Saratoga's football team by Coach Jason Daniels, because that boy dared to listen to his parents and teachers.

Shame on you, Coach Daniels, and if I may ask a pointed question, who the hell do you think you are?

You coach high school football in upstate New York. You're not a professional coach in the NFL. You're not a college coach with millions of dollars on the line each weekend. If we can all be honest with ourselves, you're not even a high school coach in central Texas, where entire towns live and die with Friday night's result – not that any of that really matters anyway, because while reasonable people may disagree over what could have been done if this player of yours was somehow neglecting his duty, he wasn't.

He hadn't missed a game. He hadn't missed a practice. And you threw him off your team anyway.

Shame on you, Coach Daniels.

One of the great center fielders in New York Yankees history was also a classical guitarist, and today, athletes from all major sports are also businessmen and actors and activists. Should they be thrown off their respective teams? Can they do two things at once? Can they do all four?

Shame on you, Coach Daniels.

I could take the time, here, to detail any number of studies from the CDC or AMA or APA that show how a varied education with diverse experiences is good for students, but I fear I lack the requisite column inches to do it well, and I fear you lack any sort of concern for the academics of it.

So instead, I'll say one more time, shame on you, Coach Daniels, and ask another time, who the hell do you think you are? How dare you deny a child this experience, or any experience, at the very time we should be encouraging children to explore who they are and what they feel, and never hide from it – to, instead, claim it and be proud of it. Why should you care if your second string running back also enjoys acting? Why is that not something to celebrate? Why is it not something to honor? Why is it not OK? Why isn't it great? Why does it make him somehow less than the others? Why should he be forced to choose?

Can you answer those questions? Do you even care to? Did you think about them at all before you made your decision? Of course you didn't. Because that would have meant you thought. About something. At all.

Shame on you, Coach Daniels.

And may we all hope that the student you dismissed is as resilient as he seems bright and ambitious, and presses on in the face of your wrongheadedness to explore everything that he is – that he never shrinks from it just because others may want him to.

Shame on you.

Chapter 21

I've always loved long car rides, and the way your mind seems to wander when it's just you, the stereo, and the streaks of a busy world whirring by. There's a promise to them, like the start of a grand adventure.

There wasn't much promise on that ride, and my mind didn't much wander. Instead, I went back to replaying that last conversation with Harry, and extended it in my mind – thinking of everything he'd said and searching for answers I still didn't have.

I'd left for the Cape before noon, but it never occurred to me that I'd be alone when I made it to the house – that the rest of my family wouldn't make it for hours. I walked in the front door expecting the house to be full, but there was only silence. I followed the foyer to the left and into the kitchen, which opens into an expansive, open layout in the back of the house, with a living room and den separated by only a few steps, each decorated in blue and white, with long, sheer curtains that billow when you open the windows.

I love that house. I used to dream of retiring in it, sitting in a chair in the middle of those flowing curtains. That day, I walked through and opened every window, and stood in the middle of the room as the curtains blew against me, trying to let those flowing sheers sweep away what I'd brought with me from the *Tribune*.

When that didn't work, I went for a swim.

The sun was warmer than you'd expect for October in the Cape, and I stood on the beach for a second soaking it up before diving into a surf that was every bit as cold as you'd expect for October in the Cape. The water felt like a thousand knives stabbing from every direction, but I forced myself to stay in until I adjusted. I laid in the water for a while, floating on my back like when I was young. In and out and up and down the water carried me, with thoughts of the *Tribune* coming and going with each wave.

I never saw the final wave coming, and didn't feel it until it was too late, when it had already lifted me up, pulled me toward the shore, and rag-dolled me into the sand. I landed hard on my ribs, the weight of the water coming down on top of me and pushing me up the beach, my side dragging along the rocks and sand. Coughing and gasping, I rolled out of the surf and crawled away from the water, flipping onto my back to examine my raw, scraped ribs.

"Perfect," I grumbled to the empty horizon, and collapsed back down, letting the sun warm me as best it could. I was still there a while later when I heard my mother calling my name from the house. I threw an arm up, feeling the cuts on my side as I did.

"What the hell happened to you?" my father asked from the porch.

"The sea was angry that day," I said. "Like an old man trying to send back soup at a deli." He laughed at the *Seinfeld* reference and told me to come up and help unpack. Slowly, I got back on my feet and headed inside, where I told my parents why I'd beaten them there, and they asked the standard questions and offered the standard mix of apology and encouragement, and I nodded the way sons do, grateful for their words, and we went on with our business as more of the family arrived and the space between the billowing curtains filled in.

A few hours later, we were a few hours into dinner and dessert and I was re-telling a story about the time our father stole a bundle of wood from our neighbor's trash heap, mumbling the whole time about what kind of idiot throws out perfectly good pine like it just grows on trees and of course it grows on trees but you must be a fool to just throw it out when it's in that condition.

It wasn't until I finished the story that I remembered when it happened. It was the weekend he took my friends and me to the house, when he was still fixing it up and we were supposed to be deciding where we wanted to be when we grew up. The house next to ours was taking out the original floors in favor of Italian marble, and built together however many years before, their old floors matched ours, so dad figured he could take the trash and build himself some baseboards.

"Mom," I said, thinking of that weekend, "Remember that essay we had to write about where we'd be in ten years? What did I write?"

She put down her coffee and thought for a minute, but it was clear she had about as much idea as I had. "You know," she said, "I can't remember. I know what the other three wrote. But not you. That's odd," and she finished with a snort.

"She doesn't remember because she doesn't love you as much," Maggie chimed in from across the table.

"But I'm clearly the favorite," I answered playfully.

"When is a middle child ever the favorite?" Ed, the oldest of us, asked.

"When it's me," Maggie and I answered together.

"I love you all equally," mom said amidst the laughing, "I know your teachers weren't happy with you, but, for the life of me, I can't remember why." That last bit was a surprise to me; I had no recollection of it at all. In fact, in all my years at school, I couldn't remember anything like it.

"Really?" I asked. "The one time they're mad at me and we can't remember?

"Oh sweetie," my mother chuckled. "That wasn't the only time."

"What?"

"Connor, your teachers didn't quite love you."

"What?" I asked through a smile.

"Well," my mother started, before my father interrupted.

"You annoyed the hell out of 'em," he said. I looked around the table, incredulous, waiting for further explanation. "They hated you."

"Hate is probably strong," my mother started. "But you did annoy them," she said. "You just never gave them a break. Ever." Mouth open and eyes wide, I looked back and forth across the now raucously laughing table until she continued. "You never stopped asking questions. They thought you were exhausting."

Chapter 22

I woke up slowly the next morning, lying in bed a while looking out toward the water and listening to the footsteps and voices of my family below. Eventually, I pulled myself up, feeling the scrapes and scabs on my ribs, and lumbered downstairs, where my sister's kids – Jack and Annie – were already running around. Maggie had already made muffins and my parents were already busy readying the house for winter – taking out the screens and packing up the kitchen.

I grabbed a muffin and thought about helping my father with the screens, but I knew what he'd say if I asked.

"Go help your mother," he would have said. "If I can't do this by myself, just put me in a home." So instead, I helped my mother and learned that Aaron and his girlfriend Bethany were in the basement checking the water heater's wiring, making sure it would last the winter. We did what we could packing up the leftover, perishable food, but with Annie and Jack running into the kitchen every few seconds, there was only so much that could be done. Eventually, the day became what it always becomes – the lot of us out on the beach.

I taught Jack how to throw a Frisbee that day, while Aaron and Annie built a small civilization around the sandcastle they'd already built. We all waded into the water, too, where I stayed long after the others had gotten out. All day long we laughed and smiled and played in picturesque perfection. It was like the first montage of every 90's movie you've ever seen – the happy one, not the sad, moping one that comes just after everything went to hell and just before everything gets fixed. It was perfect, and I remember stopping to look around every few minutes to think just that, with what I'm sure was a goofy smile on my face.

My father sat above it all on the deck, like the king of Aaron and Annie's castle looking down on his subjects. When the sun began to set, he fired up the grill one last time, and while the others went to help get dinner ready, Aaron and I stayed on the beach with the kids.

"I'm sorry about the job," Aaron said, sitting next to me a few feet from the surf, the kids running around us.

"Thanks," I said, realizing, just then, that I hadn't thought about it since the day before. "It is what it is," I sighed, maybe to myself more than him, and stood up slowly, the pain in my side keeping me from moving quite as quickly as I'd like. "How's school?" I asked him, as I plucked a stone from the surf and skipped it out across the water. Three skips.

"It's school," he said, standing up to join me and grabbing his own stone. "It's whatever." Four skips. There aren't many similarities between pre-law and mechanical engineering, but for the two of us, there was at least one: It was easy. We'd always breezed through school.

"Have mom and dad started in on what you're doing after you graduate?" Two skips. They'd started in on me during my senior year. They didn't pressure me, per say, just suggested that I start looking at law firms and planning for my future.

"A little," he said. "Nothing too bad, just asking questions. Making sure I have answers, I think." Six skips.

I threw another – five skips – and bent down to grab one more when Jack ran over from stomping on the sandcastle.

"I skip?" he said happily, and bent down to grab a stone. He wound up and threw with this whole body, rocking his arm high above his head and jumping off the ground when he brought it forward. It landed with a thud – no skips – but he didn't seem to care. So, we stood for the next few minutes, all three of us, shoulder to shoulder skipping stones. Fours and fives and sixes for Aaron and me. None for Jack. Eventually, I grabbed a small white table off the porch and we stacked it full of stones – taking turns grabbing one or two and tossing them out into the blue.

Four. Six. Two. Three. Five. And on we went until Aaron let out a short, sharp yell and ran off toward the house.

"I forgot," he came out shouting a few seconds later, carrying his flashlight. "I think I figured it out," he said breathless. He had the flashlight turned on as he ran, but standing with me now, he unscrewed it and produced a new, smaller battery, with less wiring than its previous version. "The relays were too much. It was overheating."

"So, it won't explode this time?" I asked, watching Jack pluck another stone from the table and rifle it into the surf. No skips.

"Well, it shouldn't," he answered, looking into the flashlight and noticing something that needed adjusting. He set the battery down on the table and reached inside the plastic tube to fix whatever had caught his eye.

Neither of us saw it coming. I don't know how, but it never occurred to us, not until Jack reached out and grabbed the battery like it was any other stone we'd plucked from the water. But we saw it then, and we saw it when he raised his arm up above his head. Aaron, me, and even Dad and Ed from the porch. We all saw it. And we all cried out, but it was as if no sound came out at all. It all happened in slow motion. Jack's arm came down as his feet came off the sand, and

102

the battery flew into the air – the metal cylinder spiraling end over end in a rainbow arc, cutting the thick sea air and touching down with a splash – bouncing twice and disappearing below the surface.

Two skips.

I shouted again, this time more of a guttural exclamation than anything intelligible. We stood for a second in shock, blinking hard and shaking our heads at the surprise of it before I took off sprinting toward the water and dove in head first. By the time I'd gotten in, Aaron was there too.

We each took a few frantic dives but came up empty. The last time I came up for air, I noticed Jack crying on the beach – sure he'd done something wrong but unsure what. I stepped out of the water, picked him up and held him close to my chest.

"Two skips," he whimpered into my shoulder.

"I know, buddy," I said. "It's Ok. It's OK." Ed and our father had come off the porch as a surprisingly calm Aaron climb slowly from the water, his sweatshirt and pants clinging to his body.

"Well, shit" dad said quietly, and there was almost a hint of a laugh at the absurdity of it all. But just as I started to say something to him, Ed let out a high-pitched cry.

"There!" he yelled, pointing a few feet in front of us, where the battery was floating up the beach with whatever was left of a crashing wave.

"Grab it!" we all screamed together, making dramatic lunges as the sea pulled it back toward the water and another wave threatened to break on top of it. It was Aaron who got to it first, still coming up out of the water. He dove and landed on it with his full length, like a football player recovering a fumble – not one accustomed to having the ball in his hand, but a lineman who tries to envelop it with his whole body to make sure its secure.

He came up cradling the battery, jumping through another crashing wave and sprinting up the beach, the rest of us close behind, yelling toward the house to grab some towels.

"I need a hair dryer!" Aaron yelled, bursting through the back door. I can't imagine what we all looked like at that moment. Four grown men and a sobbing toddler, two fully dressed and soaking wet, all shouting and demanding. I'd like to think we resembled those beautifully chaotic ER scenes in every hospital drama you've ever seen, but we probably just looked like bumbling fools.

"We don't have a hair dryer," Maggie answered, startled by the scene in front of her.

"Why is Jack crying?" Mom.

"Fine. Get me some towels and a bucket of rice." Aaron.

"Rice?" Mom.

"Who has a *bucket* of rice lying around?" Maggie.

"Do we not have rice?" Aaron.

"We're white." Ed.

"And why is Jack crying?" Maggie.

"He's fine." Me.

"Any quinoa?" Aaron.

"Give me my son." Maggie.

"What the hell is quinoa?" Dad.

"What kind of white people are we?" Ed.

"Where are the damn towels?!" Aaron.

"I have them!" Bethany shouted from upstairs, running down with them as I passed Aaron a few napkins and he desperately tried to dry off the battery. "What happened?" she yelled as she ran. Aaron, screwdriver in hand, recounted the story to her while opening the battery's outer casing and patting it with towels, and the two of them began talking shop about possible damage and potential fixes.

"This isn't working," he said after a few minutes. "I've got to go find a hair dryer and some other supplies."

"I'll drive you," I volunteered. Aaron wrapped the battery tightly in one of the towels and wound every one of the junk drawer's rubber bands around it, asking Bethany to sit with it like it was a sick child and we were running to the next county for help from the medicine woman.

We didn't bother to change before running out the door, and told the rest of the family to eat without us. Ed threw us a few towels to lay over the seats, and we pulled out of the driveway near sunset, heading for what we called the "everything" store just up the block.

Forgetting that we weren't in the suburbs anymore.

I hadn't even gotten out of the car when Aaron started back to the passenger side. Closed. We drove further up the road to the hardware store, but that, too, was closed. Everything was. The craft store. Closed. The home goods store. Closed. The office supply shop. Closed. On and on we drove as evening turned to night, but found nothing but the ice cream stands open for business.

Aaron sat motionless in the passenger seat – he's not the kind to vent frustration, he buries it – and I found myself wishing for him that we were back in Saratoga, where the florescent lights of any business we could possibly need would draw us in like the beacon at the base of a runway. There are none of those lights in The Cape – just dark shops abandoned in favor of a final few waves or the final few minutes of sunset.

"Alright," he eventually sighed, throwing in the towel. "Let's go home."

"You sure?"

"Yeah," he said, turning to look out the window. "I've built it twice. I'll build it again."

"I'm sorry, bud," I offered, unsure what else to say.

"It's alright. At least Jack finally got a skip out of it," and we both chuckled a little as I turned the car around and headed home.

By the time we got back, the family had scattered. Maggie and her husband were putting their kids to bed, while mom, dad, Ed, and Ed's wife sat on the porch drinking wine with Bethany asleep on the couch. Neither Aaron nor I touched the dinners that were staying warm for us in the oven. Instead, he checked the battery for anything salvageable and I updated my parents before walking past them out toward the water. I sat down on the beach and looked up, marveling at how dark it was, and how many stars you could see shining out of the black.

Chapter 23

The next morning, we all went into Chatham for brunch –
something you can only do in the fall, after the summer crowd has
thinned. After, we walked up and down Main Street, giving one last
pass through the shops and boutiques. I never buy anything on these
trips, but I always make a point of tagging along – charmed as I am
with the swept sidewalks and landscaped gardens, and the way the
church steeple rises above the rest of the town, glistening in the bright
sun like the ivory tower looking down over the city on a hill.

Contently, almost lazily, I strolled behind the others as we
made our way up a hill toward the street's East end, where you start
to smell the ocean and feel its cool breeze. The already thinned crowd
was reduced even more, there – the normal bustle replaced by just a
few straggling passersby. Maybe that's why we noticed a store we'd
never seen before. 'Vivi Nell'amore' it was called. I remember
smiling at the name as I walked through the door to that familiar ring
of a bell. Stores in towns like these always have names like that.
There's no 'Bob's Hardware,' or 'Jake's Furniture.' It's always random
sayings like 'Tale of the Cod' or something foreign.

The shop itself is set back from the street in the back corner of
a small courtyard. There's a large oak tree in the center of the square
with long, dangling branches that hang over the corner of the store,
and pink, flowered bushes lining the border.

Stepping inside, it was as colorful as it was perfectly cluttered.
The front door opened into a square room, with a hallway off the back
that ran along the edge of the courtyard. There were picture windows

on either side of the front room, with glass sculptures hanging in each – catching the light and throwing color in all directions, like the store itself was a kaleidoscope, and the glass jewelry and seashell-pressed ceramics and driftwood centerpieces were all flecks of brilliant paint inside the bright, sparkling tube. I walked in a circle around the front room and followed the trace of the store down the back hallway, which opened into a room of brilliant light, with stark white walls stocked with photographs for sale – black and whites and gorgeous color prints of what I recognized to be Cape Cod beaches and ports. There were the dunes at Nauset and the walkway at the Coast Guard Beach, and the lighthouse less than a mile away in Chatham.

Back in the main room, I could hear one of the workers telling my mother that the owner makes everything herself – the jewelry and the sculptures and the pictures. I remember imagining her life, how she spent her days hunting the beaches for the perfect piece of driftwood and going each night to a different beach to get another sunset photograph for the wall.

I continued through the photo room, scanning each image one by one, and there, in the back corner was a black and white picture of a lifeguard stand with a deep gouge running up one side, and bright sunlight shining through the hole in the wood. It was the one from the beach we went to as kids, as beautiful as I've ever seen it. A second later I heard someone walking down the hall, but by the time I'd turned, all I saw was a flick of auburn hair disappearing behind the "employees only" door. A moment later, my mother was calling to me that they were leaving. The first time all day they were ready before I was.

We drove back to the beach house after that, and while the others packed up their things and headed back to New York, I sat on the porch and looked at the driftwood on our beach and the shells in our surf, and thought about that beach where I first learned to lay in the water, and wondered how much could fit into that little shop.

Eventually, I packed my parents up, and stealing one final look out at the horizon, pulled myself into my car and drove back west, as everything I'd let myself forget gradually poured back in.

Chapter 24

"There's nothing for me here, is there?" I asked quietly, lifting my head up to look Harry in the eyes.

"No, there isn't" he answered in a soft, sad monotone. We were sitting side by side in his office, each on the visitor's side of his desk in the leather-padded chairs he had set up. This was the end of our talk. I'd come in to apologize for the way I'd left on Friday, and after that, the conversation shifted. We talked for a while that morning, longer than we should have. I had played the conversation out in my head the night before as I walked through my quiet, dark apartment, and each time, it ended there, with Harry and I exchanging those same words. "I'm sorry, Connor."

He still had nothing to apologize for, so I told him as much and restated my own apology as a shadow appeared in the door.

"You better go," he said, and I stood to leave. I stepped past Mr. Carver and his charcoal gray suit on the way out, nodding, unsure what to say and even less sure where to go next. I ended up wandering through the halls for a while, stopping to read some of the old articles hung as decoration throughout the building – like I'd taken the day off to stroll through a museum. Eventually, I ended up at my desk for the first time that day.

Before I sat down, I offered the same apology to Rick, who didn't understand what I was talking about, and instead, showed me a copy of the Sunday issue I'd left on my doormat when I'd come home the night before. There, on the front page of the opinion section, just below Wallace Williams' debut column, was a submission from

Connor Hall. Harry had run the column about the coach in full. Unedited. Under my name. I was filled with love in that moment for my gruff, rough editor, and I suddenly felt even worse about Friday, and about whatever it was I carried out to and back from the Cape.

I smiled as I re-read what I'd written, but as I got down toward the end, I found myself replaying that morning's talk with Harry.

"There's nothing for me here, is there?"

"No, there isn't."

When I finished the column, there were tears in my eyes.

Chapter 25

I took a lot of drives in the weeks that followed. Long car rides with no destination in mind, just the road and the radio. I don't remember a single word I wrote during those weeks, but I remember those rides, and I remember the talks Mack and I would have when I came home. I remember Mack asking me what I was going to do if there was no future at the paper, and I remember that I didn't have an answer, but I remember that she did. And I remember the detail with which she explained it.

"My dad wants to give you a job at the firm," she said. "And once you're there, they'll pay for you to go to law school and take the bar." There was excitement in her voice as she said it all, recounting each detail like part of a master plan.

I wanted desperately to share her excitement – wanted to feel the same energy and passion – but I couldn't, and when I told her as much, her excitement turned to exasperation. It was the third time we'd had the talk when it all boiled over, when she unloaded what must have been years of pent up frustration.

"You are 27 years old, Connor," she said standing over the stove while we made dinner. "You're turning 28 soon. When are you going to act like it?"

Again, I didn't have an answer for her, but Lord knows I spent the rest of the night searching for one.

I was still up hours later when Mike called. It was two or three in the morning when the phone rang. I was out on the couch staring into a spot just short of the TV, waiting for the call. That was the anniversary of his dad's death, and we had both taken that day off and gone to the cemetery.

I picked him up from his house that morning and we drove quietly to the graveyard. I parked a few rows away and walked with him over to his dad's headstone, but walked on like I always do while he sat beside it and spoke to his father. I thought back to the day we buried him, and that beautiful sunshine, and how wrong it all seemed. He called to me eventually and we rode back to his house in the same silence. After, we sat in his living room – half painted and half baby-proofed – until Mike came back to life a bit. He picked up one of his father's old guitars and I picked up his, and we spent the afternoon trading licks and getting back to normal until Sarah came home to him and I headed back to Mack.

I knew he'd call later that night. He almost always does, and I try to stay up to make sure I'm there to answer it.

"What if it happens to me?" he asked as soon as I'd picked up.

"What?"

"What if it happens to me?"

"It won't, Mike," I said. His voice was quivering but his breathing was calm and even, like this had been festering all night, growing inside him until he couldn't contain it, until he had to say it, even if his vocal chords couldn't stand to make the words.

"We would have both said that about my dad."

"Mike," I started, but he cut me off.

"Connor. What if I die?" I shuddered at the thought, remembering the funeral and everything Mike lived through for years. Everything he's still living through today. "I don't want my kid to be alone."

113

"He never will be," I said, the same tears welling up in my eyes that I'm sure were in his. "Ever."

"I don't want him to wake up like this."

"He won't. And if he does, we'll be there with him. I promise you." There was silence for a while, as I heard Mike's breathing quicken, but then, start to slow back down.

"I miss him, Connor. I wish he was here."

"I know you do. But he is here. I know it."

"You believe in that stuff?" he asked. His voice evening out.

"I believe fathers never leave their sons."

Chapter 26

The summer before our final year in college, I was an intern at Goldberg and Sons, a law firm in our area. It was a lot like Winter and Wall, with the same quiet, sullen floors and quiet, sullen people. I was struck by that on my first day. How quiet it was. How quiet everyone was. How little you could hear if you tuned out the ringing phones.

A junior associate charged with supervising the interns showed me to my desk that day. He led me out of the main conference area where we'd sat through hours of orientation and deeper into the building's back corner. We walked through rows and rows of cubicles, winding our way through the pods of four and six like we were navigating a maze. Finally, we turned a corner and came upon what would be my cube, with my desk bolted into the side of the wall, just in case I thought about taking it.

I stood at the desk for a minute or two after the associate had left, peaking my head over the walls to look at the rest of the floor and seeing little more than a sea of gray – cubicle after cubicle under the soft glimmer of incandescent lighting, with only glimpses of real light peeking through the open doors of the partners' offices. The only other people I saw were the three other interns, each peeking their own heads over the tops of their cubicles.

I spent my summer reading and re-reading judges' opinions and researching and re-researching a few arguments they needed fact-checked. I proofread and I copy-edited briefs and every now and then, I'd stand up and survey the landscape. I'd go cross-eyed staring for hours at the same books, then come up for air to rub my face and recharge with a change in perspective – though nothing ever did change. For all the months of my internship, it was always the same maze of gray and the same crossed eyes.

A few months after it ended, on a cold November day, I found myself thinking a lot of Goldberg and Sons. It was my senior year and I was in the basement of our college library reading a few opinions I needed for a paper I was writing. I'd read each of the decisions four or five times that summer, but I had to go over them again for the essay. I spent a while that day trying to remember what case I'd read them for, but more than that, I remember having to read each paragraph two or three times. I'd get through a paragraph, or sometimes an entire page, and realize that I didn't remember anything I'd just read.

I was sitting toward the back of the room in a small desk among dozens of others. The desks were old and wooden, with decades of doodles on not just their tops, but on the blinders that came up on three sides to help provide a little bit of privacy.

I don't know how long I'd been at it, but at some point, I remember coming to the end of another page with no clue what I'd read and leaning back in my chair to rub my eyes and regroup. I looked around the room and noticed, for the first time, I think, how large it was. Row after row of desks, with stack after stack of books and encyclopedias beyond them stretching out for miles it seemed – all under the same pale, jaundiced light that turned the already beige walls the color of a smoker's twisted smile.

One of the lights was flickering, like it was about ready to burn out but was hanging on to whatever it could for as long as it could. I watched it for a few seconds until my eyes couldn't take it any longer. I looked back to the rest of the room but after staring at the light, all I could see was gray. I blinked and rubbed my eyes again and sat back down to restart the page I'd just read, but when I finished the second time I still couldn't remember it, so I started on the third and the fourth, and on the fifth, I kicked back from my desk and up onto my feet, noticing for the first time how heavy I was breathing, and that I was still only seeing gray. I looked up at the rest of the room, which didn't look so large anymore, and looked, instead, like it was getting smaller, and before I even realized what was happening, I was moving, my feet carrying me out from behind the desk and toward the stairs at the opposite end of the room. I was running, and then sprinting, and when I hit the stairs I took them two and three at a time until I was on the main floor in the sunlight, but still sprinting out to and through the lobby, throwing open the doors and stumbling out into the cold November wind, sucking in the frigid air as fast as I could.

Chapter 27

Those next few weeks at *The Tribune*, I took walks. Long, aimless walks through parts of the building I'd somehow never been in before. I didn't tell anyone about Mack's offer, but I thought about it a lot, and thought a lot about my writing, too – and thought just as much about how I couldn't make sense of either, and even more about why.

Every now and then I'd think about it all too long and scare the hell out myself, like I'd swam down to the bottom of the deep end and stayed a little too long for comfort, and after, I'd come up gasping for air. On those days, I'd take Mack out on surprise dates or join Brady and Mike for happy hour or go home to see my parents. Some days, I did all three. I'd go to bed happy for every bit of it, but lie awake wondering why that didn't seem to be enough, and stay up even longer scolding myself that it was. I'd go back to work those next mornings refusing to wander. I'd swear I would park myself in my old, lousy chair and thank God I had that much. And each day, it worked for a while, but somewhere along the way, my feet always seemed to take over.

I was on one of those walks when I got a text from Mike. He was asking Brady and me to meet him for a drink. It was Friday afternoon and my chair wasn't looking as comfortable as a seat at Paddy Murphy's, so I left a little early that day and beat them both there, grabbing a table in the back corner of the loft section, looking out on the backyard.

The vibrant fall colors were starting to fade on the tree out the window. In the wind, the smaller branches swayed and twisted, dropping their leaves onto the browning gardens beneath them. Mike and Brady came eventually – Brady first, then Mike – and while Brady and I sipped beers, Mike drank from his soda and blurted out why he'd asked us to meet him.

"We signed!" he said after a long, bracing sip – a sip you'd expect with a drink far stiffer than Sprite, and from someone with a much harder truth to tell. "The Lizards, we signed with the record company!" he continued after Brady and I responded only with confused glances.

That second time he got more of the reaction he wanted. Apparently, they'd been in talks for a few weeks and had finally closed the deal earlier that day. They'd be heading into the studio as soon as they could and at some point, would do a small tour in the Northeast to help raise their profile – probably in the summer while he was off from school, after he and Sarah had taken time with the baby. When he mentioned Sarah, he let out a cry and jumped back from the table suddenly.

"Shit!" He said. "I totally forgot. I've got to go. But you guys should come. Call Mack and Kaitlyn, have them meet us at the house." He was speaking as quickly as I'd ever heard him, and before we could really answer he was heading toward the door. I watched him go, and noticed how loose and baggy his jacket and pants looked on him. I turned back to Brady and we smiled at each other and grabbed our coats to follow – but not without one final look outside at the fading fall foliage.

Mike and Sarah spent nearly everything they had to buy and fix up their house. They'd been looking casually since the day they married, but after they found out about the baby, they jumped at one they'd had their eyes on. They'd been fixing it up ever since, and had just finished getting the repairs done. This was the first time we got to see the whole house as a finished product.

It's a small ranch with a master bedroom upstairs and a good-sized den off the back. Though he'd left a minute or two before us, we all arrived at about the same time, and we followed Mike in through the garage and into the kitchen.

"Sarah?" he called out, turning the corner toward the den with the two of us in tow. "Whoa!" he yelled jumping back as Brady and I made the turn and saw what he'd just seen. There, in the middle of an elegantly decorated den – with an antique rocking chair and a piano and a hand-made coffee table – was our friend's wife, nearly eight months pregnant and sprawled out across the couch and that coffee table. Her upper back and head were on the middle of the sofa, while her butt and one leg rested on the table. The other leg was pointed toward the ceiling, and both arms were stretched out toward it, reaching desperately. She was almost there; her fingers were just centimeters from her foot as she rocked her chest forward in small pulses. Her tongue was hanging out the side of her mouth as she maneuvered, like it, too, was searching for something just out of reach. It was, I can honestly say, one of the most absurd things I've ever seen.

When she heard us, she shrieked and flailed her arms and legs wildly. She tried to scramble to her feet, but like a turtle on its back, there wasn't much she could do but rock gently from side to side. After a second, she ended up kicking out the table and sliding down onto the carpet with a thud.

"Hi, Sarah," Brady said matter-of-factly, as Mike stumbled toward her. "How's it going?"

"Oh, you know. Great," she sighed. "What are you guys doing here?" There wasn't any trace of anger or unrest in her voice, and certainly less than you'd expect from a pregnant woman who'd just spent the last few seconds flopping around like a fish tossed out onto the deck.

"Sorry, I forgot to call," Mike said, getting to his wife's side. Apparently, Sarah's feet had been hurting, and they'd been using a cream that had been helping. Mike usually rubbed it on her when he got home each day, and when he ran late, she decided to see if she could do it herself.

She couldn't.

Mack and Kaitlyn were on their way, and in the meantime, Mike and Sarah showed us around, narrating all they'd done with the place. The new doors, the painted trim, the wood paneling they'd removed from one of the smaller bedrooms where Mike had put some exercise equipment he'd bought a few months before. The new cabinets, the grandfather clock they'd scored at an estate sale up north.

"This is different, eh?" Brady said to me quietly. He was right. Brady lives in a small house he rents from his parents. I lived in an apartment. Mike and Sarah had a *home*. Their furniture all matched. Their walls were blue and light red, not the same lifeless pewter haphazardly rolled over the stains of a previous tenant. There was fine china displayed under professional lighting and matching custom knobs on all the cabinets – which all had locks on them to go with the artificial rounding on all the tables' corners.

When Mack and Kaitlyn arrived, they got their own tour, but while Brady stayed behind in the den, I tagged along – taking in the polished floors and wall treatments one more time. After, we sat in the den talking and drinking. Brady and Kaitlyn talked about picking out the centerpieces for the wedding and everyone got a turn feeling Sarah's belly as the baby kicked. And eventually Brady, Mike, and I ended up on the cold back deck where Mike said he was thinking of building a screen house, talking about how we loved the one at my parents', and about his new record deal and the debate over whether to shut down the failing website at Brady's office.

Chapter 28

I took even more walks that next week. I wrote my columns, but at least a few times a day I found myself wandering the Tribune's many floors, retracing past steps through familiar, well-traveled halls, and charting others I'd never explored like I was searching for buried treasure somewhere amid the brick and mortar.

At night, I stayed up late. I'd sit on the couch long after Mack had gone to bed flipping through the channels, landing on a sitcom re-run or a West Coast NHL game. When I finally did turn in, I often laid awake, enjoying the sound of Mack sleeping peacefully next to me – watching her chest rise and fall with each breath. In waves, thoughts of the Tribune would come at me, rising and crashing in a silent back and forth with thoughts of Winter and Wall behind them. In between, I counted Mack's calm, steady breaths and felt my temperature rise with each passing one, holding back a scream for not stopping the tide like I thought I could. Eventually, reality would turn to dream, until the alarm clock called me back.

Mack took Friday off that week. I remember slipping out silently to let her sleep in. I wish I could tell you what I wrote about, but I can't. I don't remember much of it, and I certainly don't remember what I was working on when Harry called me into his office, but I know it was almost the end of the day.

"Take a seat," he said when I walked in, after throwing my things into my bag with the phone I hadn't bothered to look at all day. "And close the door." My chest tightened when he said it, and I locked eyes with him as I carefully swung it shut. Harry's door was never closed. Ever. He always said we were in the business of exposing secrets, not keeping them. And as I thought about it in that split second, I realized that every time I remember that door being shut, there was someone to say goodbye to a few minutes later. I could feel my heart sink back into my chest as I sat down, nervous.

"You've got two options," Harry said sternly, cutting to the chase. As he did. "Either pick it up, or take this sheet of paper," he said, holding up his legal pad.

"What?" I asked, everything moving within me freezing at that moment.

"You've been here a couple years," he said. "Nothing you'd written had inspired anything for the Sunday cover, let alone appeared on it." He was leaning back, those thick arms crossed at his chest. "It happened four times in those few weeks we were looking for a columnist and it hasn't happened since. Why do you think that is?" The question landed with a thud between us, and all I could do was look at it and wonder, never having thought about any of it.

"I don't- I don't know," I said.

"I think I do," he said, "but that's for you to figure out," and he leaned forward and picked up his legal pad. "I've got a job idea for you," he said sternly.

"What?" I asked, incredulous and off-balance.

"CapitolBeat.com," he answered. "It's a start up covering state politics in Albany."

"Harry, I don't…" I started, with no idea where I would be finishing.

"There's nothing here for you Hall," he said, leaning back in his chair. "We've said it before. There's nothing here. But there may be there." Again, I wanted to say something, but the words escaped me. "I know the editor, and I think he'd like some of your stuff."

There was an 'A + B = C' rhythm to the way he talked. "It's nothing glamorous. It's entry level, so you'd start out proofreading and taking care of whatever they need, but keep your head down, do good work, and you'll get there eventually. If you commit to it." That last part wasn't as much like the recitation of an equation. There was almost something fatherly in it, or maybe that's just me projecting as I look back – it's hard to tell after everything that's happened.

"Harry," I finally said through a smile. In the moment, I didn't know what to make of it, but my whole body filled with gratitude for him. "Thank you. This is…I can't even describe it."

"Well, that's something you'll need to work on. Describing things would be a big part of the job," he joked without changing tone. "Don't mention it." He tore off a sheet of paper from his legal pad and scribbled on it. "This is his contact info. Give him a call, or email him or whatever, and I'll give you a recommendation," he said, extending the paper. "Now go away," he finished, grabbing his Friday cigar from the pine box he keeps on his windowsill.

I thanked him again as I stood to leave, my body working again at hyper drive as I started walking. I was planning to make the call as soon as I got back to my desk, and I was looking down at the paper as I walked, not paying any attention to where I was going. And neither, I guess, was Wallace Williams, who walked straight into me as I did the same to him. Bouncing off, we each took a step back to get our feet back underneath us.

There's a certain look you expect of a news anchor. You expect a sharp suit. You expect perfect hair. You expect great skin. Wallace Williams had all of that. A clean, sharkskin gray suit with a crisp white shirt and baby blue tie, with thick, stubborn hair that moves only when he wants it to move, and the tan of someone who'd spent the last 12 years in southern California rather than upstate New York.

There was something in him I didn't expect, though. He was young. Far younger than I'd realized – maybe just a few years older than me. It set me back a bit as I looked at him, wondering how he'd ended up with an old man's resume at a young man's age.

"Sorry about that," he said, patting me on the shoulder with what I'm sure was that week's column, on his way to Harry's office. "Didn't see you there."

"Yeah, no, I'm sorry, I stammered, still trying to ground myself.

"Wallace Williams," he announced, extending his hand. I took it, trying my best to extend a firm, hard hand.

"Connor Hall," I said, in what sounded like a sigh when it came out of my mouth.

"Oh, you're Connor!" he exclaimed. "I've been wanting to meet you. Harry gave me a bunch of your columns when I started. They're great!"

"Thanks," I said smiling, as a sonar ping of sadness and anger spread from my center. "I appreciate that."

"Hey, I've got to run," he said. "Harry wants to go over a few things, but we should get a drink some time!"

"Absolutely," I said. "That would be great."

"Awesome, we'll talk," and he turned away down the hall.

"Wallace!" I called out, and he turned around to face me, backpedaling toward Harry's office. "Welcome to the *Tribune*. We're glad to have you."

"Thanks!" and he turned back around and bounded out of view. I turned and headed back to my desk, re-reading the contact information Harry had given me a moment before. When I got back to my desk, I stood for a minute, reading it again and glancing at the phone on my desk. Eventually, I folded the note and put it in my wallet, then grabbed my bag and headed for the door.

Chapter 29

On the way home that night, I got lost – though that may not be the best way to describe it. You know how sometimes you zone out in the car and end up back home with no memory of the drive? Like the car just drove itself? That's what happened on my way home, only, I didn't end up at home. Instead, I was out on a highway, driving east, with no destination in mind.

I pulled off at the next exit after coming to, and guided the car back to my apartment complex, where I parked and lingered in the space as the last few streaks of sunlight faded to black. Eventually, I headed in, falling in step behind Doug, who was carrying inside a bag of Chinese food, shoulders slumped as he lumbered toward the door. He held the door for me and we exchanged nods before he started down the stairs and I headed up to my apartment and opened the door.

Which is when all my friends jumped out and screamed 'surprise!'

—

I've never been someone who makes a big deal of his birthday. It comes. I go out for a drink. It passes. I observe it, but rarely ever celebrate it.

To forget it, though, is something else entirely.

28. Shit.

I smiled and stood in the doorway, looking over the crowd, shaking my head and laughing. From the back, Mack bounced toward me in her black jeans and tank top and threw her arms around me.

"Happy Birthday," she whispered in my ear after kissing me on the cheek. I kissed her back and we waded into the crowd, greeting Brady and Kaitlyn and Mike and Sarah – out, even at eight months pregnant. Noah and Will had come up from D.C. It felt good to see them, I hadn't since Brady's bachelor party a few months before. They were standing in the middle of the dining room that sat just off my entryway, with the living room off one corner and the kitchen and a hallway toward the bedrooms off the other. Aaron and Bethany had come, too, standing next to Noah, talking about whatever.

But catching my eye was the skinnier guy in the back, with dark curls popping out from beneath his trademark, low-pulled beanie. Z had come.

"Happy birthday," he said to me, tipping the top of his long neck toward me.

"Hey!" I said, running toward him, seeing him for the first time in months.

"Couldn't miss your birthday," he said, as if reading my mind.

"Great to see you," I answered, pulling him into a hug. "You in town long?"

"Nah. There's some Thanksgiving craft fair they want me to shoot," he said, shaking his head. "They're putting together another 'I Love New York,' so they have me all over." Z shot and directed videos for New York State. Whatever they wanted, he did. Before swinging through Saratoga, he had been crisscrossing New York, videotaping events in Niagara Falls and Long Island, and the next day he would end up in the Adirondacks. A few weeks later, we'd see everything he shot in a commercial on TV.

"That's great," I said, smiling widely. "Touring the whole state in a few days."

"Yeah, it's cool," he said with no expression, just nodding slightly, taking a long sip of his beer. "What about you? How's work?" I filled him in as best and as quickly as I could – telling him about the columnist job, and about not getting it, and I was just starting in on the job idea Harry gave me that day when Brady, Mike, Noah, and Will joined us.

"What do you think you'll do?" Mike asked.

"I don't know," I said, shrugging my shoulders.

"Sounds like a good idea," Z said quickly.

"It definitely is," I said. "I just don't know."

"What's not to know?" Z again.

"I don't know," I said a third time, not trying to dodge his question, but truly lacking a firm answer.

"It's entry level, right?" Brady asked. "Isn't it a little beneath you?" he continued after I'd nodded.

"No, I think it's right where I am," I said honestly.

"So, what the hell?" Will asked in his own way.

"I don't know," I said again laughing, and told them about the job offer from Mack's father.

"That sounds awful," Z scoffed, looking me in the eye as we all laughed.

"It has its benefits," I answered. "You know, like…benefits. It's a career, it's stable."

"But is it what you want?" Z asked one more time, pressing the issue.

"Would you believe me if I said I don't know?" I joked, and we all laughed again, one laugh a little more nervous than the others. "I'm trying to figure it out," I continued. "I take a lot of walks at work, nowadays. Like long, meandering walks. That's not a good sign, right?" I asked it with another laugh, with nods and chuckles in response, until Noah spoke up and stopped them cold.

"I had my hand inside a baby's chest today," he said, turning toward something that caught his attention across the room. "It was awesome." None of us had any idea how to react. We stood there, mouths agape, just looking at him as he turned back toward us. "What's that?" he asked motioning, and walked away, leaving us to pick our jaws up off the floor.

A second later Mack came out of the kitchen with dinner, and our attention turned to food. We ate and drank and played games for the next few hours. Eventually, the party split into different groups. Aaron and Bethany and Noah were around the coffee table, Noah focused on what had caught his eye earlier. It was a wooden puzzle Aaron had built and brought with him – a three-dimensional star that could become a perfect cube with the right combination of moves. In the dining room were Mack, Brady, Sarah, and Kaitlyn; and in the kitchen were Mike and Will and Z – and I was bouncing between them all.

I love nights like those. I live for them. And God bless Mack, she knew exactly what she was doing when she planned that party. These friends of mine, and a block of time to do nothing but enjoy each other.

I talked with Mike for a while in the kitchen about the new songs he was writing before going into the studio with The Lizards, and sat with Aaron around the coffee table while Noah tried to figure out the puzzle. He told me about how he'd built a new battery from scratch after the last one took its dip in the ocean, and said it had been powering the flashlight for five straight days at that point.

Later that night, I came up on the dining room crew in the middle of a conversation about how Sarah managed to keep fit during her pregnancy. Sarah is a small, stick of a woman, with the frame of the cross-country runner she was in high school – the type of woman who gains baby weight only in her belly.

"I did a lot of running early on," she was saying. "Now I just do a lot of light muscle work – lots of squats, but I can only go so far." And when she said that, there beside our dining room table, with Brady and Kaitlyn and Mack and me watching, she pointed her knees to the outside, pulled up her dress, and squatted down to show us. "I have to angle my legs out so I don't hit my belly," she laughed, "but I try to do 20 of these a day." She did a second for us. And then a third. But just as she hit the bottom of her crouch on that final squat, the dining room's relative quiet was broken by a small splash on the hardwood floor.

Almost like someone had spilled their drink just below Sarah's squat.

Almost.

"Oh!" we all seemed to yell at once, jumping back a few steps. All of us, of course, but Brady.

"What the fuck?!" he shouted, with the tact and sensitivity of a carpet bomb, stumbling backward into and over one of the dining room chairs, regaining his balance in the doorway to the kitchen.

"Her water just broke," Noah called calmly from the same spot I'd left him in – without bothering to look up at us, without even taking his eyes off the puzzle he was still working on.

"WHAT?!" Mike screamed from inside the kitchen, and a fraction of a second later he was barreling into the room, not waiting for his path to clear. He ran square into Brady's back, his stride barely broken by Brady's thin frame. Brady hit the floor with a loud thud,

132

but you couldn't hear it over Mike. "But you're only at 8 months Ok ok ok what do we do are you alright baby are you in any pain what do we need to do?"

"She should go to the hospital," Noah called – again not bothering to pay us a glance from the living room.

"Fuckin' hell," Brady moaned, rolling onto his back, holding his ribs as everyone but Noah hustled into the dining room.

"Hospital right yes ok I'll get the car" Mike said after Sarah assured him she was fine, and he sprinted out of the building. I took Sarah's arm to help her out to the car, with Will stepping up to take the other one. Mack and Kaitlyn each called out instructions on how best to help her, and told Z and Aaron what to grab as they followed us out the door.

And I swear, as we reached the stairs, I heard Noah yell from behind us.

"I got it!"

Chapter 30

I stood outside a beat longer than the others, watching Mike's taillights fade into the distance. I'd offered to drive them to the hospital, but Mike was sure he could make it.

"Do me a favor," he said, after we'd helped Sarah into the car. "Call my mom. She's at the top of the phone tree; she'll take care of the rest." And with that, he was running back to his side of the car and pulling away from me.

Back inside, I did as he asked and gave his mother the good news, and the rest of us settled in. No one wanted to leave without hearing from Mike. We sat for days it seemed, waiting for one of our phones to ring. We tried as best we could to be casual, but there was a tension in the air. None of us knew what to do – how long we'd have to wait or when we should start worrying. It was a first for all of us, and none of us knew how to handle it. So, we sat around the coffee table and talked.

Noah told us why he'd had his hand in a baby's chest and Aaron told everyone about Jack throwing the battery in the ocean. As the clock ticked past midnight, we debated the merits of 'FRIENDS' as one of the great sitcoms of all time and the Eagles' place among America's greatest rock bands. And then sometime after two, while Z told us about meeting the governor, my phone rang.

"Mike?" I said, as though caller ID hadn't already confirmed it.

"IT'S A BOY!" he screamed from the other end, loud enough that the rest of the room heard and let out relieved sighs and jubilant cheers. "Andrew Reed Anderson, six pounds, one ounce."

"What a great name!" I yelled back, remembering that his father's name had been Andrew. "Congrats, Mike. How's Sarah?"

"She's great. Mother and baby are happy and healthy," he said, his voice bubbling with an excitement I'd never heard before. Ever. "Connor?" he said after a pause. "Can you and Mack come down to the hospital? We want you guys to meet him."

"Now?" I asked, surprised.

"Yeah."

"Absolutely, buddy. Anything you want."

Turning back to the group I found everyone hugging and all of a sudden, looking exhausted – like we'd all run a marathon waiting for word from Mike. I had barely hung up the phone, but as people broke from their embraces they started gathering their things to head home. Mack and I saw everyone out before hopping into my car for the hospital.

We had to talk our way past a nurse not used to 3 AM visitors in the maternity ward, but a few stern words only Mack could deliver did the trick, and a moment later we were stepping into their room.

It was a small, simple room – painted that shade of nothing hospital rooms and office buildings tend to be painted. It had a bed, a bathroom, a few folding chairs, and one heavy, leather recliner. And there, in a corner next to the bed was a crib, and inside was little Andrew Reed, who I knew I'd call Lou.

Mike had been in the recliner when we entered the room, but stood to greet us, with as wide a smile as I'd ever seen on his face. I gave him as long and as tight a hug as I could remember, and gave Sarah a tender kiss as she laid in the bed. If you looked hard enough, you could see they were exhausted – with dark bags under their eyes and greasy, unkempt hair – but their smiles did well to outshine the blemishes. I turned to the crib to get a look at the baby and did some counting, my heart swelling with each passing second. Ten fingers, ten toes, and one little dimple right in the center of his chin. A second later, Mike was by my side, picking up his son and handing him to me.

I was terrified as I held him. He was so small, smaller than I remember my niece and nephew being when they were born. I remember looking at his fingers, and holding them against mine, comparing the size, amazed at the difference. I sat down in the recliner to hold him, rocking him gently as he slept.

"Well, what do you say?" Mike asked me, and I realized that I hadn't heard whatever he'd said a second before. "We want you two to be the godparents," he said smiling. I looked up to see Mack was crying, and realized a second later that I was too.

"Absolutely," I said. "It would be an honor." I handed Lou off to Mack, and Mike and I hugged again. This time, the hug was even longer and deeper, full of two decades of history, and everything he's lived through. We cried into each other for a minute, until he pulled back and looked me in the eye.

"You were right," he said. "He never left me. I can feel him. I've felt him all night. Right here at my side." I thought back to that phone call a few months before, and about his father, and about the bond between a father and son. And felt a few more tears on my cheek. "You know," he said, "you two share a birthday. Born at 11:58." I smiled at the thought, and turned to look at him again. "I love you, Connor," he said.

"I love you, too."

Just as I said it, a nurse came in and Mack and I figured it was time to go. I shook Mike's hand and gave little Lou one final kiss, and went over to the bed to do the same to Sarah.

"Thank you," she said, pulling me close as I bent over the bed.

"It's an honor," I replied through a smile.

"No. Thank you for him," she said, nodding toward Mike. "Thank you for everything over the years." She was looking me in the eyes. "You were our only choice, you know that? Either you said yes or he didn't have a Godfather." The tears came back as she said it, and my voice failed me a second later, which is good, because I don't know what I would have said. I kissed her on the cheek and stole one last look at my Godson before taking Mack's hand and heading out the door.

Exhausted in our own, meaningless way, we didn't say anything as we walked the hospital halls. But as we stepped out into the pre-dawn darkness, I found myself looking into the black, tracing it for any signs of a coming dawn. Eventually, with my eyes still searching the sky, I broke the silence.

"McKenzie," I said. "Tell your dad I'll take the job."

Chapter 31

"Oh, Shit! Janice!"

The outburst startled me, breaking through the otherwise quiet office. I was standing in my cubicle, peering over its navy-blue walls across the tops of all the others. It was the first time Carl's yelling would startle me. It wouldn't be the last.

Carl Coughlin worked in the office closest to my cube. 20 years ago, he'd started out in that cube and rose through the company – eventually trading in felt walls for hard ones. I liked Carl immediately, and liked him more every day I worked under him.

It was noontime my first day at Winter and Wall when he called out, and I had only just been escorted to my desk after hours of orientation. I'd been standing there for a few minutes, I think, looking back on everything that had happened in the weeks since I told Mack I'd take the job.

Harry was standing behind his desk when I told him I was going back to law. He stayed quiet for a second before taking a deep, heavy breath and sighing.

"You're being an idiot," he said bluntly, with what looked like disappointment in his face. "You should reconsider," he continued, "but if you don't, good luck." He extended his large, strong hand and absorbed mine, making it look like a child's in his. It was a long handshake, with far more said by those hands than either of us spoke out loud. I hoped the whole time that he couldn't feel my pulse pounding in my palm, as the hollowness I'd felt once before in that office returned to my chest, and a question that had gone unanswered a few weeks before rang through my mind.

My parents were much more supportive when I told them. They had plenty of questions, and you could tell they had concerns, too, but while Harry doesn't have the time for it, they appreciate a good game of poker. My mother asked if I was sure the change was what I wanted, but neither she nor my father pressed when I nodded yes. Brady and Mike were somewhere in between. They didn't hide their skepticism, but they didn't force anything, either.

I didn't start at Winter and Wall until January, so more than a month went by between telling Mack I'd take the job, and when I actually started it. And that month was one of the busiest of my life. I took Mack out on dates when we had free nights, and on weekends, we went on trips to cabins in the mountains, or hotels down in the city. On other nights, I'd call Brady on my way out of *The Tribune* and meet him at Paddy Murphy's for happy hour, or for a concert at some club somewhere, or, one night, on a whim, a run out west for a Friday night at the casino a few hours away.

When neither was around, I went home to see my parents and checked in on Aaron and the battery, which was still powering that flashlight. After a few weeks, I started visiting Mike and Sarah and my godson. He grew so quickly in those first days, and yet, still seemed impossibly small. He'd been hairless when he was born, but a full head of wispy blonde hair was growing in. That dimple on his chin hadn't changed at all.

Close to Christmas, Mike asked me to come over and sit with him and the baby. Sarah was going out shopping with her mother – the first time she'd been out since giving birth. Mike didn't say it, but I think he was nervous to be home alone for the first time with his son.

"How's Lou?" I asked as I came in the door, taking in the bags under Mike's thinning face, and greeted by the familiar sound of Lou Reed singing his favorite Velvet Underground album.

"Lou?" he asked, his head cocking to the side.

"Andrew Reed Anderson?" I said, pointing up to connect the question to the music. "I know where you got Andrew, but don't tell me Reed wasn't on purpose," and a wry smile spread across his face. Lou was asleep when I got there, so Mike and I sat in the den talking quietly, with Mike gently, absentmindedly fingering one of his guitars. Later, when Lou woke up, I fed him while his dad expanded on what he'd apparently been writing while we talked. His father's son, little Lou smiled at the sound of the guitar, and hardly made a sound when I put him down in his crib and took a seat behind the piano. Remembering the lessons of my youth, I picked up what Mike was doing pretty quickly, and for the rest of the night we traded themes and melodies like we were back in school, until just as Sarah was pulling back into the driveway, we were putting the final touches on a new song.

It was a slow folk tune with an intricate guitar line supported by what I could still manage on piano. Listening to Lou softly coo as we played, we even wrote some lyrics about him, and sang in two-part harmony like it was one of our Simon and Garfunkel covers.

We played it for everyone at our annual Christmas party and Sarah cried when we finished. I remember smiling as I looked around the room at another night with most of my friends in one room. It was the same smile I had just a few days later at my parents' house as my siblings and I opened our presents.

A day later, the smile disappeared as I handwrote a goodbye letter to Harry, and it hadn't come back days later when Mack and I watched the ball drop, even as she grabbed me for a deep, passionate kiss. Instead, I thought about resolutions, and as Mack put her head on my shoulder, I watched the party in Time Square and told myself that this would be the year I finally figured this whole thing out.

"How's your first day?" Mack asked just after Carl had startled me, bounding up to me with excitement. She skipped the last few steps, and landed with both feet, like a gymnast who'd stuck the landing.

I had never seen her happier than she was in those weeks, and we were never better together. She pulled me into long, tight hugs whenever she could, and kissed me fully and ravenously almost as often. Her smiles were wider and our conversations were easier, with no more land mines buried beneath the surface, waiting to take my leg off when I couldn't help but stumble into it.

She looked incredible that day; her normally straight hair was in bouncy, subtle curls falling on either side of the glasses she only wears at work. I love it when she curls her hair, and I love those glasses.

"I haven't really done anything," I said, holding up all four inches of my orientation binder.

"Oh yeah" she snorted. "It gets better." Just as she got the words out, there was another cry from Carl's office. Apparently, he wasn't having the best day. "Don't mind Carl," she laughed, and started back toward the other side of the maze, toward her office. After she'd disappeared from view, I looked down to study mine for the first time.

The cube was bigger than I thought it would be. There was a gray, hard-plastic desk built into the corner of its walls, which were each made of that felt that lets you surround yourself with thumb-tacked memos and faxes. A plush, leather office chair was tucked under the desk, and in the opposite corner sat a wooden bookcase, stained dark and polished to a shine.

I ran my eyes across it all and sat down into the chair, the cubicles outside mine disappearing from view. I spun slowly in the chair and noticed that my doorway looked out only onto the blue of another cube, and turned back to face the desk and inspect my computer and phone, but jumped, instead, when Carl broke a silence I hadn't noticed.

"Connor Hall?" he asked quietly. "Oh, I'm sorry," he said quickly after noticing me jump. "Didn't mean to startle you."

"No, no, no," I laughed, standing and shaking his hand. "Don't worry about it." This was the first time I'd seen Carl, and he wasn't what I expected. I pictured a middle-aged, mustachioed rage factory with an expensive but unkempt dress shirt, the sleeves unbuttoned and pushed up haphazardly past his elbows. Instead, what I saw was a young, slim man who barely looked 30, let alone the 45 he was. His suit was perfectly pressed, but off the rack, not the tailored, designer three-pieces worn by the other partners. He had a thick head of hair he had grown out, so as he stood in front of me, part of the front had fallen into his face.

"Sorry I couldn't come get you from orientation," he apologized, brushing the hair back behind his ear. "I make it a point to pick up everyone in my division, but this case I'm working has gotten out of hand. Why don't you come over to my office and we'll get you settled in."

It was a spacious, sun-soaked office with a massive wooden desk and matching bookcases. A smaller, glass-topped table sat in one corner and pictures of his wife and kids were spread across each. What caught my eye, though, was the beautifully decorated surfboard standing up against the wall in the opposite corner, with a crashing wave on its top and an intricate seascape on the rest, with pinks and greens, and baby blues coloring a crowded coral scene of reef and fish and plant, all bustling below the surface of the water.

We talked for a while that day while I admired that surfboard, but I don't want to bore you more than I already am, so I'll just summarize:

Carl was my first of five bosses, and if I had any questions or concerns I should go to him directly at any time. He was sorry about the occasional yelling but he hated the intercom and he was excited to have me in the fold. And before I could get started in on a case they wanted me to get familiar with all of them, so I needed to spend the next few weeks reading up. It would be boring and he was sorry but there wasn't much he could do, and someone would be by with the boxes of paperwork later that day. And he couldn't then but eventually he'd take me to lunch and he had a conference call coming up so unpacking was probably the best thing for me to do.

So that's what I did.

Chapter 32

I read for weeks after that, pouring over filings and affidavits and motions and other court documents, getting up to speed. Each night, I'd leave the office well after the winter sun had given way to dark, and on most days, I was still visiting whomever I could until Mack wrapped up her day and met me at home. One night, when no one was free, I even took a stool at a sports bar near the office and spent an entire Ranger game talking to the guy next to me about the greatest goalies of all time.

At the end of my first week, I took Mack back to that restaurant she loves and she lit up the normally dark dining room with a wide, radiant smile, a smile that pulled a match out of me. Later, when I was finally up to speed with the old cases, we fell into a rhythm. Mack and I went out a few times a week. On weekends, Saturday nights became another date night, and Fridays, like one now-infamous Friday night at Paddy Murphy's, were for happy hour and whatever followed after.

I remember very little about that early February night, except that it started with something innocent from Brady.

"You know what I saw on one of our sites?" he asked. "Judge Amy? She makes $20 million a year."

If you grew up in the suburbs, you know Judge Amy. She's a TV judge who handles disputes over DVD players and couches with her trademark temper and resentment. Her show was required viewing on any vacation or sick day. You watched 'The Price is

Right,' then two hours of cheesy talk shows, then 'Judge Amy.' We took turns sharing our surprise, as the relative buzz of the room grew fiercer; until Brady opened a game of Questions with a Judge Amy-themed ask.

"Would you rather be Judge Amy making $20 million, or Chief Justice of the Supreme Court making 200 K?"

The question set off a furious argument that lasted the next few hours, with Brady and I battling back and forth as the bar filled up.

"You're making eight figures and you have no responsibilities whatsoever!" I remember him yelling at one point, as others in the bar began to take notice. We still had room to gesture wildly at that point, but not room enough room to do it without turning heads, particularly when you're half a foot taller than everyone else in the joint.

"You're a joke and nothing you do matters!" I know I yelled back, finishing my beer and asking for another. "You have no real impact on the world, and 200-K ain't exactly below the poverty line." Even Mack, who normally sat out our debates, weighed in. Not surprisingly, she was on my side, and argued as best she could. I know Kaitlyn jumped in too, but more than that, I remember a random woman from the group next to us leaning past her to make her case.

"Take the money and run," she said, igniting fireworks from Mack and me. Moments later, all of her friends were in on the debate, and a few minutes after that, when we were all still going toe-to-toe, I opened a tab and bought us all a round. Things get even fuzzier after that, but I know at some point, the conversation shifted to something about Congress, and shifted one more time after that to something about yo-yos and Rubik's Cubes, and I remember yelling at Brady while he and I stood in the center of a large circle.

"Congratulations, dude, you're the world's lamest street performer!" I shouted, with laughter all around and between us, the two of us flashing back to my parents' screen house and all the similar arguments we'd had before and are still having now – those arguments we love.

As the night grew later, the crowd grew larger, the bar grew hotter, the drinks grew stronger, and our stomachs grew weaker. Near last call, I pulled Mack toward the backyard and we both stepped outside, hot and weary and desperately needing to feel the cold winter air on our faces. We stood for a moment, side-by-side enjoying the cold, until we both bent over and threw up in the bushes.

It was late the next morning when I woke up, slowly rolling to my right as I always do, to stretch out into Mack's side of the bed and enjoy those perfect moments before you really wake up. But this time, instead of rolling into vanilla-scented emptiness, I turned and punched Mack in the side of the head.

She didn't even flinch when I did it; she just kept sleeping quietly with her head buried in her pillow and her arms and legs sprawled out as though at any minute investigators would come by to lay down a chalk outline.

The pounding in my head registered instantly as I quietly climbed out of bed and shuffled toward the kitchen, planning to make breakfast but instead, collapsing onto the couch. I closed my eyes and enjoyed the quiet apartment, hearing only the dueling ticks and tocks of the living room and kitchen clocks. The morning sun was warm and for a second, I thought I might fall back asleep, but instead, those ticking clocks began echoing in my head. They started quietly at first, but grew louder with each passing second – one tick then another, ping ponging back and forth and back and forth, tapping a staccato rhythm that grew louder and louder until it felt like it would drown out any sound I could make. I had been tapping my toes along with them at first, but soon, my tapping my feet were moving faster than the clocks and I was back up and down the hall to where Mack was still sleeping.

"McKenzie," I whispered, rubbing her back and kissing her cheek. "Let's go to the farmer's market."

"You're waking *me* up?" she grumbled, the irony of the situation not lost on her even though she was still only semi-conscious. It took coaxing, but eventually I got her up and we drove to the farmer's market around the corner where we were one in a sea of handholding couples enjoying their Saturday. She wanted to stay in that night, but I insisted on going out for dinner and an action movie, and the next day I spent the afternoon pulling Jack and Amy across my parents' lawn in one of our old sleds before we all ate dinner and my head hit the pillow the way it always seemed to in those months, with sleep overtaking my exhausted body just as soon as I laid down.

Chapter 33

"I can't wait to teach my kids how to surf," Carl told me over lunch, our suits clashing with the rundown interior of the hole-in-the-wall he'd picked for the occasion. When Carl insisted on taking me out, paralegals from other divisions told me to expect one of the steakhouses the firm uses to wine and dine its clients. They were wrong. And I'm glad they were.

Carl and I went to a place called Bash's; it's a burger joint that's become a legendary spot for locals. In high school, we used to sneak out during lunch when we got sick of stuffed crust pizza kept warm by a lava lamp. It's a small, dirty place, and the oil in the fryer probably hasn't been changed since in the Nixon administration, but the food is every bit as delicious as it is cheap, so you don't really care. It's not sheik or elegant, but it's got character.

"My dad first started teaching me when I was about the age of my oldest," he continued, talking about growing up outside of Los Angeles and picking out the surfboard in his office as a birthday present when he was still young. His dad saved for months to buy it, and the two of them went out every weekend. "I miss it," he finished, looking through me.

I wasn't expecting an emotional review of my boss's childhood, but it was impossible not to be charmed. Carl was funny and smart, and you have to admire a guy who can eat a double bacon cheeseburger with extra onions and not get a single stain on his dress shirt.

I asked about his wife and kids and he asked me about Mack and my niece and nephew as we waited for our lunch and lingered longer than we should have after we'd eaten it. Later, as I unrolled the sleeves I'd slid up while eating, he asked one final question.

"So, what are you hoping to accomplish here at Winter and Wall?"

"Honestly," I said, after thinking it through. "I'm not sure. I guess I just want to do well and carve out a home." Carl nodded, pursing his lips, as if deciding something.

"Let me ask you something, and please feel free to tell me I've gone too far," he said. "Why are you here?"

"What do you mean?" I asked, not offended, just confused, and maybe stalling as I considered how to answer.

"McKenzie used to come around and make me read the stuff you wrote in *The Tribune*," he said, revealing something I never knew about Mack, and swelling my heart with a rush of love for her. "It was really good. Why aren't you doing something like that?"

"I guess I wanted something more certain," I said, deciding only after I said it that I'd found the right answer.

"I can understand that," he replied, nodding his head. "Just make sure it's enough to get you through." He was looking through me again as he said it. "It's a good job, but you need to have your head in it. It can be frustrating and hectic sometimes, as you'll sometimes hear – I don't know if you've heard me yelling." We both laughed when he made the joke, and he told me again to come to him with any questions and said one more time how happy he was to have me in the firm. When we got back to the office, we shook hands and he promised to make sure we did it again sometime soon, and he slipped through his open door and sat down behind his desk. I stole a glance at his surfboard before turning to walk over to my cubicle, as a memory flashed in my mind, a memory from college, one I spent the rest of the day thinking about.

Chapter 34

The night I ran out of the library, I was lost. Everyone was. I wound up back at our college apartment explaining what happened and wondering aloud what I'd do next. No one had an answer. For the most part, everyone just looked confused.

Except Z. Z called it the 'first day of the rest of my life.'

Much of that night is a blur. I remember spending it with Mack, our first night together. I remember tossing and turning while she slept next to me, and not knowing what to do after she'd left, because when Z appeared at my door with a crazy idea, I couldn't figure out how to say no.

Neither of us had ever been to Atlantic City before that day, and as we came over a long bridge and drove down into its heart, we were both surprised by the glitz. It was midafternoon when we rolled in, but even as the sun beat down, the lights on the casino marquees were as bright as they were gaudy. There was hustle and excitement as we approached Atlantic Avenue, with neon signs and paid hype-men assaulting our senses, promising deals and shows and glamour. It was overwhelming for us both, and we were happy to find the parking garage.

When the elevator doors opened on the casino floor, there was a change in the air. It was different. It was heavier – with decades of cigarette and cigar smoke hanging in the atmosphere, mixing with whatever freshener they were pumping in to create something I'd never smelled before, and something I knew I'd forever identify with what happened that weekend.

Stepping through the doors and onto the floor, we both expected more. We expected the interior to match the siding we'd seen outside. We expected what you see in movies, with massive crowds around every table and jackpots every few pulls at the slot machines. We expected high rollers and cocktail waitresses everywhere we turned. Instead, that metallic jangling sound echoed out from the slots across the empty casino floor, and it felt like there was a thin layer of dust or ash on the hard surfaces that weren't covered by Hawaiian shirts and ill-fitting jeans.

It was dirty. It was grimy. It was perfect.

We settled in at a blackjack table where an older woman was sitting alone with her pack of Marlboros open next to her chips, waiting for her to pull one from its sheath and step away to enjoy a few drags between decks. She looked like she was in her 70's, but maybe that was just the nicotine showing in her skin the same way it made itself heard through the rattle in her laugh – something we heard often. She thought we were fun and excitable, and she liked how we yelled when we won a hand, and how nervous we were when we doubled down.

Her name was Ruth, and we sat together for a while at that table as others came and went around us, joining and leaving an endless conversation about the city's best diner, her craziest casino stories, and plenty more in between. But after a few hours, a shift change brought us a dealer we hadn't seen before, and two busts later Ruth was on her way out. We decided to pull up stakes as well, wishing her luck as she lit up a cigarette and headed for the slots.

We walked the quickly filling casino floor for a few minutes, not quite sure where to go next, until we stopped at a crowded craps table where a tall, middle-aged man was yelling over everyone around him.

"Come on, four!" he yelled over and over as the dice flew through the air. When a seven turned up instead, he cursed loudly and turned away from the table in disgust, spotting the two of us as we watched. "You boys looking to get in?!" he shouted, pointing our way.

"We've never played," I responded, a little overwhelmed.

"So, what? You come stand next to me," he said, slapping an open spot at the table. "I'll teach you." Z moved first, striding straight over, smiling. I followed a step later, taking a spot at the rail. "Billy," the man said, extending his hand. "From Philly." I took his hand and gave him our names before he continued. "Now, you want to learn to play craps? Here's how ya learn. You have a $100?" he asked, not waiting for us to respond. "You take $100 and you lose it, then you know how to play." He threw his head back and laughed wildly, the deep baritone of it bouncing off the ceiling and vibrating in my bones, the chain he wore peeking out from underneath the unfastened buttons of his shirt. He was still laughing when he turned to the dealer. "Ramon!" he yelled. "Get these boys some chips, and get me my dice!"

Billy's presence was overpowering. We put our money down with no argument and watched as Ramon pushed six dye Billy's way, chuckling to himself as he did. They knew each other, you could tell. In fact, you could tell Billy knew all the dealers, pit bosses, and waitresses around him. He called them all by their names, and they all called him by his. He joked with them all and they all joked back, all sharing stories from tables past. Still laughing, Billy picked up two of the dye and blew on them slightly before splashing them down the table.

Eleven. Winner.

Though we didn't know that until everyone else reacted.

Over the next hour, Billy explained every facet and every bet, and we lost every single cent of our hundred dollars. But with no hesitation, we each threw down another 100 as the dice moved around the table.

"Here we go now, shooter!" Z said clapping his hands.

"Open all night, shooter, seven-eleven," I added, as Billy stepped behind and between us, and threw his arms around our shoulders.

"This is what I'm talking about!" he yelled. "Let's go shooter!" As he yelled it, the man at the table's end bent over the dice and rubbed the felt with his hand, never lifting his head. He made four slow, small circles with his right hand, and after the fifth, he snagged the dice and floated them forward. Seven. Winner.

This time, we didn't wait for the table's reaction to tell us what had happened. We cheered just as loud as the others while Ramon stacked our winnings and the shooter bent back down to rub the table and start again.

There was a lot of cheering and a lot of stacking over those next few hours. By now, some of it has blended together, but certain moments stick out – like Z yelling at a shooter for rolling a three, and the table booing me when I threw the dye off the table and into a woman's drink, and hugging Billy when the dice turned up that hard six we were both looking for. And some of the things we casually talked about while waiting for the dealers to color up a few big winners.

"So, what do you do, kid?" he asked.

"I'm pre-law," I answered after a moment, choosing the easier answer over the longer, more complicated one involving the quarter-life crisis I'd had in the library the night before.

"A lawyer!" he exclaimed. "Me too!" He tossed some chips on the table and asked for a bet I hadn't yet learned. "You didn't see that coming, did you," he said, sipping his drink, seeing the surprise register in my face. "I guess I wouldn't too. I don't really seem like the type." He took a new drink from a passing waitress and handed her a large tip, casually calling her 'darling' as he did. "I'm not like this in the office," he continued. "I come out here each weekend to get it out of my system." At that, he laughed loudly again and took a large sip of his drink, then practically spit it out a second later. "Another three?!" he yelled. "You've got to stop rolling prime numbers! From now on, this is a no prime number table!"

We didn't know it, but day turned into night at that table as the dice spun past us all like we were hands on a clock. Hour after hour we played, as on and on the dice went round.

And it was all building to one moment late that night.

The dice were in my hand and Billy was throwing around money like a guy who had plenty to spend, and a guy who'd had plenty to drink. He was making bets all across the board and putting big money down behind them. From what I could tell, he'd already won a few thousand dollars at that point, but stood to make even more if I rolled well, and more still if, to simplify it, I rolled the same number twice, and did that six different times.

When I did it the first time, we cheered like we had all night, and when I did it again, we did the same. When I hit the third pair, the cheers were loud enough to draw looks of curiosity from other tables across the floor. On the fourth, as they grew louder still, we even started pulling a few of those curious heads over to us. But with the excitement came a tension we all started to feel. Lord knows I did.

I love rolling the dice. I love to feel them rattle around in my hand and hear the noise they make as they do. I love the feeling you

155

get when you release them at just the right angle and watch them flutter through the air. That night, it had quickly become my favorite part of the game. I'd even picked up the felt-rubbing habit from the guy down the table, and had developed my own little routine. I rubbed the felt six times, paused for two counts, and then tapped the table twice with my knuckles before grabbing and throwing the dice in one, quick motion. I focused as much as I could on the routine, and tried to tune out everything else around me. But as I continued to roll, my grip on those dice got tighter and tighter as the stakes got higher and higher, and everything grew more and more intense. When I completed the fifth pair, it was overwhelming.

"You magical bastard!" Billy yelled, barely audible over the rest of the table. "One more, kid! One more!" His voice cracked with excitement when he said that last part – sounding like we all did as teenagers. Word of what was happening must have gotten out, because when I looked up from the table, a large crowd had gathered around us. I could feel my pulse through my fingertips as I rubbed them across the table, and I could hear the excitement and energy in the voices of everyone in earshot as I paused for those two beats. Out of the corner of my eye, I could see Billy and Z take deep breaths as I tapped the table and let the dye fly. We watched as they floated through the air, no one daring to exhale, fearing that a slight push this way or that would give us a seven rather than the eight we were looking for.

4. Nothing.

I rolled for ten minutes, hoping and praying and pushing for the eight, and dreading anything else. Each time, the breaths were held and my pulse pounded furiously in my fingers.

Six. Nothing.

10. Nothing.

5. 9. 2. 6. 9. 5. 3. 11. 10. 3. 4. 11. Nothing.

8.

Winner.

The explosion was like nothing I'd ever heard before. It was a deafening, smothering roar that wrapped around and over us like a blanket. Billy threw his arms around me and planted a long, forceful kiss on my cheek, as strangers patted me on the back and Z threw his beanie in the air while high-fiving everyone else around the table. For minutes, it seemed, the entire section celebrated, led by Billy, who wandered a few feet away and screamed about how much he'd just won. And even when things settled down, there was still a buzz in the air – one that ran through you like a current, like what you feel in a baseball stadium after a big home run, when fans are almost grateful for the third out, like they needed the chance to catch their breath. For us, the third out came on the next roll, when I finally crapped out.

"Who's got a cigarette?" Billy asked, sighing. "I think I'm done." He grabbed a $500 chip and tossed it to the dealers as he took the rest and stepped back from the table, fanning himself with the collar of his button up shirt, looking over the rest of the casino.

"Can't top that, right?" Z laughed, grabbing his own pile of chips and smiling at Billy. He waited for an answer, but one didn't come right away, and just as his smile started to fade and he looked at me with a question in his eyes, Billy turned back toward us.

"Maybe," he said, winking. And with that, he walked away, striding toward a crowded roulette table. He pushed his way to the front and slammed his chips down on the table, sparing another $500 chip that he tossed my way before turning back toward the dealers. "Martha," he said. "15 thousand on red."

"Billy! No!" I screamed, as a wave of shock spread across the crowd. "No! Stop!" I yelled again, trying to push my way to him. But it was too late. The pit boss had already accepted the action and the bet was on.

"What the hell?" Z said more to himself than anyone else, which said just about everything that needed to be said. It's hard to explain what I felt in that moment. It was a powerful, intoxicating mix of panic and anticipation. Again, I could feel my pulse, but this time, it was straight from my chest and stomach. I wanted to run as fast as I could for as far as I could, but I was rooted to the ground, needing to see where that little white ball ended up.

The tension of it all taking hold, silence slowly spread across the dozens gathered around as the dealer spun the ball and we waited to see where it would land. You could hear the ball hit the plastic and metal, bouncing this way and that. With each little hop and jump it took, our eyes darted with it, until finally, mercifully, it settled.

Black.

"Oh! Damn!" Billy let out through the heavy sighs of everyone assembled. "Well, what can you do?" he finished matter-of-factly, throwing up his hands and turning back toward us.

"Billy, what the fuck?!" I yelled. "That was $15 thousand. Why would you do that?" He smiled at the question and looked me square in the eye.

"Cause sometimes you gotta add a little life to your life," he said. "Every now and then, you gotta let yourself feel your heartbeat. Just to make sure it's still there," he continued, poking my chest with his finger to show me where. He looked up past me after that, looking somewhere distant and smiled. "I love having all my chips in the pot." And with that, he patted us both on the shoulder and walked past us. A second later he had disappeared into the crowd.

"I can't believe that just happened," Z said a few minutes later as the two of us walked the boardwalk in the cool, November wind. And for a while, we walked silently after that, listening to the sound of the crashing waves, until finally, Z spoke up. "I'm happy for you," he said. "For yesterday. You did the right thing." As he finished the sentence, I thought again about the library and something cold ran through my body. "You're scared, aren't you?" he said when I didn't respond. "Don't be. You need more life in your life," he joked, and we both laughed. "I'm freezing. I'm going back to the room."

I let Z go ahead, and as he turned to go back inside, I turned the other direction and headed out onto the beach. I walked out close to the surf but stopped just short and fell back into the sand, tucking my knees up near my chest and wrapping my arms around them.

Z was right. I was scared. Terrified. But as I felt the cold, salty air on my face, I found myself thinking of Billy, and seconds later I was standing again and walking back inside. I cut through the casino floor to the elevator and up to our room where Z was already asleep. I climbed into the empty bed and drifted away quickly, and slept long into the morning.

Chapter 35

The day after my first lunch with Carl, we got a new case. It was a years-old labor dispute involving a local grocery chain, and we were taking it over from another firm. We all took the next few days getting up to speed, and as I sat in my cube reading page after page, I couldn't shake the feeling that somehow, it was familiar. We worked for weeks on that case, and the feeling hung with me the whole time, like an ever-present ghost hanging just over my shoulder. I spent plenty of time thinking about it between research binges and coffee breaks in the kitchen, but I could never place it, and at some point, I forced myself to forget it and focus on the work – which wasn't always easy.

I was beginning to understand why the office wasn't livelier – why, when I visited Mack before I'd taken the job, it was always so quiet. On my floor, the work was mostly reading and fact-checking. It was pouring over transcripts and searching for anything that had been missed or overlooked. It's monotonous work, and it takes a certain level of concentration to stay as focused as you need to be, so while it's not shoveling gravel or working construction, it takes something out of you, and you end up another quiet, sullen person in a quiet, sullen office.

Carl and I got lunch a few more times during those next weeks – each time at that same greasy burger joint, and each time taking a little longer than we had the time before. He told me more about his wife and kids and about his favorite little surf shop back home, and I told him a lot of what I've told you so far, about my family and friends and Mack. I was growing to like Carl a lot and I think he was growing to like me, too – even if the shouts from his office were coming a little more frequently.

We came back from one of those lunches late in February to find Mack waiting by my cube. She was there to tell me that she had to travel to Boston that weekend, and as I considered spending the weekend alone, I thought about asking Carl to grab a drink. Brady was spending the weekend at a pre-wedding class in Rochester and I assumed Mike was watching Reed, but before I could get up from my desk, my cell phone lit up with messages from the group chat my friends and I have, usually reserved for random movie quotes and sports talk.

NOAH: I got the weekend off! Come to D.C!

BRADY: Cant. I have to go learn how to leave room for the holy ghost

WILL: Gross. Isn't it supposed to snow this weekend?

MIKE: How'd you get a weekend off

NOAH: I'm in quarantine

WILL: WHAT?!

NOAH: We had a plague scare so they quarantined the whole wing for 48 hours. We're getting released tomorrow but since we've been here for 2 days straight theyre giving us the weekend.

MIKE: I wish I could but the band is in the studio this weekend

WILL: THE PLAGUE?!

I ignored Will's last text and mulled over Noah's offer, but before I settled on an answer, I got a call from Mike.

"Hey, what's up?" I said, picking up.

"Hey, I only have a second between classes, but the texts just reminded me," he said. "On Friday, we're going to record that tune we wrote a few weeks ago. Do you want to sit in?" he asked.

"Seriously?" I said, shocked and excited. "Absolutely."

"Awesome," he said. "Can you be at the studio around 5:30? We'll do that first."

"Yeah, I can do that," I said, smiling, suddenly even more excited for the end of the week.

"Great! I'll get you more details tonight," he said quickly. "My class is here, I gotta run," and a second later the line was dead, and I was left alone with my work.

There are four small cities in our area, with sprawling suburbs between them like the musculature connecting one joint to another. If you had asked me before I knew any better, I would have guessed that the area's most successful record studio built their office in one of those four, maybe in the middle of some hip, trendy neighborhood with plenty of bars they could troll for undiscovered talent. And if not there, I would have guessed they'd chosen one of the brand new, sparkling strip malls spreading like a virus into what little green space is left.

They didn't. Instead, Solid Gold Productions chose an old, run down office building next to the airport. Mike must have been as surprised as I was, because he was waiting outside to help me find the place, in the middle of the snowstorm Will mentioned. He brought me inside with an arm around my shoulder and a short speech about how happy he was that I had come. Stepping into the lobby, you could see where the studio had put the money they hadn't spent on location. It was smooth and polished, and decorated in some kind of new age, trendy Feng shui I wasn't nearly cool enough to understand. The studio, too, was smooth and polished, but brighter than I expected, with intense light reflecting off the hardwood floors.

The rest of the band was already set up, scattered across the space like strangers making small talk while they waited for a bus. I waved to the crowd as Mike led me in, but before I could strike up any conversation, their producer popped onto the microphone from the booth next door. His voice signaled it was time to start, and Mike brought me over next to him and handed me one of his guitars.

"Sorry we're a little rushed," he said, picking up a banjo I'd forgotten he knew how to play. "Just hang tight for a second, we'll get you going soon." A second later he was counting the band in and the uneasy silence of the acoustically perfect studio exploded into sound – both familiar and new. This was the song Mike and I had written, but in a different, more full form. It was the realization of a potential I didn't even know existed. Our slow folk tune was now an energetic bluegrass rocker – the type you hear playing in the background when the main character finally comes of age. My little piano line had grown into something dense and complex in the hands of the professional who sat behind the keyboard, and Mike's guitar line was somehow even more intricate on the banjo, with an energy that dragged the song forward. On the third time through the tune, I joined in on rhythm guitar, channeling what Mike had taught me years before, adding another layer of texture, but not much more. I struggled to keep up the first times through, but I had the hang of it soon enough.

Mike and I had played together countless times, but outside the few times he'd pulled me onto one of their smaller stages, I'd never played with a full band, and not that it didn't before, but in a whole new way, the allure of rock stardom made a ton of sense. There's no way I made it look as good as Mike, but I felt myself copying every front man I'd ever seen, rocking my body back and forth to the beat, and throwing my head back when it got especially good, silently singing the lyrics Mike and I had written a few weeks prior.

We must have played the tune through a dozen times before Ben, the producer, called us into the booth to listen to what we'd laid down. Mike sat behind the soundboard staring into its lights and knobs as we listened to the playback. If he moved at all, it wasn't noticeable.

"This is going to be a great tune," he said after the last time through, turning to face me with a wide smile on his face. He jumped out of his seat and pulled me back toward the studio, his mix of confidence and control and excitement becoming contagious. "Come on, let's get the vocals done." He led me into one of the room's corner booths and sang his part before turning to me. "Just like at my house," and he shut the door and left me to it. Nerves got the better of me on the first time through, but with Mike's words ringing through my head, they melted away on the second. I listened to what we'd played together just minutes before, and admired how Mike's vocal line laid above it, and did my best to fit between the two, singing the harmony we'd written together. On one of the final takes, when I found my spot and it all clicked in, I gave myself chills.

After, we listened to a crude, slap-dash version of what would end up the final product after Mike and Ben spent a few hours agonizing over every possible tweak. I looked at Mike the whole time it played and watched the water well in his eyes and fall gently down his cheek. He turned to me after, smiling, and nodded ever so slightly as Ben declared the tune wrapped for the day.

I thanked everyone for letting me come in and turned to Mike to say it again to him.

"I couldn't imagine recording this song without you," he said before I could open my mouth, wiping away a final tear. "I want to get it all done and play it at the baptism in a few weeks."

"That sounds great," I said to him quietly, something lodging in my throat as I did. And before we could say anything else, he was being ushered back into the studio to start the next tune. I stayed for a few minutes listening to them work, and watching Mike realize a dream he's had almost as long as I've known him. I felt myself smile as I thought about it, so proud and so happy for him, awed by everything he'd done after living through a nightmare that would have killed me. But as I sat with Ben, I could feel him growing tired of my eyes behind him, so I decided it was time to go home and see Mack. I nodded to Mike through the window, noticing how good and happy he looked, and thanked Ben again on my way out to the car – where I remembered that Mack was in Boston.

I sighed as I remembered and stood against the car trying to think of what to do next – certain, only, that an empty apartment didn't interest me at all. I leaned my head back on the roof and felt the snow coming down, when the quiet, winter night was rattled with the warning of an incoming plane. I watched a large jet fly straight over the studio and touch down at the airport. And just as that plane cleared the runway, I watched another taxi out and blast off into the clouds a second later, destination and destiny unknown. Another followed behind it, but I didn't see that one take off. I was already behind the wheel of my car, parking it a second later. I grabbed my iPod and ran inside a second after that.

"One ticket to Washington D.C.," I said to the agent.

"Any baggage?" she asked.

Chapter 36

You're a stranger in my arms,
But there's something in your eyes,
The blue of clearer skies,

It's a blue that was there before my time,
The same blue I see in mine,
The blue that's lingered through the line,

I know I don't know you but,
I know I love you and,
I know that you and I will go,
Hand in hand the world in tow,

And I'll teach you what I know,
And you'll show me what I don't,
And melt this heart I worry won't,

'Cause I still feel what I have lost,
But I see what I have gained,
See why I'll never be the same,

I know I don't know you but,
I know I love you and,
I know that you and I will go,
Hand in hand the world in tow

Chapter 37

"Judge Amy sucked anyway," Will said loudly, standing with Noah and me at the back of their favorite D.C. bar. They'd both come to pick me up at the airport, and on the train ride back into the city we'd dispensed with "I thought you weren't coming?" and "why don't you have any luggage?" and "what was it like in the studio?", leaving me to bring up the Judge Amy conversation once we got to the bar.

As it turned out, I was on the last flight into Washington that night. It had started snowing harder just after I took off, and it was coming down fiercely in D.C. when I landed, blanketing the streets with a new, pure layer of white overtop the already browning morning coat.

The bar was in the basement of an older-looking building. It made features of its original stone walls and was decorated with leather lounge seating. It felt a lot like an upscale version of a dive bar we used to visit in college, a dive bar my mind kept drifting back to as we drank round after round and played round after round of Questions. Through the street-level windows you could see the snow piling up outside, and I remembered how Brady, Mike and I used to close the bar down during snowstorms in college, hoping that classes would be cancelled the next day.

It was late when we stepped out into the rapidly piling snow, still finishing whatever conversation we'd started inside, and wandered up the block looking for food. Up the road, you could see the Capitol shining like a beacon in the black of the night, and I couldn't help but notice how gorgeous it looked. I've always loved D.C., just for moments like that. You're always just a turn or two away from something picturesque.

We ate at a burrito place on the corner, and as Will and I talked about the new Speaker of the House, Noah interrupted, as only Noah could.

"I've always wanted to go sledding on Capitol Hill," he said, looking outside as the snow continued to fall.

"Brilliant," Will mocked, finishing his burrito and standing up to clear his plastic tray. "It's after three, what do you say we go home and get some sleep." He waited for a response but Noah's gaze never shifted from the street. He didn't say anything; he just kept looking outside, and before I could even consider what Will was saying, I spoke up.

"No," I said standing, clearing my own tray but not returning it back to the store. "Let's go sledding."

Will complained the whole walk up the block to the top of the Capitol lawn, but everything he said could pretty much be summed up by his first and last statement.

"This is a really shitty idea."

Still, while he may have been whining, there he was, standing between us, tray in hand, set to sled down Capitol Hill. We stood there for a minute together, as though we all needed a moment to take in what was happening. It was just as cold and wet as you'd expect it to be in the middle of a snowstorm, and we were on the grounds of the Congressional building, with the length and breadth of the National Mall laid out in front of us, each monument lit up and sparkling through the snow. And we were drunk. And ready to go sledding.

Noah and I stepped back to take a running start, and though he was still complaining, so did Will. And when we ran forward and threw ourselves chest-first onto our plastic trays and down the hill, so did Will. And as we yelled like we used to when we careened down to the bottom of that hill behind my house, so did Will.

"I don't know how long it's been since I've done this," I said as we stood back up. "High school?

"Ramp!" Noah yelled a second later, ignoring me. He was pointing a few feet to our right at a small jump at the bottom of the hill – probably left over from some kids earlier in the day. We ran up to the top of hill and got set for another run, this time aiming for the jump.

"Let's do it as a train," Will said as we got set. "If we're going to do it, let's fucking do it." Noah and I needed no convincing, and silently, we moved into order. Noah went first, with me next and Will following up – smallest to largest. We each took a few extra steps back this time for maximum speed, and on the count of three, we were back on the run, each right behind the other.

We'd done this countless times as kids – we spent entire days doing it in middle and high school. But that was then, and so many years later, we were out of practice. It went to hell before we even landed. Will had taken off with too much speed, and instead of landing behind me, he crashed into my legs, pushing me forward into the back of Noah. Somehow, the tangled mess we were, we still landed on our trays and managed to slide down the hill together, hitting the ramp as one large mass of man.

Which is when it got worse.

There's a reason grown men don't do this sort of thing.

Airborne, we abandoned our trays and flailed our arms and legs wildly, desperately searching for the ground. None of us found it

169

right away. Instead, Will ended up finding only me, grabbing two fistfuls of my hair as we fell back to earth. We both landed on top of Noah, my knee finding a soft spot in his back. There were cries of pain from all of us as we rolled to our respective stops, but moments later, the screams had become laughs as we laid on our backs, ignoring the snow that was burrowing its way into our jeans and loafers. Slowly, we stood back up, still laughing, until we saw the flashlights from around the corner at the top of the hill.

"Fuck," Will said, loudly again. Too loudly. "We should go. Now."

"Who's there!?" a voice yelled out of the blackness. We left the trays scattered where they'd landed and scrambled out to the street, sprinting off toward the first cab we could find, still laughing as we ran.

In the middle of our senior year of college, the news called for a huge, three-night snowstorm. Overall, it didn't end up being too bad, but the first night was exactly as advertised. Will and Noah were on a break and back up with us that night, and we spent the whole night out drinking at the dive bar, walking home in knee deep snow well after last call.

We woke up early the next morning, but after finding out that classes were cancelled, we didn't go back to sleep. Instead, we planned a party. The meteorologists were calling for more snow, so we called everyone we liked and opened our apartment.

Not a single flake dropped that night. Not one.

After 36 hours in the bottle, it wasn't easy getting up that next morning, but we all made it to class.

Years later, down in Noah's D.C. apartment, it was a different story. I could hardly move, let alone get to a class if I had to.

I barely made it to the bathroom that morning. The walls were swaying back and forth when I rolled off the couch, and my head felt like it was in a vice. It took me a second to realize I was in Noah's clothes, and another to remember why. Will was asleep on the other side of the coffee table, curled up in a ball without a blanket or pillow, also in Noah's clothes, which were stretched comically crossed his broad chest.

I found our clothes from the night before hung across the bathroom, still soaking wet. Slowly, I walked back to the living room, looking around Noah's place as I went. It was a small, city apartment, but the type that made everyone else our age jealous. He had a fireplace and new furniture, and from his porch, you could see the Potomac and the top of the Washington monument in the distance. When I got back to the living room, Noah had taken my place on the couch, and I stood in front of the fireplace looking at the pictures on his mantle. Mostly, they were of us when we were younger, but there was one of a girl I'd never seen before. We talked quietly about her for a few minutes, waiting for Will to come back to life. Apparently, her name was Karen, and he'd been seeing her for a while. It was already late morning at that point, and nearly noon when we walked down the street for brunch and thought about what to do that day.

We considered going back out to a bar, or even getting ticket's to G.W.'s basketball game that night using Noah's student discount. We even thought of throwing a house party for whoever wasn't on call, but one-by-one the ideas were dismissed as our energy failed to rebound. Instead, we took a drive around the National Mall with a clean slate of driven white snow blanketing it, and went back to Noah's to order a pizza, watch the game on TV, and talk about the things you talk about while watching basketball and eating pizza.

The next morning, I put my own clothes back on and they took me to the airport, the smallest trace of snow still in my shoes, squishing with every step as I boarded the plane home.

Chapter 38

When I got back to work on Monday, I couldn't get comfortable. All day, it was like there was lump buried beneath the leather of my chair. I leaned back and forth and shifted this way and that, but nothing worked. Nothing worked all week. Every time I sat down that lump was still there, a nagging knot of pain pushing its way into a pressure point. On Thursday afternoon, I tried balling up my jacket and stuffing it up against my lower back, hoping for some small measure of relief. Slowly I leaned into it, holding my breath as I eased back into the chair. When I'd finally settled, I sat perfectly still, relieved to feel nothing. And then Carl ruined it.

"God dammit! That won't work!" Carl yelled from his office, probably reading an email from a client. Startled, I jumped in my seat, and when I leaned into it again, the lump was back.

"He's under a lot of stress," Mack said that night when I told her the same story I just told you. She was standing at the stove, sautéing vegetables. "Your new client has him on a deadline."

"We've only had the case a few weeks," I argued, cutting up lettuce for a salad.

"But they want it taken care of," she said, "and his bosses want whatever the client wants."

"They're putting pressure on him?"

"Not in those words, but they've made their point," she said stepping across the kitchen. "We're supposed to go to that conference together, but I'm not sure he's going to make it. It's bad." As she finished, she leaned up against me. "What do you think, Mr. Hall?

173

Can you handle the pressure?" and she kissed me, running a hand through my hair and using the other to pull my body against hers. We stood like that for minutes – hours maybe – until the smell and sound of burning onion pulled Mack away, giggling as she went back to the stove.

There were a lot of kisses like that in those early winter months, and a lot of giggling, too. We spent nearly every night together, meeting back at my apartment to make dinner while we chatted about our day, before eating on the dining room table I'd barely ever used before and settling down to watch TV with her head resting on my lap.

Coming home had become the best part of my day, after either staying long enough to leave with Mack, or visiting Mike or Mom or Brady and finding her car in the parking lot when I pulled in at night. I was putting in 50 or 60 hours a week, and Mack was turning in 70 or 80, but she was happier then than I'd ever seen her. And looking back on it, maybe at times, I was, too. Those nights were straight out of a daydream, with easy conversation darting between hilarity and sincerity and flirtation without effort. The little arguments all fell away, and left in their place was only the good made great in the vacuum.

Some nights we went to shows or museums, and on weekends we were still taking trips, spending Saturday nights at bed and breakfasts or on the sides of ski mountains. The kissing and the giggling followed us everywhere, even to the office, when she was certain no one was around. When they came, the office kisses were always a highlight of my day, and a refreshing break from the pages I was reading so often I'd started to memorize them.

Somewhere along the way, Carl came to tell me that he was happy with my work, and needed to start giving me more. So, over the days, my cube of blue filled up with stacks of white, tacked onto the fabric of each wall, surrounding me on every front and waiting to advance. There were stacks on my bookcase, too, covering up the scratches and notches I'd just started to notice.

But while he'd given me more, it was just more of the same. It was a lot like first grade math. The specific numbers changed, but it was still just addition and subtraction. I read the same kind of details in the same kinds of cases, then did the same research I always did, made the same notes on the same precedent-setting cases, proof read the same arguments, and took the same walks around the office, often ending in the same break room to have the same kinds of conversations about the topic of the day.

I remember a particularly heated conversation about the greatest albums of all time and another about whether one of our clients could move his money offshore to avoid taxes. I remember debating whether a local grocer could refuse to make a wedding cake for a same-sex couple, and I remember it leading to a shorter debate over proper shopping-cart etiquette. One afternoon, I remember walking in while a junior partner described a politician's lawsuit against a TV station for running a video of him talking about an affair. We talked about privacy and celebrity for longer than we should have, and then, someone else brought up an Oscar nominee and her feud with the paparazzi, and we ended up talking about her movies, too.

Walking back to my desk that day, I could hear Carl yelling. I slid past his office toward my cube and tried to settle into my lumpy chair, but a second later, my phone rang, its high-pitch ring cutting a path through my head. The caller ID told me it was Carl.

"Hey," he said when I picked up. "Can you come in here a second?" There wasn't any anger in his voice, and when I stepped through his door, he was standing in the corner, leaning his chin on his surfboard and looking out the window at the waning winter and the coming spring.

"Carl?" I said after a second.

"Hey," he answered, jumping a little. "So, you know McKenzie and I are supposed to go to a conference next week in Chicago?" He waited for me to nod before continuing. "Well, things are getting a little crazy around here, and I don't think it makes sense for me to leave. So, I figured you could take my place."

"Carl," I said, stepping further into the office. "That sounds great, but shouldn't someone more senior be going?" He laughed when I said it, shaking his head.

"It's no big deal," he said. "I'm not sending you in an official capacity. Just call the airline, take my ticket and cancel my room. Go, have fun, sit in on some seminars, drink at the hotel bar. If you want, sit with McKenzie at the job fair. I don't care. It's easy, and at least you and McKenzie can enjoy it." Carl was the only one in the office Mack talked to about our relationship. "Go have fun," he finished, carefully setting the board back against the wall and slumping back into his chair.

"Thanks, Carl," I said, and I turned to leave, but stopped just short of the door. "Carl," I said turning back around. "Is everything Ok? Is there anything I can do to help?" He looked up and smiled, looking me square in the eye.

"No, it's alright" he said, turning away and looking back toward the corner. "It'll be fine."

Chapter 39

Mack barley stopped talking the entire flight to Chicago. The company flew us first class, and while I sunk deep into the leather and did my best to leave an imprint in the seat, Mack leaned forward over the tray tables, the schedule she'd made for herself stretched across both hers and mine.

She had a detailed itinerary laid out for the whole weekend. She knew which seminars she wanted to see most, the quickest routes between them, and even when and where she'd sneak in a snack break – and what the snack would be.

Somewhere over Buffalo, she asked me about my itinerary, like she had a few times before we left. I didn't have an answer on the plane, and I hadn't any of the other times, either. Mentally, I readied myself to combat her coming exasperation, but she didn't seem to mind, and just made a suggestion or two before continuing her search through the schedule.

As we circled O'Hare, I leaned past Mack to look out the window and wonder what I always do above big cities: why do people choose to live there?

The concrete and asphalt sprawled out in every direction below us. From the sky, it was nothing more than a drab slab of gray set starkly against the vivid, gorgeous blue of Lake Michigan. I searched the gray for any specks of early spring green and began to wonder how weathermen track the sunset times there. Are they broken down by neighborhood? According to when the sun disappears behind each tower or apartment building?

It was a cold late March day when we arrived at the hotel, but climbing out of the cab, you couldn't feel it. Instead, there was a blast of heat from the bright lights hanging under the awning, as a doorman helped Mack from the car and grabbed our bags out of the trunk.

Stepping into the hotel, it was like stepping back in time, or stepping back into a few different times, really.

Huge, stone columns ran the length of the lobby, like the Parthenon had been dropped into the Windy City. Two grand, marble staircases stood on opposite sides of the room, and intricate, ornate trim work covered everything we could see, like at any moment the Romanovs were going to walk in and signal the start of the grand ball.

We both took a second to look it over, but couldn't take more than that; the lobby was abuzz. It was early Friday morning when we arrived, but the conference was already in full swing across the hotel's many – really, far too many if we're being honest – ballrooms. A blur of blue, black, and gray whirred all around us as suits and pantsuits scurried back and forth across the lobby.

"This is like a dream," Mack said as I opened the door to our room a few minutes after we checked in. The room was small, but slickly designed in rich, dark brown – the desk and TV directly across from the bed. "I love you," she smiled, pulling me onto the bed and wrapping herself around me. But a second later she was standing again, slipping into her suit and heading downstairs to sign in and make sure she got a good spot for the first seminar on her schedule. "Remember," she said as she started out the door. "I'll meet you downstairs at four for coffee," and she jumped back into the room to kiss me before bounding out the door to leave me alone in the room.

I stayed there for a while on the bed, enjoying the way her taste lingered on my lips, before putting on my own suit and making my way downstairs to sign myself in. After, with my badge around my neck, I sat down to study the seminar schedule included in the complimentary conference tote bag. I sat in a stray chair left against the wall and skimmed the book, hoping something would jump from the page and point me in any given direction, but nothing did. Neither 'Environmental Due Diligence' nor 'Class Action Case Law' did the job. 'Public Records and Litigation' didn't move me either. Neither did 'Proving Landslide Claims.'

After two passes through the book, I decided to move myself, and set off toward nowhere in particular, exploring the never-ending rows of banquet halls and ballrooms in the hotel's basement. Through twists and turns, dead-ends and double backs, I probed what felt like an impossibly complicated maze, below that all-too familiar fluorescent light and above that plush carpet of color and pattern.

At every turn was another room; each fully packed with those power suits. 'Patents and Paternity.' 'Act of God or Personal Liability?' 'Taking and Defending Depositions.' I walked past each and what felt like two dozen more just like them, with associates and junior partners listening with rhapsodic anticipation to the senior partners and professors who'd written all their textbooks. You could see it on their faces. They'd all left their hotel rooms the way Mack had. They'd all thrown open the door and skipped down the hallways, excited to sit with whomever they'd sit with and listen to whomever they were going to listen to. The energy was everywhere, and when you didn't hear it in applause and laughter, you could feel it – even passing by the open door to 'Will Reading and Estate Executing'.

More than once, I came close to stepping into one and standing in the back, but I never quite made it through the door. Instead, I kept walking, quicker and quicker as I went, wondering why the partners and professors hadn't included in their books and opinions whatever it was that was so damn funny.

After a few more twists and turns, I happened into a large, open space the size of a small auditorium. On all sides were other seminar rooms. There were four or five on each wall and they were each like all the others: standing room only. I walked into the space's center and spun slowly in a circle, spending a few seconds looking into each room before moving onto the next. I was only about halfway through when there was a great rush of noise from all angles. All the seminars were starting to empty, like some high school bell I hadn't heard had started to ding. A second later, the quiet, empty space was a hurricane of dark wool, and I was at the eye. Hundreds of lawyers and paralegals spun around me, moving from one place to another, each so sure where they were headed, taking direct lines and walking quickly, with purpose.

I did the only thing you can do in a storm like that. I waited. I watched as it spun, hoping it would wear itself out and I would come through on the other side still intact. It was chaos for what felt like minutes, as debris of flesh and fabric flew past me. But soon enough, just as quickly as it had started, it cleared, with a new round of seminars under way. I thought of Mack somewhere in the bowels of the hotel with a sparkling white smile, and decided that the coffee shop upstairs sounded good.

Chapter 40

"I'm sorry I'm talking too much," Mack said after what might have been minutes without a breath. She was, but I didn't mind. In fact, I liked listening to it, and wished I was on her side of the conversation. We were at the table I'd been taking up for too long, surrounded by other pairs having similar, but more 2-sided conversations. "So," she said, putting down her coffee and wiping her mouth with her napkin. "I got you a surprise." She reached into her bag and handed me an envelope. "I looked and the conference didn't have much scheduled for tonight," she continued as I opened it, confused. "So, I thought you and I could go see the Rangers. They're playing a few blocks away." I knew they were playing, I'd looked it up almost as soon as Carl told me I was going, but I never brought it up. To me, this was a weekend for Mack, but I guess she thought differently, because I was staring at two tickets right next to the Rangers' bench. When I looked back up, Mack had a sheepish, almost shy smile.

"Thank you," I said, smiling, as she stood up and took my hand.

"Come on, we've got about an hour and a half before we need to leave."

It was just about 90 minutes later when we both stepped out of the room freshly showered, with fresh clothes on our backs and our sheets no longer freshly folded and tucked. We held hands as we walked to the elevator, and inside, she pinned me to the back wall, her lips and tongue finding mine with force, breaking away only a second before the doors opened at the lobby.

Our arms were locked for the length of the game, while Mack jumped back every time the boards in front of us shook at the force of a hit, and while I marveled, as I always do, at the punishment those guys take in the name of hockey – wondering what could make someone want to get their teeth knocked out and come back for more just minutes later.

Twice a period, I think, I thanked Mack for the tickets, enough that during the third, she told me to stop. Still, I said it at least one more time on our way out of the arena, holding hands while I hailed a cab, and sitting closely together in the backseat, and kissing again in the elevator ride back up to our room, and tumbling back into bed when we got there – where we stayed late into the night before either of us drifted off to sleep.

When Mack's alarm went off the next morning, I was already up. I'd been up for a while. I was sitting at the desk studying the Saturday portion of the schedule, picking one seminar per session and planning to spend my day in the middle of the maze, but with a map this time around.

"Excuse me," a voice said from somewhere nearby. "Excuse me!" This time it was more forceful, catching my attention. I looked up, curious, and found a ballroom full of eyes focused squarely on me.

It was hours after Mack rolled out of bed, and even though I had my map, I was every bit as lost as I had been the day before.

That was the third of the three seminars I had picked out, and one of the few clear memories I have of that morning. I can't remember any of the topics I'd gone to see, but I remember the polka dotted tie the presenter wore in the first, and how it blurred the more I stared at it. And I remember him joking about his law school days and the way *everything* started to blur after that. I remember trying to pull it all back into focus at the start of the second session only to end up bouncing in my mind between a *Times* article I'd read on the plane and a movie Brady and I had seen the week before. And I remember trying to focus again at the start of the third, but more than that, I remember needing to try and try and try again as it continued, and I remember thinking about a blog I'd written just after I'd started at the *Tribune*. It was a think piece on what made for boring TV. All those years later, I could still remember most of it, and as the white noise grew deafening, I started running through it in my mind, reworking and rewriting.

"You're mumbling to yourself, and it's quite distracting," the presenter said, shifting her feet and leaning into her microphone. I felt my heart thumping somewhere deep and low as I looked around the room and found myself struggling to stand.

"Well, that must have been annoying," I stammered, finally making it to my feet and gathering my bag into my arms, pulling it tight against my chest. "I'm so, so sorry everyone. I...excuse me." I trailed off as I stepped out of my row.

I walked as quickly as I could without running, and kept walking once I'd made the hallway. I was hoping to find the stairs out to the lobby and street but got turned around in the maze and settled for a random chair away from the other seminars, back where the hotel staff stashes the excess equipment.

I tossed my bag onto the floor and leaned my head against the wall, breathing long, deep breaths. I tried to remember how I'd gotten so distracted, and thought about the stories everyone else in that room would tell later about the crazy guy who had a meltdown and started talking to himself.

It took too long to get my breathing under control, and longer than that figure out what had happened – because I don't think I understood it for months. I tried to that morning, though. I tried to understand what had gone wrong, and chastised myself for letting it happen. When no answer came, I decided that I'd never know exactly what happened, but found that conclusion unacceptable, and started spinning the cycle all over again.

I thought through the entire morning, and eventually, I found myself thinking back beyond it, about my walk through the halls the day before and my indifference over the schedule the week before that, and even back to my cubicle and the break room.

I don't know how long I sat there, but I know I my breathing was starting to quicken again and my feet were starting to move again just as the sound of conversation and shifting feet filled the basement, and I remembered that Mack needed help at the job fair.

I smiled and kissed her when I met her to help set up, and told her that everything was great – lying, unsure how to explain why it wasn't. Throughout the afternoon, the memory of the morning hung with me. I shook hands and sat quietly while Mack peppered with questions each college senior that came looking for a job, but as I looked at their fresh faces, I thought about how so much like kids they seemed, and how far removed I felt from them. It felt like there was an entire ocean of time between us, like they were on the shore and I was suddenly somewhere adrift on the open sea, with nothing but blue above and below and all around, the winds and the waves pushing me this way and that, but never any closer to land. I thought about how full of purpose they all seemed, and imagined one of them as a face in the crowd watching me mumble to myself. It took everything I had not to find the door, but I managed to stay still and stay seated – until Mack shook me loose to tell me it was over and take me to the cocktail reception, where I found a way to talk about anything but the morning with anyone who would listen. The next day, I ran Mack all across the city to every tourist trap she'd let us explore, and that night, we got to our plane just in time to board. We were both exhausted after the long day, and I fell asleep before we pushed back from the gate.

Chapter 41

My cubicle was smaller that next morning. Or maybe it just looked smaller. I stood in the doorway and rubbed my eyes trying to figure out which it was, telling myself it was just the effect of the hours I'd spent awake the night before.

When we landed back in New York, Mack woke me up with a kiss on my cheek and a whisper in my ear.

"Thank you for this," she said. "I love this life we've made."

Back at my apartment, she fell asleep quickly on my shoulder while I laid awake, maybe energized by the nap I'd taken on the plane, but maybe not.

From my bed, I saw the night sky start to brighten and watched the alarm clock click closer to its set time – less of a wakeup call that day, and more a warning.

As I stood in my cubicle, I shook off as much of the exhaustion as I could and collapsed into my chair to bury myself in work, ignoring a few scratches I'd never noticed before on my desk. I skipped lunch that day, working through it as I did the rest of the week, too, fighting off the occasional flashback to that seminar, with all those faces staring back at mine. They came to me every now and then when my attention wasn't taken.

When I came up for air at the end of those days, I went anywhere but home – until Friday, when I had nowhere to go. Mack was back in Boston for work, Brady was back in Rochester for more wedding prep, and everyone else I would have run to was out living their own lives.

For a while that night, I let my car drive me wherever it wanted, but eventually, it found its way back home, just as Doug was walking in with another bag of Chinese food in his hand. I watched him waddle toward the building and waited for his basement window to light up. When it did, I looked closer at the painting I'd seen a few months before. It was just like I remembered: unremarkable, yet intriguing. A man in a dress shirt in a field of swirling pink and purple. I wanted badly to get a better look at it, but decided, instead, that it must be a replica of some impressionist I didn't know – probably something they sell at a museum gift shop.

I watched three or four movies that night, and stayed up late reading the *Tribune* on my laptop. I read Wallace Williams' last few columns, noting with surprise how his writing had improved. I read a few other editorials, too, and wondered whether the byline could be trusted – whether they'd hired someone else to invent their own stable of characters. I drifted off to sleep still judging each article in my mind, and thinking through how I would have written those columns if it had still been up to me to do it.

When I woke up the next morning, I was still on the couch with my laptop still sitting on top of me. And suddenly, I was desperate to get out of my apartment.

I jumped in my car and drove without target, and somehow ended up at the mall, though I can't tell you why. I hate the mall, with its cold concrete and beige color scheme. I always end up exhausted after just a few minutes inside, like the same black hole that sucked out the building's character and charm instantly claims my energy, too.

So maybe I was hoping it would put me back to sleep, or maybe I just thought with so many people around, I'd have plenty to distract me from whatever drove me there. I walked each of the mall's three floors that day, stopping in a few stores here and there – like the pet store with the puppies, and the toy store with the train sets my nephew loves, and the indie record shop that deserved better than being stuck between a pretzel stand a shoe warehouse. All the while, I let everyone around me take control of my imagination. I made small talk with more than a few, and imagined entire lives of the others who passed my view, based only on the clothes they wore and the bags they carried. For hours, I didn't think at all about work or what happened the weekend before – at least not until I stopped in one final store. Though as I think about it now, maybe I was thinking about it all along, because how else would I have ended up leaning over the engagement rings in one of the mall's dozen jewelry stores?

I'd thought about it before. Of course, I had. At my age, you're supposed to be thinking about it – if you haven't already sorted it out. So, when one of your best friends gets married, you think about it. And when another gets engaged, you think about it more. And as the train you're on keeps hurtling toward parts unknown, you occasionally blow through a station that makes you think about all the ones you haven't seen yet, and whether or not you even boarded the right train to begin with – whether or not you have any idea where you are, let alone where you're headed.

I looked over princess cuts and heart shapes, solitaires and squares, and all the while, I was replaying Mack's words in my head. 'I love this life we've made.' She was keeping track of each stop we made, and knew exactly where we were and exactly what should be coming next. I knew only that the train was running behind.

"Can I help you?" a woman asked from behind the counter. She was an older, bigger woman, with younger but somehow bigger hair. It was bottle blonde with red streaks blown out wide. She jingled as she extended her hand, showing off the entire bracelet section on her wrist, and a good portion of the ring display on her fingers.

"That one," I said, shaking her hand with one hand and pointing to a square-cut, solitaire diamond with the other. I don't know anything about engagement rings, but I know everything about Mack. Classic. Elegant. But not ornate.

"Oh, honey," the woman cooed, reaching under the glass. "This is absolutely one of my favorites." She started telling me about karats and clarity, but I didn't hear any of it. I took the ring and turned it over in my hand, inspecting it and imagining it on Mack's finger as she showed it off to her parents and friends – picturing the look on her face as I pushed the matching wedding band up alongside it. A shock ran through my body as the two rings touched for the first time in my mind, and I closed my hand around the ring as it did. "I can tell you like it," the woman said. "Put it on. I always tell my male customers to try it on. It gives them a whole new perspective." She insisted for longer than I could resist, and I did as she asked, sliding it onto my pinky and holding out my hand the way I knew Mack would.

It was a gorgeous ring. But as the saleswoman told me that again, I was already looking past it, at another one that had caught my eye. It had an intricate, twisted band with diamonds embedded in it, and a larger, heart shaped diamond above it.

"Can I also see that one?" I asked, leaning in.

"This is another one of my favorites," she said, jingling again as she went back under the display. Again, she talked to me about the statistics, and again, I tuned her out. I thought, instead, about the differences between the two – between the braided band and the tiffany one, the multiple diamonds against the solitaire, the heart versus the square. "Are you looking to buy today?" the woman asked, breaking my concentration.

"Oh, no," I said. "I'm just starting to look." She'd sent that shudder through me again when she asked the question, and at that point, I knew it was time to go. I handed her the second ring and grabbed the first, which was still on my pinky. Where it stayed, even as I pulled at it.

We exchanged a laugh as I pulled again. Mine was more nervous than hers, and got even more nervous after that when it still didn't budge.

"Don't worry, honey. It happens all the time," she said, still laughing. She took my hand in hers and started twisting and pulling at the ring, but it didn't move at all. "Oh, boy, that's really on there." She was still laughing, but there was less behind it this time. She squeezed my hand with hers and I felt a wave of heat wash over me as my hand went clammy. She pulled and twisted again as I began pulling backward, like we were on opposite ends of a tug-o-war. But nothing happened.

I was breathing faster now, noticing the others in the store looking on as I continued to pull and twist the ring. The saleswoman wasn't laughing anymore, but she wore a wide smile as she spread grease on my finger and started telling a story about cutting a ring off a bride's hand. I envied that bride, and wished I'd never come into the store.

With another wave of heat crashing over me, again we twisted and pulled, harder this time, praying it would budge. And finally, it did. With a pop, the ring broke loose and we both flew backward. I stumbled into a column behind me and she fell loudly back against the wall and plopped down into one of the stools they keep on their side of the counter. She laughed again, uproariously this time as she climbed back up to her feet, sliding her business card across the glass.

I never bothered to pick it up. I just apologized and went for the door.

Chapter 42

I've never seen a train conductor in my life. I take the train down the city once or twice a year, but to this day, I've never seen the person behind the controls. There's only one guy at the deli I trust to get my order right, but hurtling forward at 80 or 90 miles an hour, I guess I've always just believed that the tracks will get me wherever I'm supposed to go.

My nephew and I were playing with the train set I'd just bought him when I first thought about that. He was at my parents' house when I showed up after leaving the jewelry store, the indent of the engagement ring still visible in the soft flesh of my pinky. I ran my hand over it all day, until it finally faded after dinner.

I slept there that night, after a late night talking with Aaron about the still-working battery and God knows what else. The next day, everyone came over for Sunday dinner and I stayed until Mack came back from Boston.

Carl looked like hell when I saw him Monday morning. His hair was greasy and tousled, and his shirt was wrinkled and loose. When I walked past his office, he had both hands on his head, leaning over his desk. Word around the office was he had been there all weekend, and had only gone home for a few hours Sunday night.

The grocery chain we were representing was coming in for an update and we were hoping to wrap everything up. It was the case we'd been assigned just after I got to the firm, and I still hadn't figured out why it sounded so familiar.

I thought about it more as I settled into my cubicle, but didn't have long to ponder it. Carl called shortly after I sat down with a long list of work he needed done, and quickly, we all started to feel what Carl was showing. That whole week was a struggle. We were working long, hard days and there was still something wrong with my chair. And every now and then I was still seeing those faces from Chicago. And once a day or so, even amid everything else, I was still absentmindedly running my fingers over my pinky, like the mark of the engagement ring hadn't faded days before. It was a fight to stay focused. A fight I was losing going into the final round, when I got knocked the fuck out.

My cubicle was a mess, with textbooks and encyclopedias strewn across every hard surface. Most everyone else had switched over to electronic copies, but I like the feel of a book, and like being able to make notes in the margins.

Sometime that Friday afternoon, buried beneath the papers I was reading for Carl, I reached for a book I'd used in college and started in on one final review of an old decision that affected our case – one final review that proved one too many. It was the end of that long week and Carl and I had both skipped lunch again that day, and I just couldn't keep my head in the book. I'd start in on a paragraph or page and lose track of what I was reading. I'd get to the end and realize that my fingers had gone back to my pinky and I hadn't done any real *reading* while I read. I started and restarted the same page three or four times before kicking back from my desk to lean back in my lumpy chair and rub my eyes.

But as I did, it all came back to me like a tidal wave that hit me square in the chest and carried me inland as it charged on to flood the town.

Suddenly, I was back in that basement library watching the walls turn gray and feeling my legs carry me as fast as they could away from it all. Except I wasn't moving this time, and I wasn't at school, either. I was still in my cubicle. My first one.

Suddenly, I was back at Goldberg & Sons, reading that same opinion – the one I would read a few months later in my college library's basement.

And suddenly, I remembered why the case was so familiar. I'd worked on it all those years before as a summer intern.

I fumbled across my desk searching for the original file and flipped through it, looking for something specific this time. I found it quickly, and felt the air leave my chest as I did. We were the third firm to work this case, the second since Goldberg & Sons.

I didn't realize it, but I was standing as I read the file, wondering how I'd missed it for so long. I looked at the paper for what felt like hours, until I wasn't reading it anymore, just staring into its negative space. Eventually, it slipped from my hand and I looked up over the top of my cubicle across the rest of Winter and Wall, or the college library, or Goldberg & Sons, or wherever the hell I was, had been, or would be. I felt my legs carrying me again, and this time, I really was moving, and a second later I was outside, catching my breath next to my car, wondering where I was going to go from there.

Chapter 43

Imagine being an astronaut. Imagine drifting through outer space, pulled or pushed by forces unseen. Imagine how small and insignificant everything must seem from up there – your hometown just one spec on a massive orb, everyone you know just one person amid seven billion others.

Do you think it scares them? Do you think they float to the other side of the ship and look out into the darkness to wonder what comes after those millions of stars burning billions of miles away? Do you think they know the answer? And if they don't, do you think the sheer size of it all frightens them?

Because it scares the shit out of me. It always has.

When we were younger, Noah would wonder aloud about what might come after the end of the universe, and I'd always change the subject. Now, even the blue of the ocean is too much. Sometimes, when I'm sitting on the beach, I think of how far that blue stretches out beyond the horizon, and how small this life truly is. I try not to think of it, but still it comes to me in waves, like it did while I was sitting on the sand in Atlantic City as the sun rose after a long Friday night there with Brady.

I'd called Z first, just after I'd peeled out of the Winter and Wall parking lot with only one direction in my mind. Away. He didn't answer – which I should have expected – so instead, I called Brady, who picked up after the first ring.

"You have plans tonight?" I asked a second later.

"None yet," he said. "Kaitlyn is going out with her sorority sisters. I was actually just going to call you now. Mack's back in Boston, right?" She was, but I didn't say that. I just told him I'd be there in five.

I hung up before he answered and drove faster than I normally do – the strip malls and office complexes becoming only a blur outside my window. My turns felt sharp and my breaking was harsh. When I pulled up, Brady was already outside, curious, I'm guessing, about the call.

"What was that about?" he said, his long arms out and turned up, more confused than anything.

"I'll explain in a minute, just get in," I said, unlocking the door. "You have money?" I asked.

"Yeah, why?"

"Let's go to A.C."

"Sounds good," he agreed, like I knew he would. "Any reason?"

I told him the story about Goldberg and Sons and the case I'd worked before, and as I did, I could feel a guilt building inside.

"We don't have to go," I said, giving him a chance to back out.

"I mean, I'm already in the car," he said. "We've come too far."

We talked through the whole ride down, the conversation spinning on as it always does. I don't remember everything we talked about, but I remember Brady asking about Lou's baptism and how we needed to be back for it on Sunday, and I remember asking about his wedding planning and the nerves that were bubbling up every now and then. I remember him mentioning that one of the websites he'd designed was being shut down and that GNS would eventually start a

196

search for another, and I remember us sharing our newest ideas for our own site again – and again getting nowhere. And then I remember the smell of sea air creeping into the car as the Atlantic City skyline appeared in the distance.

Driving down into it, it was like I was back in college with Z. I'd made a few other trips since that first one, but even driving in at night like Brady and I were, I was always taken back to that afternoon in college.

We drove through the bright lights of the casino marquees and ended up in the same garage Z and I had parked in so many years before. And as the door opened on the casino floor, that same casino smell came flooding back, with the stale ashtray smell filling my lungs and just a hint of air freshener lingering on it. It smelled so right.

I love gambling. There's a camaraderie with it you don't get anywhere else. When we were little, my dad would take us to the racetrack and I always loved the way every walk of life came together. We'd stand in our khakis next to a thousand-dollar suit wearer working on Wall Street and a ditch digger in jean shorts, and differences aside, all our conversations would run together. You can go a lot of different places without leaving the finish line, or without leaving your seat at a blackjack table, which is where Brady and I found ourselves that night.

We played for a few hours at that table, high fiving our dealer and fist bumping with the rotating cast that came and went around us. First, there was a clean-cut businessman who'd come down from the city and talked with us about why the real estate market was due for a rebound. He left only when his wife came to get him. In his place came a young girl who threw down a diamond platinum membership card before warning Brady not to split nines against a seven and complaining about the latest album of that pop star Mack

197

and I had seen a few months before. And just as Brady and I were both ready to propose, a seat at a more expensive table opened up and she was gone, replaced by an older man in his sixties who told us why Muhammad Ali was the greatest U.S. athlete of all time, and how he'd scored a ticket to the Thrilla in Manilla while he was in the Navy. He turned blackjack on three separate hands before the dealer turned two of his own and we took that as a sign to go.

The three of us went to a craps table across the pit where we sparred over the state of boxing. We were clueless, he said, but weren't as bad as the "punks" next to us talking about mixed martial arts or "whatever the hell that wrestling crap is."

He was still there a few minutes later when the "punks" were replaced by a group of women our age, in town for a bachelorette party. They were all dressed for the clubs in fluorescent, skin-tight dresses with heels too high to make sense. Except for one. She stood beside them in a flowing, floor-length dress that started sky blue at the bottom and slowly faded to navy at its top.

Her name was Hailey, and she slid up next to me with a smile and a quick "hey," like we'd been friends forever. She had dirty blonde hair she let fall wherever it wanted to, but she flicked it behind her shoulder as she turned to me.

"So how do we do this," she asked, looking down at the table in front of us. "You know how to play, right?"

"I do," I said, charmed.

"Good. Teach me," she said, her voice bubbling. "How'd you learn?"

"I lost a hundred dollars," I said, deadpanning, remembering Billy from Philly.

"You're fired," she quipped quickly. "Who else can teach me?" she asked the rest of the table, not caring about or maybe not even noticing the sideways glances she got back.

"Just do what I do," I laughed, making my bets and explaining what they meant.

A second later, the dice started spinning, and soon after, so did everything else. Her friends moved on to other tables, but Hailey stayed at ours and took it over. She picked up the game quickly and fell into its rhythm, betting and rolling and in the time between, jumping into the middle of whatever was being talked about around the table. We talked first about what we all did and where we were staying. And as the night continued and our voices grew louder, we talked about far more than that – given new ideas by passing words from another player or even just the change of the song playing on the casino speakers. She was from Daytona originally, but had just moved out to Seattle where she didn't mind the weather because she's always loved the way things shimmer in the sunlight that comes just after a rainstorm. She hated romantic comedies and couldn't stand the president, and we had never heard of her favorite band but she assured us we would soon enough.

The table got more and more crowded and the conversation kept expanding as it did, and all the while, Hailey, Brady and me were at the center, and I thought more than once about how well she could have fit in the screen house.

Hailey's laugh was high but full, and after a while, I swear it started to harmonize with ours. We played a trio late into that night as the dye bounced about and while we gave them only half our attention. Hailey had wit and charm and no fear about spreading both, even long after her friends had left the casino floor.

"No, I feel like staying," is all she'd said when they asked her to leave, sending them away with a flick of a hand that put a smile on my face. Because somehow, with this woman I'd just met, at this musty old craps table in a state I only visit for gambling, I'd found a touch of something I hadn't felt in too long and wasn't ready to let go of yet. So I let myself enjoy it fully, ignoring and forgetting so much else until hours later, when I finally looked down and remembered that the house always wins.

I'd started out with a few hundred dollars in chips and somewhere along the way, I'd been all but cleaned out. I guess I hadn't noticed it through everything else, but when someone down at the end of the table crapped out, I stepped back and looked at Brady and Hailey.

"How much did you lose?" Brady asked, his own stack looking just as weak.

"The horror," was all I said in reply, whispering it just loud enough for them to hear, with my eyes wide and alarmed, even as a smile was starting to spread from my lips.

I know how awful this sounds, but I've never really worried about money. I don't have *real* problems; I just have the fake ones that seem real to brats like me. But either way, when you lose $500 in a few hours, you take notice.

"We've just got to win it back," Hailey said, so full of confidence it was as though there was no other choice.

"Or I could just be done," I said, picking up the rest of my chips and stepping away from the table.

"Are you having fun?" she asked. I smiled at the question, the simple, uncomplicated answer clear on my face, along with the satisfaction of having a simple, uncomplicated answer. I nodded and started to answer, but she jumped in before I could. "Then why be done? How much did you lose?" She took me by the hand started leading me across the floor as I answered.

"500," I said.

"Do you have 250 on you?" she asked without turning around, forcing me to tell the dirty blonde back of her head that I did. "Good," she said, stopping abruptly and turning around. "Red or black?" she asked looking me straight in the eye.

"Oh, no," I protested, taking another step back from her.

"Come on," she said, pulling me by the hand. "Live a little." She locked her eyes on me again and nodded her head ever so slightly, and the rest of the casino melted away around us, until it was just her, those eyes, and the pounding of my heart growing stronger in my chest. It all came back a second later as my hand found my pockets, and before Brady could tell me what a terrible idea this was, the money was on the table.

"Red," I said, my eyes still on Hailey's, but my mind on my heart, and that feeling you get when you've got all your chips in the pot.

There was electricity running through my body, a current flowing out from my chest in every direction, carried through my veins to every extremity, jolting my whole body out of a sleep I didn't know it was in.

My heart played a heavy metal drummer's rhythm across my chest, impossibly hard and impossibly fast. My breaths quickened and every part of me seemed to vibrate. A blast of energy raced through me, like that feeling you get when the lights finally dim and your favorite band takes the stage – except multiplied by a factor of ten.

"Oh, this is a great idea," Brady mumbled with his trademark sarcasm. "One of your best."

"Come on," Hailey interjected. "How often do you get excitement like this?" She leaned over the table as she said it, ignoring her friends as they walked back toward us. She squeezed my hand as we saw the dealer set the ball in motion and watched it bounce across the wheel. I swear I could have rocketed to the moon if I could have just channeled the energy racing through me and blasted it out the bottom of my feet. Slowly, the ball began to settle, with my pounding heart skipping a beat with each bounce. Until finally, it stopped.

Red.

"You lucky bastard," Brady laughed as Hailey let out an excited cry and the dealers stacked my winnings. A wave of what I took as relief washed over me, cooling my blood and settling my body. But even as the chips were piled and pushed my way, and even as I heard Hailey say something about what she wanted to do next, my cooling blood turned downright cold, the relief turned to something else, and my legs started to move again.

Hailey's friends were all around us now and she was saying something about a late-night pizza place, but all I could do was shake my head.

"All right, well, maybe we'll catch up later," she said, and she fell in behind the neon dresses and stilettos and was gone a moment later, never turning back as she went.

When she'd left our view, I turned the other way and started across the casino floor.

"Come on," I called to Brady, who stepped up alongside and walked with me out the casino doors and onto the boardwalk. The early April wind was whipping hard off the water as we looked into the darkness that surrounded us. It was late and the boardwalk was empty, with only the glow of the lampposts providing any light. I took deep breath after deep breath waiting for everything inside me to settle back down. It never did.

"I like it out here at night," I managed, looking down the boardwalk laid out like a long road that twisted and disappeared into the black.

"It's nice. As long as you don't get stabbed," Brady said, yawning. "Everything OK?"

"Yeah," I said, turning back toward the beach, looking into a different bit of black. "Go to bed; you're beat," and I handed him my chips to take with him.

"You coming?" He asked, already moving back toward the door.

"No," I said, stepping toward the beach. "I'll be up a little later." Brady said something else but I can't remember what, and maybe I didn't even hear it then.

The wind howled harder as the wood turned to sand and I kicked off my shoes, letting my toes feel each grain as they slid away in mass each time my foot searched for ground.

I walked out just inches from where the surf was advancing up the beach and stood for a second before my legs gave out and I plopped down. I sat there for a while that night, too long. The wind whipped around me and the waves crashed loudly and spectacularly in front of me. They were all I heard as I sat, and the water was all I could see – at least for as long as I could make it out before it met the horizon in darkness.

The sand was cool against me and there was a chill on my cheeks from the mist exploding off the water. My body grew colder and colder as I sat there, thinking of how I'd seemed to radiate heat earlier that night, and of the energy and excitement around the roulette wheel.

I thought about how rare those moments are, and how you always wish they'd come along more often. I thought, too, about whether they're rare for everyone, or just for me, and as that crossed my mind, I started looking back on the times I remember being so aflutter. I remembered the day of the school shooting, when I wrote those columns, and I remembered the first time I saw the grass at Yankee Stadium. I remembered writing my column on swearing and running out of the apartment that morning after reading what had inspired it, and I remembered when our parents took us to the beach house for the first time and told us it was ours. And I remembered the first time I rolled craps and won all that money for Billy.

And just as soon as he'd entered my mind, Billy took it over, like I was just another table for him to dominate. I started wondering about where he was at that moment, and whether he still came into Atlantic City every weekend, and if I could find him at the tables if I went back in and searched. I wondered if he'd remember me, or that night, and wondered if he was still a lawyer, and then whether I could still be one at his age.

The black turned to navy blue as I thought about it, and as oranges and pinks shot across the sky, I started to think that I didn't have an answer.

But as the bright blue of a brilliant morning sky took hold, the waves began lapping at my feet, and soon enough the rising tide had my toes not in sand, but in the water, and I remember watching the blue wash over them as something else washed over me.

I've always been someone who thinks that if you're open to them, you're sent signs by the universe – or by God or Allah or whoever you believe in. Thinking about it now, maybe the only signs we get are the ones we convince ourselves we're seeing. But either way, with my toes dipped in the water on that beach, I was sure I was getting one.

I didn't move them an inch, and kept my eyes fixed on the way the ocean came up to cover them before sliding away again and exposing them once more – and I remember thinking how perfectly that described my life. Up until then, all I'd ever done was dip my toes, I thought. And as I watched the sun rise, I thought about everyone for whom it had already risen, and everyone else for whom it was just starting to rise, and everyone else still in the darkness. A jolt ran through me as the size of it hit and I considered my place in it all, and thought that maybe it was time that I just accepted it.

"Take a god damn swim and get over it," I remember saying out loud, the sound of my own voice surprising me, just as footsteps crept up behind me.

"Have you been out here all night?" Brady asked, shielding his eyes from the sun.

"No," I lied. "I came up to the room but you were asleep and I didn't want to wake you." We both knew I was lying, but we both knew why, and we both knew enough to leave it alone. He stood silently for a minute or two, watching the sun climb higher while my eyes went back to my toes. But high tide had passed by then, and the water had already started receding.

"Let's get some breakfast," Brady said. I didn't argue.

Chapter 44

"Do you reject Satan?"

"I do," I said, standing next to Mike and in front of the entire church. Mack was on my other side, beaming in the white dress she'd bought just for Lou's baptism. Mike was beaming too, we all were, really, as we all aged a little with each passing question.

"And all of his works?"

"I do."

It's not natural to feel yourself growing older, and do it the way I was doing it. I never thought I'd be a Godparent before becoming a parent. But standing up there, strange as it felt, it also felt right, like I was finally where I should be – better late than never.

"And all of his empty promises?"

"I do."

And more than anything, I just felt happy for Mike and Sarah as I watched their eyes tear up more than a few times during the ceremony.

"Do you believe in God the Father almighty, creator of heaven and earth?"

"I do."

We'd waited around for much of that Saturday before leaving the casino, so when Brady and I got back into town, Mack was already back from Boston.

"Why Atlantic City?" she asked when I told her where I'd been.

"I don't know," I answered. Truthfully, I think. "It just felt like the thing to do."

"Anything exciting happen?" she asked, and when I thought back to everything that had, I wasn't sure I wanted to be truthful anymore.

"Not really," I said quietly, and we went about a normal Saturday night, Hailey and the roulette table and the beach spinning through my head, but never mentioned aloud.

"Do you believe in Jesus Christ, His only Son, our Lord, who was born of the Virgin Mary, was crucified, died, and was buried, rose from the dead, and is now seated at the right hand of the Father?"

"I do."

When we got to the church Sunday morning before the baptism, Mike was standing in the garden with Lou. He was in a brand new gray suit, tailored to show off all the weight he'd lost and all the muscle he'd built. It stunned me as I saw him, my friend looking so much smaller and fitter than I could ever remember him, and his son looking so much bigger than when I'd seen him last.

There's a path just outside the church door with a memorial brick laid for members of the parish who have passed away. He was standing over his father's, rocking his son in his arms.

"His funeral was here," he said, his eyes still down on the ground.

"I remember."

"It was sunny, just like today," he said, looking at me for the first time, without an ounce of sadness in his eyes. "Remember that?"

"I do."

"What do you think that means?"

"I don't know. What do you think?"

"I don't know, either. Probably nothing," he said. "But I like it."

"Do you believe in the Holy Spirit the holy catholic Church, the communion of saints, the forgiveness of sins, the resurrection of the body, and life everlasting?"

"I do."

"Why do you think you stopped going to church?" Mike asked as he turned to start walking back inside. We all used to go with our families when we were young, but none of us made it past confirmation.

"I don't know," I said. "I guess I just never felt a great connection. You?"

"I blamed God for my dad," he said, tilting his eyes toward the sky. "But I think I want to start going again."

"Is it your will that Andrew Reed Anderson be baptized in the faith of the church which we have all professed with you?

"I do."

Chapter 45

It was just halfway through the day when I started watching the clock that next Monday. It was noontime and Carl had already been in one of the boardrooms for hours. He was trying to settle the grocery chain lawsuit and wasn't sure either side was ready to deal, and as the afternoon began, we still had no word one way or the other.

We pretended to do our work while we waited. At least I did. I pointed myself toward my computer and absently clicked through emails, not bothering to read any of them. Every few clicks, I'd peak my head above the walls and take a look around, then go back to the clicks when there was nothing new. It was a routine I'd perfected without realizing in the weeks before, but a habit I was determined to break. I'd decided that much in Atlantic City, but I was too nervous to try that day.

I knew what was at stake for Carl; I understood the pressure he was under. So, when I finally saw him turn the corner with our clients, I stood up out of my lumpy chair and searched his face for any sign of what had happened. He saw me, but stayed stone-faced while he shook their hands and turned toward his office while someone else led them to the lobby.

Most everyone had left for lunch, so as I stepped out of my cubicle I quickly caught his eye again. Without breaking stride, he motioned to me. I followed him into the office and his whole body seemed to exhale as he shut the door behind us. His shoulders slumped as he dropped his head, but just as I started fearing the worst, he looked up with relief on his face.

"It's done," he said, stepping past me and falling into his chair. He pointed toward the seat across from him and let out another sigh as I sat. "They had a ton of questions, but they went for it," he said, sitting up straight, and he let out one final sigh before continuing. "Thanks for all the work you did on it," he said.

"My pleasure," I said, relief washing over me, too, as something else began showing on his.

"Is it?" he asked, looking me straight in the eye, as mine drifted away. "Do you like the work you're doing?"

"I want to be here," I said, and I swear I felt that Atlantic City surf come up and splash against my toes. He smiled as I said it. A knowing smile.

"Those aren't the same things," he said, "but I know what you mean. And if you're determined to be here, I can give you more to do while you are." Over the next few minutes, he told me about the firm's 'back to school' program, and how it would help me get my law degree the way it helped him get his. "Is all of that that something you'd want?" he asked, as I thanked him and thought about how much I wanted to want it.

"I do," I said.

"Good," he answered, leaning back and looking away, "because you shouldn't do this work – shouldn't be here or anywhere really – unless you want to be." He stole a glance toward the corner as he said it and sighed one more time before continuing on about how it would all work and sending me back to my desk.

My chair was as lumpy as ever when I sat back down in it, and stayed that way for weeks. My desk got more notches and scratches over those weeks too, and my bookcase lost more of its shine – but I tried to not pay them any mind. Instead, I threw myself at my work. I worked even longer, more extended hours listening to Carl call out to everyone and no one at the same time, each new day ticking by much like the one before it, with little change but the words Carl yelled and the colors of my shirt and tie. I was quiet in my cube; I was quiet most of the time, really – just another body in that quiet, sullen office. I concentrated on the spreading stacks of white in my cube, trying as best as I could not to drift away in my mind to that Atlantic City beach. Even weeks later, that beach and its water and my toes were still crystal clear in my memory, appearing occasionally in the pages of any given book when my eyes would go cross before bouncing back to focus. Even as the days grew longer and spring bloomed in full, it was almost always dark when I went home, and just as always, the work came home with me. It sat lurking in the back of my mind – the familiar pages and the familiar arguments and the familiar shouts all ever-present and ever-ready to spring to the front. I didn't sleep well in those weeks, and when I laid awake at night I often found Winter and Wall advancing forward. But sleep always came eventually, and my lumpy chair was always waiting for me the morning after.

And so I sat, and so I worked. Determined to do right by everything I'd lucked into. Determined to do what I should. Determined to do what everyone else could. Determined to dive in.

Chapter 46

The crowd roared when the Lizards were announced, and we bowed our heads toward the center of our circle, our arms pulling each other close.

"May the good Lord shine a light on you," Mike said, as the crowd kept cheering.

"Make every song you sing your favorite tune," we answered before breaking the circle and heading up the few steps that led to the stage. They roared again as they saw us – as we stepped behind our instruments to start the show.

The bar was packed; it was standing room only on both levels, and I couldn't help but smile as I sat down behind the piano and Mike counted us in.

It was a straight-ahead rock tune we opened with, and my fingers moved fast and with exact precision, racing up and down the keyboard like I'd been playing for decades. The crowd before us bounced and swayed, and so did all of us on stage, rocking and writhing to the rhythm.

It was an exhilarating feeling, hearing my piano line mix with the bass and the guitar and the drums, and seeing so many react so excitedly to it all. It was unlike anything I'd ever felt. We played through two or three songs – each one more exciting than the last, each one drawing more from both the crowd and the band. Mike was the same masterful showman he always is on stage, but somehow, I was hanging with him, dancing and playing and connecting with as many faces as I could in the crowd, all there to see us. It was incredible. But then it all stopped.

I was still playing, but no one else was, and everything else in the bar had ground to a halt. The crowd had stopped dancing and instead was standing still, looking up at the ceiling, confused. I turned to look at Mike and saw fear spreading across his face.

"What's that sound?!" he shouted. I didn't hear anything, but when I turned back toward the crowd, it was clear they did, as the confusion turned to panic and they all started to scramble.

I blinked, and a second later the roof and back wall were gone, and the bar now opened onto a beach, with a wave building high above our heads, ready to break on top of us.

I was sitting at the piano when it crashed, while most everyone in the crowd was still trying to get away. The water was heavy as it came down, and for a moment, my whole body was under, squeezed tight on all sides by the pressure.

When the water receded, the bar and the people were gone, and all that was left was me, my piano, and Mike – and a second wave building even higher in the distance. There was horror in his eyes and I wanted to run to him, but I never moved from my stool.

The wave made no noise as it came again, but crashed even harder than the first. This time, the squeeze was too much, and I couldn't breathe as I waited for the water to rush back out to sea.

When it did, I was the only thing left. Mike and the piano had washed away like the bar and the band and the crowd before them. In the distance, I could see another wave, but this time, I could hear it too. It was a deafening roar that shook my bones. This next wave was twice the size of the last, coming closer and closer, charging toward me like a skyscraper of blue and green ready to crumble at any second. I cried out wildly for help but the sound was lost against the thunder of the ocean as the blue turned black just feet away from me. I watched with terror as its top rolled over and started back toward ground. But the closer it came, the more that fear began to ease into something else, and one final scream came out as little more than a sigh. It was coming for me, and there was no escape.

I took one last deep breath, closed my eyes, and waited until the water hit, and felt it lift my feet up off the ground.

Chapter 47

When I woke up, I was already sitting, jolted out of sleep by the dream. I was out of breath and I'd broken into a cold sweat. There was just enough moonlight reflecting in off the pond to see Mack lying next to me, and as I scanned the rest of the room, I rubbed my eyes and focused on slowing my breathing.

Slowly, I rolled toward my phone to check the time. It was three in the morning and I'd only been asleep for two hours, after lying awake for two hours before that – which, as I've said, had become standard.

I was exhausted all the time, but not that good type of exhausted you feel at the end of a long day spent walking the city or skiing your favorite mountain – and not the type that comes just before you catch your next wind, either, or even after you've caught it so many times that there are none more catch. I was just flat out tired. But I was OK with it.

Carl and I had gotten even closer over those weeks. We went to lunch when we could and were still working late together almost every night. Other than Mack, he was the only person I talked to at the office, and one of the few people I talked to at all. I didn't go out much after work in those weeks. Most nights, I stayed home with Mack and spent hours in front of the TV, not all that interested in doing much else – but I didn't have a choice the weekend after I had that dream.

My family throws a lot of parties, but no parties are like our graduation parties – because they're not parties, they're weekend retreats. Mack and I left work on time that Friday and drove straight to my parents' house. The 'Congratulations Aaron' banner was already hanging up outside. I smiled as we walked past it and in through the open garage door, stopping to steal a glance at the battery, still sitting on the workbench. Still on.

"Connor!" the family yelled as we stepped into the kitchen. My mother was already taking lasagna – Aaron's favorite – out of the oven, and the others were already taking the rest of dinner out to the dining room. The weekend was in full swing. Hung throughout the house were pictures of Aaron at all different ages. I scanned each of the ones I could see from my spot in the kitchen, each one flooding me with memories of the whole life we'd spent together. The next day, there would be dozens of extended family members there celebrating with us, but that night it was just us – and Aaron was already hiding. While we headed to the table, my little brother was tinkering in the corner with one of our nephew's malfunctioning toys.

I walked his way, but my mother cut me off and ushered me toward the dining room where we took our normal spots and my father stood as the rest of us sat.

"This is a very special weekend," he started, raising his glass but putting it down a second later, realizing that one of us wasn't in his seat. "Where the hell is Aaron?"

"What? Sorry!" he called from the other room, dropping the toy and jogging into the dining room.

"You know, the rest of us were here for the start of our graduation dinners," Maggie said with smile before our father continued.

"Everyone here? Good," he laughed. "And Margaret makes a good point," he continued, ignoring her sneer when he used her full name. "This is the fourth time we've celebrated a college graduation, and I hope we never lose track of how special they are. We are so proud of you, Aaron, and so impressed with all you've done, and so excited for your future." My mother wiped away a tear as he raised his glass a little higher and we all did the same. "Alright, let's eat," he finished.

We were all sleeping there that night, each of us back in our old bedrooms. And after hours around the table we moved to the living room, and eventually, one by one, everyone started moving upstairs until it was just Aaron and me.

"Are you excited?" I asked just after Dad had given up and gone to bed.

"I guess," he said simply, shrugging his shoulders and stretching out into the end of that couch Dad had been keeping warm.

"It just feels like the next thing you have to do, right?" I asked, remembering the night before my own college graduation, when Mike and Brady came to the screen house after the rest of my family had gone to bed. Four years before that, all six of us spent the night before our high school graduation in that screen house – like it was just any of the other nights that had come before it. For a second, our whole history in that room popped into my mind and I thought about how much I missed it, until I settled again on the two nights before those graduations. On those nights, everyone else had been so excited and energetic as we played graduation-themed Questions, but I remember feeling nothing, and thinking that something must have been wrong with me.

"Yeah," he said, reaching down to pick up the toy he'd been tinkering with earlier. "I just want to get to Monday."

"Do you know what you'll do?" Aaron had offers from a few different engineering firms and had spent the last weeks of school figuring out what would come next. He finally had it all planned out.

217

Some lawyers our father knew had helped him apply for a patent on the battery and he was going to take six months to try and sell it. If that worked, he'd use the money to open up a studio and keep tinkering and inventing and selling, using Mom and Dad's garage as his office until he made enough to rent a warehouse space. If it didn't, he'd accept an offer from a smaller engineering firm, thinking it would give him more flexibility.

He told me all of this without looking up, eyes down on the toy in his hand, poking at it with the screw driver he'd pulled from his pocket, the small one he keeps on his keychain.

"There," he said, and with one final twist the toy exploded into a fit of noise – with wailing sirens and beeps. "Alright," he said, standing. "I should go. It'll be crazy here in the morning and I have to get out first." We exchanged 'good nights' and he headed up the stairs, leaving me alone with the toy, a little fire engine with a face on its grill and 24 different sayings to cycle through.

"Be prepared, not scared," it cried before it shut down. I took that as a cue to do the same.

Chapter 48

There was chaos across the house when I woke up the next morning, startled from sleep by Maggie's voice.

"Ed, move your ass," she yelled to our brother from down the hall. "Do you know how much hair I have to dry?"

"Hey, I have to get in there next," Aaron called to her, and I stepped out of my room just as Ed came out of the bathroom across from me, and just as Maggie and Aaron met us from opposite ends of the hallway. And for a moment, it was only the four of us. Just like when we were younger.

We used to meet like this every holiday, jockeying for position, trying to make sure we got in before the hot water ran out. Ed and I smiled while Maggie and Aaron argued across us, maybe both thinking that same thing. A second later, the argument was broken up by Maggie's daughter, who ran up to us already dressed in a cute little sundress with her hair held in a ponytail by a barrette that matched the daises on her dress.

"Mommy, I have to pee," she announced, and Aaron used the moment to slip into the bathroom.

"This is my life," Maggie sighed, bending down to pick up her daughter. She sighed again when she noticed Aaron, who'd taken up a defensive position in front of the vanity. "Fine, I'll take her downstairs and dry my hair down there."

"Aaron wins. That's an upset," Ed said, following Maggie down the hall as Mack stepped past them both and came toward me.

"Morning!" she said, bouncing up onto her toes to kiss me. She was dressed in a matching pair of pajamas she hadn't gone to bed in the night before. "I am not looking forward to potty training our kids," she said, stepping toward her suitcase to prepare the outfit she'd wear to the ceremony. We sat together for a few minutes in my room, that quip about our kids playing on a loop in my mind. Eventually, Aaron stepped out of the bathroom and we both turned to see him. He was freshly shaved and his hair was gelled into place the same way he's done it since high school: parted on the left, swept over to the right. He looked so young.

"See you on the other side," he said, heading off down the hall, and something caught in my throat as I watched him walk into his future, while Mack took his place in the bathroom and stepped into the shower.

I listened to the water run over her and thought again about Aaron and how young he looked, and then again about what Mack had said, and how big a lie it was. She couldn't wait to potty train her kids. I'm sure she already had a strategy on how to do it. And just as I started to consider which one she'd prefer, I heard short, little steps running down the hall.

"Mommy?" my nephew said, scooting past my door in a little gray suit with his little curls bouncing in his eyes.

"She's in the bathroom, buddy" I called to him from my bed. I heard his feet stop in their tracks and a second later he appeared in the doorway, looking at me with no expression, like he was still considering what I'd said. Then, without warning, he turned on a dime and threw open the bathroom door.

"Mommy?" he asked as he ran in and grabbed a fistful of the shower curtain. He threw it open with one twist of his arm and revealed Mack's naked body bent over as she held the detachable showerhead in her hand, rinsing off her legs.

She shrieked and jumped back as she did, pulling the nozzle with her and spraying water across the walls until it slipped out of her hand and fell back to the wall with a loud thud. It bounced a few times, spraying wildly in every direction, including straight into Jack's face.

He screamed when the water hit him, the same second Mack's flailing feet slipped out from under her and she slid down the shower wall onto her butt and then onto her back, with both feet straight up in the air. Jack was able to keep his feet under him, but only for a second, because suddenly, as the water kept spraying, he turned to run out of the room. But rubbing his soaking wet face as he went, he misjudged the door and sprinted head first into the wall.

At some point during the mess I had stood up, but I hadn't actually moved. I was on my feet, but in a passive way, like when a police car shows up across the street and you try to see what's going on without getting too close. I looked at the twisted wreckage that had become the bathroom – my girlfriend's legs as she thrashed back and forth trying to grab the loose nozzle which was still spraying water all over the bathroom, and my nephew, sprawled out on his back in the hallway where he'd come to rest after pin-balling off both sides of the door frame.

I wanted to laugh, and I knew I should already have been scrambling to help at least one of them, but instead, I stood for at least another full second, dazed, wishing I'd been more specific about where Maggie was, and deciding that before I'd consider having kids, I'd buy a house with locks on the bathroom doors.

Jack was quiet for that second, like he was asking himself how he'd ended up on the ground. But he quickly gave that up and started wailing. At the sound of his scream, I finally started moving, picking him up and pulling him tight against my chest, letting him wipe his wet face against my shirt. By the time I looked up, Mack had gotten back to her feet and corralled the showerhead, which she was now holding by her side with one hand while the other rubbed her back.

She looked dumbfounded while I asked if she was OK, and sounded just as stunned as she answered. By the time Maggie made it upstairs, Jack had already stopped crying, but she charged down the hall nonetheless, asking what had happened. She didn't wait for an answer; she took Jack from me and checked his bumps and bruises, then turned and looked into the bathroom for the first time.

"Woah!" she yelled, spinning on a dime and looking away. This was the first time I'd really taken stock of the whole thing. There was water all across the room. It was everywhere. The ceiling, the walls, the windows, the floors. There was a small stream running out into the hallway and pooling against the carpet. Half the curtain had been torn off the rod and all the soaps that normally sit on the side of the tub were scattered across the tile, including one small bar that was floating in the stream, slowly making its way out of the room. The force with which Jack hit the wall knocked some of the pictures crooked, and there, in the middle of it all, was Mack's naked body, dripping wet and just now working to get behind what was left of the curtain.

It was like a small hurricane had rolled through our bathroom, and as the damage assessment and clean up began, I tried my best to display the appropriate somber attitude, but all hope of that was lost pretty quickly.

"Look mommy, boobies," Jack said, pointing over her shoulder toward Mack, who had just wrapped herself in her towel and was starting to step out of the shower. I laughed out loud when he said it, but I guess I was the only one who found it funny.

"Oh, grow up, Connor," Maggie said as she started down the hall, but I just kept laughing. Harder than I had in weeks.

Chapter 49

Teachers get a lot of criticism, but if you want to complain about job security, you should focus on politicians. It's our own fault, but when I think about the ones that are really good at their jobs, I'm always reminded of the Pope. They're there, they're infallible, and they're around until God decides to retire them.

"I'd give anything to trade places with each of you," the Senator said, giving the same commencement speech he'd given a few years before at my graduation – because why would you bother writing another one when you've been around long enough to know that no matter what you do, you'll be around forever? I could still remember parts of it, short on imagination but long on cliché.

"These last four years, you've been driving down a long, winding road," he said. The graduation was being held in an amphitheater tucked into the state park near our house. It's the same theater we'd seen countless concerts in, and the very same I'd graduated in a few years before.

"And now, you're at the end and you're faced with a choice. A fork. Left? Or Right? As a democrat, obviously I'd like you to choose left."

That line got the same polite chuckle it had the first time around, but it seemed to trigger a squirminess in both Jack and me, so as the speech continued, I took my nephew up onto the outdoor lawn at the back of the theater.

"You can choose either path, or any path, really. And you've got miles in front of you."

As soon as I set Jack down, he took off running in aimless, endless circles – the way kids do when they've got energy to burn and an imagination to help. There was no one around us and he wasn't making too much noise, so I let him run while I leaned against a tree.

"What's great is that no matter what path, even now at 20 or 21 or 22, you can be whatever you want to be. You can choose."

Something flashed in me as I heard that line again, and I started thinking about how Mike, Brady and I had met under one of those trees after our graduations and talked about what paths we would choose.

"I've always remembered a piece of advice I got when I was young, and I'd like to pass it along to you. 'Do good, and you'll do well.'"

Mike talked about needing to replace a few guys in the Lizards and Brady told us for the first time that he'd turned his internship at GNS into a job offer. He told me about a writing position they were also hiring for, but I'd just started the blog at *The Tribune* and I was still trying to figure things out. So instead, I talked about a column I'd written: 15 TV Crossovers the World Needs.

"I guess the important thing is that this is not the end. It may feel like you've reached the end, but this is only the beginning."

I was so sure that I'd figure everything out. Back then, I thought I'd do the blog for a few months until I came up with a better plan, and soon after, I'd be moving on to bigger and better things. But as I watched Jack run in his little circles with that free, easy feeling you're so full of when you're young but never feel again, I wondered if I'd ever come up with one.

"This is the first day of the rest of your life."

I looked up when he said that, and whatever had flashed in me a second before sparked into something else entirely, something strong I don't think I understood then. It burned a hole through my

225

insides and I felt something cold fill it in as panic and anger spread through my chest.

"This diploma is a launching pad to greatness."

And I wondered if I'd ever found the launching pad or chosen my path.

Or worse yet, if I'd ever bothered to look for either.

Chapter 50

"Are you alright?"

I got that question a lot over the next month. It started with everyone at Aaron's graduation party.

"You just seem quieter than normal." They all said it. Aunts and uncles and cousins at the party, then Mack every couple of days after that. I told them all the same thing.

"Yeah, I'm fine. I'm sorry. I'm just tired."

It wasn't a lie; I was exhausted. I was sleeping less than ever – falling asleep later and waking up more often. I went to work every day without the energy to do much more than sit and silently work while quietly cursing the lumps in that goddamn chair, until one Thursday, I couldn't take it anymore.

I'd been struggling with it all morning, until just before noon I stood up sharply, the chair rolling backward and loudly crashing into my bookcase. With my hands, I started pushing against the back and bottom, leaning into the leather, hoping to smooth out whatever laid below the surface. When I sat back down and realized it hadn't worked, I started twisting and pulling on each of the levers on the bottom, shifting the lumbar and height in all the ways I'd tried before. When that didn't work, I tried something more drastic.

I stormed out to the lobby to where the maintenance crew was fixing the fountain that had broken earlier that morning. I helped myself to one of their screwdrivers and marched back to my desk to flip the chair over and start in on the screws. Looking back, I don't know what I was trying to accomplish. There was no plan, just a craziness that needed indulging.

I can't imagine what I looked like to Carl when he came by the cube a half hour later looking to get lunch. I was on the floor, sitting cross-legged in my suit, surrounded by screws and plastic pieces, more than I would have thought went into a chair. I was sweating and my hair was a tangled mess. I looked up at him and wondered what he was thinking, and wondered what everyone who'd walked by had thought, too, and realized that I didn't actually care.

It felt good to take that thing apart.

Calmly, I stood up and saw for the first time the full scope of what I'd done. There was no real chair left at all. Just parts.

"My chair is broken," I said.

"We'll get you a new one."

"You alright?" Carl asked after we'd ordered our customary burgers at our customary table. It had been a pretty quiet ride over. He called his secretary to get me a new chair and I told him to make sure they left my mess for me when we got back.

"Yeah, I'm fine." I said, beating back the part of me that wanted to say anything else. "I'm sorry. I'm just tired."

"This job will do that to you," he said, leaning back, putting his arm up around the back of the empty chair next to him.

"It's not the job," I said, and meant to go on but he cut me off.

"You know, I told myself that for a long time," and he leaned in before continuing. "Now, you don't need me to tell you how to live, but speaking from experience, you can pretend like it's not, or you can fix it."

As he said it, I realized for the first time that Carl's office had been awfully quiet.

"Did you fix it?" I asked.

"Not yet. But soon."

After lunch, I dragged the parts of my old chair down to the dumpster and came back up to try out its replacement. I leaned into the new leather and my whole body relaxed into it, feeling nothing but relief. I enjoyed its comfort for a second, but was roused out of it a second later.

"Good luck, Carl," someone said from his office.

Curious, I stood up and saw McKenzie's father walking away. My feet moved on their own, taking me toward him. I got to the doorway and saw Carl standing by the windows, looking out to the trees – or maybe past them. On his desk, there were cardboard boxes; each packed with the pictures and children's art projects that had littered every hard surface.

He turned when he realized I was there and shot me a smile.

"Sorry I couldn't tell you before, but...Fixed it."

I didn't have time to say anything, behind me came Mr. Wall, the firm's other founder. I gave them the room and took my confusion back to my cubicle and sat down in my chair.

And felt a lump.

Chapter 51

My graduation robe didn't fit well. It was way too long, with inches of fabric collected in bunches at my feet. I was standing in a long line with a faceless stranger both ahead and behind me, and as I tried to pull up the robe, I realized they were both standing on parts of it.

"Excuse me," I said, and gave each side a tug, but neither of them moved. I pulled again, harder this time, but still, neither budged – and neither did the robe. After a third failed try, I gave up and looked around. We were standing in the front of that familiar amphitheater with the stage above us and the assembled crowd in the seats in front – the lawn and those trees out beyond them. I scanned the grass and remembered all the concerts I'd seen from it, until my eyes came across something I didn't expect. There in the middle of the green was my parents' Saratoga house, seen as it is from the back, with the screen house looming large and drawing my attention.

I could hear a band playing 'Pomp and Circumstance,' but it wasn't the one in the front three rows. That band hadn't even picked up their instruments. Still, the music grew louder as the line started to move and I shuffled along to keep up with it, my robe still trapped under my neighbors.

I looked for any signs of another band, trying to find the source of the sound, but my concentration was broken by cries and yells from those faceless others in line with me. When I looked back to them, they were jumping and hiking up their robes. I watched them struggle, trying to figure out why, until I finally looked down and noticed it. We were standing in ankle deep water. Once more I tried to pull at my robe, but again it wouldn't move, still trapped beneath the feet of the two around me – the only two in line not bothering to struggle against the water.

The music started to grow louder as the line moved forward, not one of us stepping out despite the rising tide. I sloshed through the water as we made our way toward a staircase that led up to the stage, and started to hear a new noise above the music. There were names being read off one by one, and for the first time I looked up onto the stage and saw a podium, and another faceless man standing behind it. Quicker and quicker the water was getting deeper and deeper, as my robe was getting wetter and wetter and heavier and heavier, starting to weigh me down.

When we made it up onto the stage, there was still no sign of a band, but as I kept searching, I saw the source of the water. The lawn had been flooded by a sea of blue, splashing against my parent's house, and spilling into the seating below.

The crowd in those seats scrambled to get out of the way, some running forward and jumping onto the far side of the stage – all while the music continued and the names kept being read. I searched the crowd for my family, and finally found Aaron and Mack standing on the stage past the podium, smiling at me.

More and more, people climbed on and still the reading continued, and still the line shuffled toward the podium, with my soaking wet robe still trapped.

But suddenly, there was a loud howl and I looked out to see the water not just spilling over, but crashing waves into the seats. The water charged forward from the back of the lawn and I watched as it slammed into my parent's house before continuing on toward the stage and exploding against it, spraying foam across us all.

Some ran for cover as the water receded, running backstage and out of view while I stayed stuck in line shuffling toward the podium, dragged by whoever was in front of me and pushed by whoever was behind. All I could do was watch with horror as wave after wave came, until finally, the house and the screen house gave way, disappearing beneath the blue.

231

And still another wave came and another name was read, and on it went. More of the crowd ran from view, until all I could find was Aaron and Mack, still standing across the stage from me, waiting. But as another wave came and I took another step forward, I saw someone step between them. I strained to see him through the mist, but soon, I recognized Carl, who looked me square in the eye as another wave and another name brought me up to the podium, the music growing as loud as the crashing waves.

There was no expression on Carl's face as he raised his arm and pointed out to the water. I turned to look just as another wave built bigger than all the rest, bigger than the theater itself.

It was a tower of water careening toward me, blotting out the sun as it came.

"Connor Hall," I heard.

And then the wave broke. And then it all went dark. And then I felt my feet lifted off the ground.

Chapter 52

It was just after 1 AM when I woke up in a cold sweat, with the blankets pulled out from the bottom of the bed, bunched up around my hips. Mack had spent the day in Boston and I had gone to bed before she'd gotten home, but she was there when I rolled to my right, her hair still wet from the shower she must have taken.

The room still smelled like her lotion, and the way it filled the air helped pull me out of the dream. I tried to lie back down but soon I was up again. Quietly, I stepped out of the room and kept walking, and before I realized it, I was outside, feeling the breeze on my face.

It was the kind of night I love, with a brisk cold replacing the heat of the day. I walked out to the parking lot and turned back to the building. All the windows were as dark you'd expect well after 1. All but one.

Doug's basement light was still on, and I could make out the top of his head in the middle of the room, facing what looked like a large canvas. Above him was that painting of pink and blue that always caught my eye. I tried to make out more of it, but its blurred edges kept it unclear. All it did was lull me back toward sleep, so I went back in to bed and my body gave in.

"He's an idiot," Mack said the next morning as I poured my cereal. This was the first time we'd gotten to talk about Carl, who'd turned in his two weeks notice after our lunch and was told not to come back after Friday. "Why would anyone throw away what he has? Every junior partner in the firm would kill to trade places with him and he just quits? Can you believe it?" she asked, mostly to herself, barely taking a breath as she went.

She talked all throughout breakfast and into her shower. I didn't have to say much during that time, and that was fine with me, because I didn't know what to say anyway, and when I finally did, I regretted it immediately – but that wasn't until later that morning.

When I got into work, Carl's door was open and he was sitting behind his desk, maybe sneaking one last look around.

"This is exactly how the office looked when they first gave me the job," he said as I stepped through the door. "I never thought I'd see it like this again."

"What will you do now?" I asked. He and I hadn't talked since the day before.

"My dad and I just closed on a little shack in Malibu, right on the coast. We're going to open a surf shop." He broke out into a wild smile as he said it, looking back at the surfboard in the corner, the last piece of his furniture left in the room.

"So, you're leaving the business?" I asked, leaning up against his empty bookcase.

"It's not for me, Connor," he said, the smile leaving as quickly as it came. "It's not what I want."

"Nervous?" I asked quickly, nodding.

"A little, or maybe I'm just excited." He stood up and came over to me, extending his hand. We shook like we had on my first day, and I told him about a Lizards show that night and suggested he come. He told me he'd try, and with that, he tucked his surfboard under his arm and walked into a new life, shutting the door behind him.

I took my first walk around the office in weeks after watching him go, and ended up stepping through the doors of Mack's office

234

and up to her desk, noticing a picture we'd all taken a few months back at one of Mike's gigs. To anyone else, it looked like a group of friends, but to her, it was a portrait of the two of us, with a few human frames.

"Connor, hi. What's up?" she said when she picked her nose up out of the memo she was reading. She was hunched over, highlighter in hand, hard at work.

"What if I didn't do this?" I asked quietly.

"What?" she said, rocking back and up to her feet. "What does that mean? Where is this coming from?" she demanded.

"I don't know. Nowhere," I said, surprised but not sure why.

"Stop it," she said, but didn't get out another word. Her phone rang as she was starting in on her response and it was a call she'd been waiting for. She picked up the phone but before she said anything, she grabbed me by the tie, pulled me over her desk, and planted a forceful kiss on my lips. Pulling away, she shot me a stern look as she answered.

Chapter 53

You busy?

That's all Brady's text read. The answer was complicated, except it wasn't really at all. Was I busy? No. Mostly, I'd been staring into my computer since I left Mack's office, replaying Carl's exit in my mind and thinking about what I'd say to Mack when I saw her next. But should I have been busy? Absolutely. Our bosses were still deciding who would replace Carl, but when a successor was picked, they'd need to be brought up to speed on our cases. I should have been preparing what they'd need. But I wasn't, so I chose the first answer.

No. What's up?

Any chance you can be at Paddy Murphy's in 20 minutes? Again, my answer should have been more complicated than I made it.

How bout 10?

It took me about that long to make it to the bar. It was early, but it was a Friday afternoon so things were already filling up. I grabbed a small table in a corner of the backyard, where I let the waitress talk me into starting early as I waited for Brady.

It felt strange, sitting in a lawn chair under the warm June sun, drinking a beer while everyone else in my office was still in their cubicles. No doubt, they were wondering where I was, but my direct supervisor had just quit, so I didn't see a downside. And either way, I had a good idea what this was about, and I needed to be at that bar.

"Am I doing the right thing?" Brady asked as he sat down. He'd asked me the same thing a week before he proposed to Kaitlyn, and now, a week before their wedding, he was doing it again. He'd also asked it just before he started his job at GNS. All three times we ended up at Paddy Murphy's. This time, I didn't say anything when he sat down, I'd learned enough not to.

When you know people well enough, you know how to deal with things like that. For Mike, you counter everything he says with something reassuring. For Brady, you basically just wait.

He wasn't panicked or jittery. Instead, he was calm, and talked like it was any other day. He went for a while as we drank, slowly tracing circles in his mind about the finality of marriage and what he saw for himself in 10 and 20 and 30 years.

Brady and Kaitlyn grew up next to each other; their parents are still neighbors. They've known each other as long as they've been alive, and have been friends for just as long. Even during grade school, when we all went through that 'girls are gross' phase, Brady had Kaitlyn. They were great friends, with a history and a bond every bit as strong as the one Mike and I share with him now. It was a surprise when they started dating during college, but when we sat back and thought about it, it made perfect sense – which is what I reminded him when he finished.

"Who's your oldest friend?" I asked quietly over my drink.

"She is," he answered.

"And who's your best friend?"

"You are," he said after a second, but shifted in his seat as I smirked. "She is."

"Then what's the problem?" I asked, and a smile of a different kind spread across his face.

"There isn't one." He knew the answer all along, and had probably convinced himself before I said anything, but sometimes, when Brady is done, he just needs one final push in the right direction.

"Besides," I said, "marriage isn't final. Get a mistress, let her divorce your ass and move back in with your parents. That'll wipe the slate clean."

His smile turned to laughter after that, and we ordered another beer and watched afternoon turn to evening.

When it turned to night, we walked the few blocks to where the Lizards were playing their concert. Mack and Kaitlyn were already there, and as Brady pulled his fiancée into a tight hug, Mack and I stepped away to talk.

"What was that today?" she asked, a mix of anger, fear, and genuine concern, I think, on her face.

"It was nothing," I said, pulling her into my own hug. "I'm sorry."

"Are you sure?" she asked, pulling back, the concern winning out in her expression. "You scared, me. I didn't know what you meant. 'What if I didn't do this?'" she quoted. "I thought you meant you wanted to leave the firm."

I didn't say anything in response, just kissed her forehead and pulled her toward where Sarah had just arrived with our Godson on her hip. I gave little Lou his own kiss and swung him around in my arms as he laughed. I looked at Mack over his head, and she managed a smile as I handed him back to his mother. A second later, Mike came up behind us, already in mid-show form.

"This is gonna be a good one," he said, throwing his arms around Sarah and me, and leaning in to kiss his son. He bounded away after that, revealing his parents behind him, who took Lou home with them, leaving Sarah to her first childless Friday night in weeks.

She ordered a glass of wine from the first waitress that passed by, and Brady and I ordered our fourth or fifth beer from another as the lights dimmed and the Lizards took the stage.

Mike was right; this was a good one. They sounded great through the first few songs, and like the rest of the bar, we were on our feet as we listened, Mack and I dancing close like we rarely did.

They played a little longer as we danced on, until Mike stepped up to the mic and pointed to the back of the bar toward us.

"We've got one more before we take a little break," he said. "But to play it, we need a little help from the guy who helped me write it. Connor Hall, get up here." The whole bar seemed to turn my way as I froze, surprised and dumbstruck. I managed to smile and shake my head, but he called for me again and a wave of applause swelled up under me as Brady and Mack each pulled me by an arm until I was starting through the crowd on my way to the stage.

Mike came down to pull me up, handing me his guitar and grabbing his banjo.

"I couldn't debut Reed's song without you," he beamed, and urged the crowd to give me another round of applause as I slung the six-string over my shoulder. I looked over the crowd and found Mack and Brady in the back, and watched as Carl stepped in behind them, greeting Mack before stopping dead in his tracks when he noticed me on stage. "Here we go!" Mike yelled out to me, pulling me back to the moment and counting us in.

I fumbled through the first few bars, but found my way before too long, and quickly got lost in the song. I bucked and swayed with each chord and thought for a second about that dream I'd had, and watched Mike as he sang our words, then called me up to join him.

We sang together into his mic like one of those cheesy scenes in a 90's sitcom, and for a moment, I couldn't see the rest of the band. It was just him and me, like we were a good version of our middle school selves playing at that dance, and I remembered how much fun I had that night, and how I never mention that when I tell that story – even when I told it to you a while ago.

I watched the crowd dance as we sang, and heard that odd quiet you hear when a band starts a new song get replaced with the raucous cheers you hear during an old favorite. I found Sarah in the crowd and watched her wipe away a tear, then turned back to Mike to see one form in his eye and felt as close to both of them as I did distant, if that makes sense.

Lost as I was, I nearly missed the end of the song, but I managed to catch on just in time, and join in on that big finish you get at the end of a set. Mike put down his banjo and hugged me, then grabbed me by the hand and threw our arms in the air like I'd just won a prizefight. The crowd roared loud as we stood there, wrapping us all in a blanket of warmth as applause and laughter can. We ran off stage before it died out and Mike and I leaned against the wall catching our breath – not saying anything, just smiling at one another, savoring every second we could, afraid that anything else might break whatever spell had been cast on us.

"That was unexpected," Carl said a few minutes later when I'd made my way back to my friends. They were all sitting together at a table – Mack next to Carl, playing nice while in a crowd. Sarah jumped up to greet me as I came close, throwing her thin arms around me and whispering into my ear.

"I love that song," she said, and squeezed me tightly for a few seconds.

"You were great," Mack said, stepping to us. Brady didn't stand up, he just handed me a fresh beer and pulled the chair next to him back away from the table.

"Unexpected?" I said, taking my spot between Brady and Carl, circling back to what my former boss had just said. "Like you resigning and moving to California?"

He smiled before answering and exchanged a look with Mack. I knew hers well. It said "you're wrong, but whatever." It's her way of agreeing to disagree.

"Was that really a surprise?" he said when he turned back. "I wasn't happy," he continued. "And I couldn't even keep it a secret. You had to know." In a second, I thought back over my months outside Carl's office – on the times I'd heard him yell out and all the long stares out the window or at his surfboard. Of course I knew, but maybe I figured it all melted away on nights and weekends. Maybe he left it all behind when he walked out the door and maybe that was enough. Or maybe I thought it was just how it works. Or maybe I was just in denial. "I fought it for a long time," he said, dragging me out of my head, "but I couldn't anymore. I wanted more than that." The lights dimmed as soon as he finished that sentence and the crowd rose to their feet to welcome the band back on stage. The room erupted around us but we stayed in our seats as I considered what he said and explored its deepest, darkest corners.

"Come on," I finally said, leaning in toward him. "Let's go get another drink."

The Lizards' second set was even better than the first. At least I'm assuming it was, if the crowd noise can be taken as any indication. I didn't hear much of it myself. I bought Carl a beer as the set began and one quickly turned to two, and two became three, and three become more, and more become the two of us in the back of the bar talking about the perfect piece of land he and his father bought on the coast, and how he'd get up in the morning and surf as the sun rose, then close down the shop and surf again at sunset, and about the house he was going to buy, and how this was all my fault.

"What?" I asked, incredulous.

"Maybe not your fault," he said, throwing up his hands, "but you had something to do with it."

"How?"

"Do you remember that thing you wrote about that asshole football coach who wouldn't let the kid do the play?" I nodded. I remembered every word, but you already know that. "McKenzie gave it to me to read, and I thought about what you said about experiencing everything, and it got inside my head. I thought a lot about whether the kid version of me would be happy to see what I was doing now. And the answer was pretty clear."

"Well, I'm glad I could help?" I said, still nodding, finding new deep, dark corners to explore.

"That was one of your best," he said, unaware of how he'd just knocked me off balance. "But I liked the fuck one better."

"You read that one too?"

"I read a lot of them." By this point, Carl was pretty drunk, and talking pretty fast, rambling almost. "You were great at that. Why aren't you doing that still?" I was pretty drunk, too, but not so drunk that I couldn't feel the weight of the question.

"I don't know," I said as the band brought the house down on my chest, it seemed, and we slipped out with the crowd into the warm, nearly-summer night. There was a haze in the air hanging over the street. It was like the whole world was translucent, and I was looking past it into something else, something unknown.

"Good luck," Carl said, shaking my hand one more time and hailing a cab.

"Congratulations," I managed, still looking through him. "You too." I hugged him and watched his cab slip beyond the vale, bound for parts unknown, then climbed into Mack's car as she steered it past all the blurred fluorescent lights and back to my apartment.

Chapter 54

The sunset was as bright and beautiful as it was colorful. There were pinks and purples and oranges spread across the sky with a thick brush. I was standing in the sand watching it all, seeing the sun shift subtly through the hole worn in the wood of the lifeguard stand.

I was back on the beach we used to play on when I was young. Because I was young. Six or seven or eight, maybe. I looked up and down the beach looking for anyone else in my family, but there was no sign of them, and no sign of anyone else, either. For as far as I could see, there was nothing but sand and water, no sound but the wind and the crashing waves.

I kept watching the sun set over the ocean like I knew it couldn't on the east coast, and stepped out from behind the lifeguard stand to take a closer look – when a splashing caught my eye.

There was a surfer out in the waves, slashing across them as they broke. I watched him for what felt like hours. He rode each one expertly, never once falling off the board, even as they started to build higher.

The light was lingering longer than it should, long enough to show storm clouds building in the distance, stirring up the water and building the waves higher and higher with each passing set. They were crashing further up the beach, too, and before long they were bigger than any wave I'd ever seen.

The water was crashing against my feet, but still I watched, and still he rode. But still they continued to grow. They were monsters, thrashing hard against my legs, and then my waist.

"Connor!" someone shouted behind me. "Get out of there!" I turned to see who'd yelled, expecting to see Maggie or Mack, but instead, saw

someone else, someone I never thought I'd see again. It was Hailey, in the same dress she'd worn that night in Atlantic City, her hair blowing in the wind.

I wanted to run to her, but my feet stayed still. "They're getting too big!" Get away!" she yelled, but I didn't move toward her, not until a wave did what my legs wouldn't. It hit me square in the chest and threw me down on to my back, then carried me up the beach until I was sitting in the sand.

The waves kept coming after that, breaking bigger and stronger, crashing into and around me. Hailey was still yelling but I couldn't see her anymore; I couldn't see anything but the water and the darkening sky. The sound of the waves was thunderous as it grew louder, and broken only by Hailey's shouting, and one terrified scream that pierced through it all.

I looked up toward that scream to find the surfer airborne, finally thrown from his board and flying over my head. Through the water, I could see him clearly, just for a split second, just long enough to see Carl's face starring back at mine. He was younger than I know him to be, with long hair dropping past his eyes.

He disappeared out of my view and behind him came the wave that had tossed him, and as I heard his body hit the sand, I heard Hailey let out another scream and saw the world turn black as the water hit my head, and felt my whole body leave the ground.

Chapter 55

I didn't deserve my job at Winter and Wall. I knew it when I worked there and I know it now – and you've known it this whole time you've been reading about it. The job was a gift from the CEO to his daughter and future son-in-law – one I'd hoped to earn. It was an unspoken gift, but everyone I worked with knew it, too, which is probably why Mack's father never stopped at my cube the few times a week he passed it. We saw each other plenty, but in the office, we never spoke. Not until a week after Carl's last day, the Friday before Brady's wedding.

"Connor," he said stepping into the doorway of my cubicle, startling me. "Can I borrow you for a minute? I'm not interrupting anything, am I?"

"Mr. Winter," I said, standing and straightening my tie before turning back to shuffle some papers on my desk and pretend like I hadn't just been staring into the void just short of my computer. "Not at all. What can I do for you?"

Wilson Winter is a smaller man who I imagine looks like a child behind his massive desk. On sight alone, he's not a man you'd expect to be atop a major law firm. But where his colleagues built their empires with brute board and courtroom force, Mr. Winter built his on relationships. He knows people. He knows when his clients need to be convinced or settled down, and he knows when his employees need a few words of encouragement from the boss.

"Not here," he said, motioning over his shoulder and turning toward Carl's unoccupied office. He'd left his suit jacket upstairs, and as I walked behind him, I looked over his monogrammed suspenders and wondered if I'd ever seen him so casually dressed. I hadn't – at least not at work. "How are you, son?" he said as he shut the door behind us.

We sat together in the chairs that Carl had left behind, and as I started to answer, my eyes found a worn-out spot on the carpet where Carl's surfboard used to sit. It was strange being in there. It had been a week since Carl cleaned it out, but I hadn't so much as looked in the office since.

It was bright that day. The sun was streaming in through the windows and as it shined on the desk and the bookcases, you could see the outline of where there had once been pictures and paintings, with a thin film of dust collected everywhere else. In those spots, the wood was still polished and perfect, fresh and rich.

"I'm doing alright," I said, pulling my eyes away from that spot in the carpet – if only for a second. "How are you?"

"You know, you surprised me when you took this job, and I'm not someone who gets surprised very often" he said, ignoring the question we both knew I'd asked just to be polite. He leaned forward with his elbows on his thighs and continued. "Mackenzie wanted me to make you an offer and she's not an easy woman to say no to," he said with a chuckle. "But even as I agreed, I didn't think you'd ever accept."

"Well, Mr. Winter, I'm glad you did," I said. Shortly after Mack and I started dating, he told me I could call him Wilson. Years later, I had still never done it, and wasn't about to start.

"I am, too," he said. "Carl spoke highly of your work, especially after you'd first started.

"He was a good boss to work for," I said, my head turning itself toward the corner, my mind wondering why I'd been such a surprise.

"He was," he said, his whole body rocking back and forth in agreement. "And I know it must be hard for you, which is why I wanted to check in and see if you were still with us." He waited for a beat and I nodded. "And I promise you that soon enough, we'll have someone in this office who will be another good boss to work for. And I know he had talked to you about law school and a long-term future here, and I want you to know that if it's still what you want, it's still all there for you. You have a home here, Connor."

"Thank you, sir," I said still turned away, until my head snapped back toward him. "Mr. Winter, why were you so sure I wasn't going to take the job?"

He sighed heavily as he leaned back in the chair.

"I just didn't think it was what you wanted anymore," he said, his own eyes finding the middle distance. "But I'm glad it was." And with that, he reached over and patted the side of my leg as he stood to leave. I followed him with my eyes as he walked in front of me, but stopped when he walked past that corner of the room where the surfboard had been. I heard him open the door and step out into the hallway, but for a while, I didn't move. Not until a familiar voice broke my concentration.

"What are you doing in here?" It was Mack; she was standing in the doorway, her bags in her hand and her head cocked to the side. I didn't have an answer for her, but she didn't make me come up with one. "I feel like you haven't been at your desk all week."

She was right. I'd gone back to taking walks. The back room, the patent division, the executive wing, the smoking area out back, I hit them all during that week.

"Are you Ok?" she said, dropping the bags and stepping toward me as I straightened up in the chair. "You've been off all week. At least."

She was right about that, too. It was like I hadn't woken up from that dream, from any of them. It was like I could feel the waves pounding in my chest, and I could feel the water rising higher and higher, lifting me off the ground.

"Connor?" she said, stepping closer. I still hadn't looked at her. I didn't want her to see that I didn't have an answer.

"Huh?" I finally said, pretending to be startled, like I hadn't heard everything she'd just said. "Did you say something?"

"Are you OK?" she said sternly, crossing her arms.

"Yeah, I'm fine," I answered as nonchalantly as I could, finally turning to her and kissing her on the cheek. "I'm sorry. I'm just tired. And I can't believe he left." And with that, I took her by the hand and started toward the door. "Let's get going," I said, eager to get on the road and get away from as many of the waves as I could.

Chapter 56

I hate traveling north. It always feels like I'm running uphill, like it takes longer to get wherever I'm going because I'm working against gravity. I know that doesn't make sense, but either way, I always drive a little faster when I'm going north, just in case.

That day, I drove a *lot* faster, Mack warning me once or twice to slow down as we made the 90-minute drive to the lakeside hotel hosting Brady and Kaitlyn's Adirondack wedding.

The resort is a popular destination for weddings, famous for the lush green lawn I found shortly after we arrived. It jutted out into the lake and led down to a private beach ringed by blue water and green mountains. The whole complex was nestled into a horseshoe bend in the shoreline, so as I stood on the lawn, I could see how wide and large the lake was, and see ripples roll across its surface, disturbed by either wind or wake. The mountains rose like a wall above the water, looking light years away but somehow right on top of me as I wondered about the last time I last went hiking.

You could see three or four of the Adirondack's 46 high peaks from where I was standing, and I remember thinking about the SUV we followed up the highway, with a "46" sticker on the bumper bragging that she'd climbed them all – reminding me that I was still at 0. Brady and Kaitlyn had climbed their 9th that morning.

"Connor!" they both yelled behind me, greeting me with an arm around my back before I could turn. Kaitlyn was in a white sundress looking every bit the bride, with a flower in her hair helping pull it back away from her face. Brady was in white, too, a sharp, well-ironed button up over Navy blue dress pants.

Mack and I had just checked in to our corner suite on the resort's top floor – the room the hotel recommended when they heard the best man and maid of honor were coming together. It was a large room of white and chocolate brown, with a tub built for two and a bed nestled in the corner, facing a wall of windows that looked out across the full length of the lake and the full height of the mountains.

"This place is gorgeous," I said to both of them, throwing my arms over their shoulders. "This is going to be an incredible weekend. Congrats again." I smiled at Brady and gave Kaitlyn a kiss on the cheek before she skipped off to meet up with Mack, who'd already jumped into her maid of honor duties and started talking with the wedding planner about the flatware or the napkins or something I'm sure only she had noticed.

Brady watched her jog off while I watched him watch her with a smile that stretched out from one ear to another. He was grinning in a way he never does, and when he turned back toward me my grip around his shoulders got a little tighter, and we walked down to the beach to wait for dinner. While we waited, Brady talked about their morning hike and another they had planned for the day after the wedding, and the boat trip he'd set up for the groomsmen the next morning while the ladies were in the spa. As he talked, the sun slid lower and the resort filled up with their guests – some who came down to say hello, and some who didn't. And a few who came down to stay. Four, to be exact.

Mike came first, walking down the hill to the beach with his son in his arms. It had only been days since I saw him, but for some reason, as he cooed happily in his father's arms, Lou looked so much bigger than he had at the Lizard's show – wearing a tuxedo t-shirt as he reached for my sunglasses.

He'd pulled them off my face and was holding them tight in his tiny fist when Noah and Will came bounding down to the lake, fresh off their flight up from D.C. Z came a few minutes behind them, strolling through the grass, the first time any of us had seen him in months.

We greeted each other with hugs and handshakes, and as we stood on the beach with the lake and the mountains around and above us, I thought back to the last night we were together: My birthday, and Lou's birthday, too. I looked again at Lou and one more time I marveled at how much he'd grown and wondered how much the rest of us had grown with him. There was something building there, deep in the dark hallows of my chest, but it never had time to pick up any steam. We weren't all together two minutes before Mack's voice called us up to the resort for dinner, where we laughed and drank like we used to, except with better food and more expensive drinks, and with a reasonable bedtime, rather than one that dared the sunrise.

When that sun did rise the next morning, the girls were already at the spa. It wasn't until a few hours later that the six of us rolled out of our beds and onto the pontoon boat the resort was loaning us for the day.

It was a choppy ride on the lake, with a strong wind blowing under a bright blue sky, with thin, wispy clouds scattered across it. I was behind the captain's wheel but had no clue where I was going, so I steered the boat aimlessly as we talked, meandering lazily across the water, against and with the blowing breeze and everything it stirred up in the water.

It always surprises me how fast we bounce back – how quickly we go from strangers learning about the lives we've been living to the same high school kids we knew so well.

Noah talked about his last few dates with Karen, and Z told us about his latest shoot. I told them all about Carl, and Will had us debating the latest budget battle in Washington. And soon after that we were back talking about chemistry class and Shelly Linderman's skirts. It all came so fast, the jokes and the laughs, like we'd been waiting those months for that exact conversation, when we could all quit whatever con we'd been running and just let it all out.

I steered the boat into a little bay as Brady started a game of Questions, asking how many tanks we thought it would take to defeat the Roman army. We all gave our answers as I tossed out the anchor, and hours later we were dozens of questions in, enjoying the time out of the wind. We laid out in the sun and soaked in its warmth, the conversation and the questions still coming. Every now and then there'd be a lull and I'd find myself staring up at the mountains or thinking of Carl and whether or not he was surfing. But then something would pull me back to the boat and the laughs and the memories would take hold – until someone looked at their phone and realized it was time to go make another one. So as the clouds started to thicken, I steered us out of that bay and back into the wind.

That one flower had a become at least a dozen in Kaitlyn's hair, worn in long curls and met at her shoulders by the simple, elegant dress she wore. A string quartet played as she walked up the aisle on a white carpet laid out atop the lawn, leading to a birch arbor they'd put on top of a small hill that looked straight down onto the water's edge, in between two mighty oak trees that towered over the whole wedding, with those mountains behind them.

As the crowd stood to welcome her, I turned to look at Mack who'd just taken her place up front. She smiled wide at me for a second, and then turned back to watch Kaitlyn. But as she did, I lingered on her, until my eyes caught Brady's smile.

Brady has always been the sarcastic one, who's just as quick to joke and laugh as the rest of us, but who has never been one for wide, sparkling smiles. But even more than the night before, he was glowing as he watched his bride make her way toward him. And as the minister welcomed us all, my eyes stayed with him and that smile. They declared their intent and no one voiced any objections, and through it all, that smile was there. It was there through the vows and into the exchange of the rings, when he turned to me with a tear in his eye and I handed them over, a lump forming in my throat and a wide smile of my own taking shape. Mike must have noticed Brady, too, because he nudged me slightly when the groom turned back to Kaitlyn, and I thought about the way Mike had smiled just as wide at his wedding, and how he'd cried when his son was born. And suddenly I was searching for Lou in the crowd, looking again at how big he was.

I shook myself out of it for a second, just in time for the minister to tell Brady to kiss his bride. I helped lead the applause as the two turned to face the crowd and skip off to a new life, leaving Mack and I behind at the arbor.

Chapter 57

Brady didn't want to do any big entrances, so instead of a cocktail hour and a formal reception, he and Kaitlyn walked right off the white carpet and onto the dance floor for their first dance.

Mack and I held hands as we watched them slowly twirl in the center of the floor, their eyes locked on each other, their grins both bright and brilliant. Mack was leaning against me as they danced. I put my head on top of hers and felt her hands weave into mine, and saw a starburst as she faced me. I turned and kissed her, hoping to spark some kind of big bang and worrying it would end up more like a black hole. When it was neither, I hugged her tightly and turned back to Brady and Kaitlyn. They were gorgeous, and I felt a love and happiness for them that grew with each passing second. As the music wound down we all clapped and cheered, and Brady called us all onto the dance floor to "get the party started" as he put it. I squeezed Mack's hand and pulled her out to meet them, jumping in before the others – before even the frat boys we'd met at Brady's bachelor party and spent his wedding night trying to avoid – just as the band kicked into one of those upbeat dance tunes you love to hear at a wedding but click away from on your stereo.

The sun was just starting to set over the lake as the first chorus started. It was incredible, with a whole palette of color sprayed across the still-thickening clouds. I turned my back on it and faced the resort, and joined in as we all sung along to the song we knew by heart, hoping a chorus could help drown out whatever whispers were building in my mind.

I refused to listen to them. I refused to hear them. Not that night. Instead, I focused on the reception and forced them to fade away, needing to try harder at certain times, like when Mack and I we were quietly called away to pose for pictures with Brady and Sarah beneath the arbor, or when just the guys went down to the beach for a few photographs in the final seconds of sunset.

Or when I took the microphone, raised my glass, and started improvising.

"Hi, my name is Connor Hall, and I appreciate romantic comedies." I was standing at the head table in front of nearly two hundred friends, family members and complete strangers. I'd worked on a speech all week, but had thrown it out during the ceremony, and standing at the front of the luxurious dining room decorated in whites and pinks, I was just thinking about what I already knew I'd remember forever from the ceremony.

"Now I know that's a strange way to open a toast," I said, "but stay with me, I promise this is going somewhere." I paused as the crowd laughed, and I smiled at Brady, whose own smile was almost as large as it had been all night. "There's this one rom-com in particular. I don't remember which one so don't ask me," another laugh, "and it talks about weddings and looking at the groom when everyone else turns to watch the bride walk in. It's a terrible movie," I continued, but stopped when that line was greeted by groans. "What? I appreciate them, I don't like them," I joked. "I didn't even want to see it. She made me," and I pointed to Mack for another cheap laugh.

"I bring it up because tonight, as Kaitlyn started down the aisle and each and every one of you turned to looked at how beautiful she is, I looked at my friend Brady, and I watched him light up like I've never seen him light up before." I looked down and saw Kaitlyn lean over and kiss him. "Now, I've known him a long time, and we've been together for the best moments of our lives. But I can assure you, this was different. This was something new. This was something more. This was something better. And you know, it's a cliché to talk about a groom marrying their best friend, but I'm going to do it anyway, because it's true tonight. Because Kaitlyn is the only person in the world who has known Brady longer and better than Mike and me. And it's another cliché to talk about having found a soul mate, but maybe I've seen too many rom-coms, because I'm going to say that too. Because again, it's true tonight, and I saw it in that smile, and, with the benefit of hindsight, I think we all realize we've been seeing it our whole lives. Playmates and friends and then best friends long before their relationship grew into something different. Something new. Something more. Something better. Now I promised myself to pretend to be brief tonight, so let me tie this all together by saying this: Brady, Kaitlyn: what you have, what you have become, is something so beautiful and something so special. And I've known it long before tonight, but I saw it again in that smile, and I'm so honored to have been here to share this incredible weekend with you, and I'm so excited to celebrate the life you two have built and see what you build in the future. And I look forward to the lifetime of happiness you bring out in one another. Good luck and great love to you both. To Brady and Kaitlyn."

They were both crying when they stood up to hug me, Kaitlyn making it to me before Brady could. I gave them both long, tight hugs, then sat back down next to Mack, and stealing one final look at the mountains before the last of the light faded to black, I took a deep breath and thought about soul mates and best friends and that smile. And just as I started to shudder, I exhaled it all away and jumped into whatever was happening around our table.

Things had already gotten loud amongst the lot of us, and they stayed that way for a while. We ate dinner and drank and joked and when the food was gone and the drinks were low, we went back out to the dance floor and lost ourselves in the music. We danced wildly like no one was watching – like our parents weren't all seated together in the crowd, looking on and judging us for a while before they headed back to their houses and left the resort to the kids who weren't really kids anymore. The band played through the upbeat Stevie Wonder and Jackson 5 tunes and moved on to the slower Van Morrison and Louie Armstrong songs so we could pull each other close and sway sweetly in our intimate circles and forget the world outside – a world you couldn't see unless you tried.

Clouds had taken over by then, so the night sky was even darker than usual, and I as I danced with Mack and watched Brady dance with Kaitlyn and Mike dance with Sarah, I convinced myself that there was nothing beyond the dance floor – that there was only that band, those friends, and that girl dancing in front of and on top of me. But sometime after "Shout!" I stepped off that floor to catch my breath and it all changed.

"Hey," I said to Z, who'd stepped away just before I had. "What a day, right?" I asked, chuckling, looking back on it all.

"Yeah," he said, turning toward me and leaning up against a thick maple tree off to the side of the lawn. I could hear the water quietly lapping against the shore below us. "I miss days like this. With all of us together, like the old days in that screen house."

"I know," I said, thinking back to that morning in the bay, and those brief few seconds on the beach the night before. "We need more days like today," and we both paused in silent consideration of what that might be like before I went on and ruined it. "That's awesome about the Met," I said, referencing a story he'd told about the behind the scenes look he'd gotten while filming a new commercial.

"Yeah, it's good," he said, almost sighing, and we spent the next few minutes talking about working for the state, and the people he'd met and the places he'd seen, and the summer travel commercial he'd directed with a jingle we all had stuck in our heads for weeks. He was quiet and calm, even for Z, and it was almost as though we were standing on opposite sides of the lake as we talked.

"It's so great, seeing your stuff on TV," I said smiling. "Sometimes we still can't believe it. I'm happy it's working out. We're proud of you." He looked away when I said it.

"How's the family?" he asked, still turned away, eyes toward the water below us.

I told him about Aaron and the battery and about Maggie and the kids, and we talked for a few minutes until things circled back to Carl and the law firm. I laughingly told him about the chair I'd taken apart and about going back to get my law degree, and about how lucky I was to have the job, and when we got through it all, Z turned back to me for the first time and looked me square in the eye, and asked me a question that took away the breath I'd only just managed to catch.

"Are you happy?"

Something faltered inside me when he asked it. Carl and I had danced around it more than once, but this was different. This wasn't Carl. This was someone who knows me – someone who already knew the answer.

"Are you happy?" he asked again when I managed only a shrug.

My blood ran cold the second time and there was a hollowness in my chest that felt all too familiar as it spread through the rest of my

259

body. Z took a step forward, and there was pain on his face as he continued.

"What are you doing, Connor?" he asked. "Because can I be honest with you? I'm not proud of you." Whatever was left in me drained out of my shoes as he turned away for a second, but then spun back to me. "I love you buddy, but you hated law. There's a reason you walked away from it. And to see you back in it, trying to convince yourself it's ok. It's tough."

I started to answer, but no words came out, so Z leaned back against the tree again and continued.

"I'm sorry, he said, and he looked up toward the starless sky, the band playing some dance tune in the background, the raucous party sound-tracking Z's destruction of any sense of contentment I may have been clinging to. "We can pretend like you're not, but we both know you're miserable, and I've had this vision of you since I heard you'd gone back. It's you, 20 years from now in Atlantic City. And you're betting the house on black just to 'add some life to your life.'" Somehow, he drew a smile there as I remembered Billy from Philly, but it faded as quickly as it came, as I started seeing it too, seeing myself drained of anything but desperation and denial.

"What am I supposed to do?" I said, surprised I had the strength to pick up my head. "I'm being lapped." Z's head tilted to the side like he didn't know what I meant. "Look around," I said. "Everyone here has it all put together. You've all got jobs doing what you love. Mike's got a kid. Brady's married. I'm too far behind to start back at the starting line. And what right do I have? So, I don't like my job. I'm in a better spot than plenty of people out there."

"But you're miserable," he countered quickly. "And look closer. You think I wanted to be doing tourism videos? You think Brady wouldn't rather be in a loft somewhere painting? Or hanging

260

murals in a museum? We're hanging on to a piece of it, and you're not even doing that." A cold wind kicked up just then, and for the first time, I noticed how the temperature had dropped. I looked back to the reception and watched Mack dance on without me.

"What am I supposed to do?" I asked again. Still watching her.

"I don't know," Z said. "But we both know it's not this."

We kept talking for a few more minutes, but I don't remember any more of it. I just remember him apologizing for bringing it up and me telling him he didn't need to, and I remember sometime later, pulling him into a hug and thinking to myself 'because you're right.'

Chapter 58

The stack of papers on my desk got higher and higher each time I looked at it. I rubbed my weary eyes with both hands and when I opened them again, the pile had doubled, and when I reached for something on my bookcase they doubled again.

I sighed and collapsed into the leather of my chair, but jumped to my feet when I felt something sharp in my back. I inspected the chair but found nothing. Still, I was afraid to sit back down, so instead, I stayed standing and took stock.

My cubicle walls were cleaner than ever before. The reminders and important documents I'd tacked to them were all gone, and all that was left was that blue felt, which, as I looked closer, didn't quite look the same. It was brighter than before – clearer, with a shine. I bent over for a better look, and as I leaned in even closer, I saw that they were moving. I picked up my hand and ran it slowly along one wall. It was smoother than the old, familiar felt, and when I pulled my fingers away, they were wet.

I rubbed them together, feeling the wetness, examining it, and leaned back in over my desk to feel it again, but something caught my eye in the hallway. A large man was lumbering through the office, his head down, his arms swinging back and forth with each step. I recognized the walk immediately.

"Harry!" I called, but he didn't seem to hear me, and just kept storming down the hall, the way he did at The Tribune. I yelled again but it was lost amid the noise of Carl's office door as it swung open loudly, my former boss stepping out from behind it to slide into step behind Harry. This time I called to them both, but neither broke stride.

I turned to follow them, but when I spun toward the entrance to my cubicle, I found only another wall. It was like the others; light blue and shimmering under the fluorescent lights. I turned again, searching my cube for a way out, but as I turned and turned, I found nothing but walls. I yelled to them both again, but they just kept going, beginning to fade into the office maze.

I could feel my heart in my chest as panic took hold and I turned back to where my door should be. I put my hand to the wall and again felt the water. Desperate, I pushed hard and watched my hand sink into it before turning my head to find Harry and Carl, making out only their silhouettes in the distance.

I pushed harder still and started to step through the wall, but just before my foot broke through, the whole cubicle shook, and with a loud boom, the smooth, glimmering wall of water became a rushing river, cascading down like a waterfall.

I jumped back and frantically looked around. All four walls were flowing now, with water gushing down from top to bottom. Terrified, I stepped toward my computer to look again for a way out, and felt my heart jump as I heard a splash when my foot hit the ground.

I looked down and saw the water pooling at my feet, getting deeper with each passing second. I screamed for anyone who could hear me, yelling toward the distant shadows I knew to be Carl and Harry. They turned my way this time but didn't come back toward me; they just stood still and silent as the back wall of the office crumbled and gave way to bright, blinding light.

The water was at my knees now and still rising. I threw myself into each wall but they wouldn't budge, like there was something solid behind them. Before long, the water was at my hips as I thrashed about, desperate for a way out. I threw my hands up to wave for help, and only then noticed the clear blue wall above me, too, connected to the others.

I was trapped, with the water at my chest, rising more and more as I struggled. Soon, it was at my throat and then my nose, and just before it rose above my eyes, I caught one last glimpse of Harry and Carl, and watched them disappear into the white.

I fought to break through the walls again but it was no use. I felt the water overtake the top of my head, and I felt my feet lifted off the ground.

Chapter 59

I woke up screaming this time, sitting straight up, sweating and panting. Mack was awake, too, her eyes filled with questions.

"What's wrong?" she asked, sitting up. There was a flash of light from outside and a second later, a monstrous crash of thunder that shook us both. It was pouring outside, with rain whipping loudly against the windows.

"Nothing," I said, still looking out the window. "I think the thunder just startled me." I turned to her and forced a smile. She looked at me unconvinced, but her frown faded when another crash of thunder rattled the walls. She rolled closer to me as thunder clapped again, and pulled me in tight against her body. With another boom, she kissed me deeply and wrapped her body around mine, and we took on Mother Nature as the storm raged just beyond our walls. A while later, she fell back asleep on my shoulder, tucked into a familiar position with a satisfied smile on her face. I closed my eyes to do the same but sleep never came. Instead, I searched for the lake and mountains with each flash of lightning and wondered when morning would come. When it finally did, we laid in bed together, taking in the sweeping views and looking back on the night.

"It was gorgeous, wasn't it? Mack said. "I love weddings."

"I know you do," I laughed, searching her tone for a deeper meaning. "And it was."

"What were you and Z talking about last night?" she asked. We were still talking by that tree when the reception ended. Mack found me there and pulled my body up to the room, but my mind stayed right on the lawn. It still there Sunday morning as I assured her that we were just catching up.

It was there through breakfast, too, and while we packed the car and said our goodbyes. There were hugs and handshakes for Mike and Noah and Will, with Brady and Kaitlyn up and out early, climbing their 10ᵗʰ mountain before the next storm rolled in.

You could see the clouds threatening rain when the valet pulled my fathers' car around, but I left the car there for a second and searched for the one friend I hadn't found yet, who I finally saw down on the beach.

"Hey," I called, striding down the lawn. Z turned and smiled. "We're taking off."

"It was good seeing you," he said, shaking my hand, and there was a silence between us as we considered what came next. "I'm sorry about last night," he said after a minute.

"Don't be," I said, still shaking his hand, until he pulled me into a hug. We didn't say more after that, we just hugged for a second longer before I climbed back up on the lawn and took one last look at the lake – the mountains hidden in the dark clouds that looked ready to collapse at any second.

"If you could do anything with your life, what would you do?" I asked Mack after we'd been on the road for a while.

"Exactly what we're doing," she said without hesitation. "You know that. Why?"

"I've been taking a lot of walks, lately" I answered.

"What? Why? What does that mean?"

"There are times, a few times a day, where I just zone out. So I take a walk and just wander around the office. To clear my head, I think. Do you ever do that?"

266

"No," she said, something different in her voice, something I hadn't heard in months.

"What do you think that means?" I asked, curious for her response.

"I think that means you're still getting used to the work. You'll be fine." That was the answer I expected.

"What if it means I hate it, and I shouldn't be doing it?" I asked, eyes on the road, head under that maple tree.

"Connor, stop it," she said sharply. I could feel her eyes digging into me while mine stayed on the road, sure that there was more in my face than I wanted her to see. "What's going on?"

"What if this isn't what I want to be when I grow up?" I asked with a forced chuckle, hoping it would break up the building tension.

"Well, it is what you're doing and you're already grown up." Those words sent another shockwave through me, like Z's had the night before. "You'll get into a rhythm with the work but it takes time. Be patient. You're in a great spot." I started to answer, but after a few words in she cut me off. "Connor. You always talked about wanting to have it all figured out early. You do. Just accept it. Maybe it's not the best right now, but you'll go back to school, you'll move up in the company, and it'll get better."

"I couldn't make it through undergrad without a full-on freak out," I pointed out, still refusing to turn my head.

"You're older now."

Finally, I took my eyes off the road and saw her expression soften as she registered whatever was in my face, but before either of us could say anything, her phone rang. It was the office and they needed her to go to Boston that night to be in place for an early meeting the next day.

We rode in silence for a while after that, and somewhere along the way another storm rolled through. The sky grew darker as thunder roared and lightning sparked across the sky, and it was as though the whole highway might explode. The lightning was moving almost as fast as my mind, which was bouncing back and forth between everything Z had said and everything Mack had said, and everything I was feeling then and everything I'd felt before over a whole life in the suburbs.

It felt like my whole head might explode along with the road as I dropped Mack off and she implored me to relax, and it felt like the whole neighborhood might explode, too, as I turned into Meadowbrook Estates to return the car, and wound my way through the trees and the lawns and the proud parents who I'm sure would have talked to me for hours about their kids and all they'd accomplished if I slowed down enough to let them.

And as I turned onto Cobbler's Court, it looked like my parents' whole house was already exploding, with at least a dozen cars parked around the cul-de-sac, and some party I didn't expect already in full swing.

Chapter 60

"What's going on?" I said after parking on the street and walking into a flurry of activity, with aunts and uncles and cousins spread throughout the house.

"Go ask you brother," my mother said, bubbling with energy, walking past the front door with a plate of food. "He's in the garage."

Confused, I waded through the crowd, saying my hellos as I went.

"What's going on?" I asked again, this time stepping into the garage to find Aaron at his workbench, the battery in his hand. He turned around slowly, smiling as he did.

"I sold it," he said, holding it up. I rocked back stunned and confused, not sure I'd heard him right.

"What?"

"I sold it," he said again, standing up off the stool he'd been leaning on. "It happened so fast. We agreed to the deal this morning. G.E. is giving me six figures for it."

"Are you kidding me?" I asked, even more stunned than just seconds before, my brain still lagging behind as I processed. "Are you kidding me!?" I asked one more time, but louder, my mind slowly catching up. "That's incredible!" I practically screamed and leapt the few feet between us to hug him. "Congratulations!" I yelled through a laugh, still hugging him before finally stepping back. "So, it works?" I asked, my voice dropping a few decibels. "I mean, it's really a self-sustaining battery?"

"Oh God no," Aaron laughed. "That was never really going to work. But they think it will help them lengthen battery life, so they bought the design and it'll give me enough money to open my own studio."

"Wow," I said simply. I leaned back against the fridge to catch my breath and found that every part of me was shaking, and after only a few seconds pressed against the cold metal of the door, I was pulling Aaron back into another hug. "Congrats," I said again. "You're amazing, brother," and he pulled back with a smirk.

"And it's not over yet," he said cryptically, handing me the battery and heading back inside. I stayed behind for a few minutes, turning it over in my hands. For a moment, I thought I felt that cylinder heating up again, like it was about to explode the way the first one had, but I realized after a second that it wasn't the battery at all, it was just me.

I closed my eyes and took a few deep breaths, hoping to settle my body before going back in, hoping to forget about everything that had run roughshod through my mind all morning. With one more shake of the head, I put the battery back on the bench and followed Aaron into the house and took a seat at the table next to Maggie and Ed, where we told our favorite stories about the family baby – like the one about the t-shirt cannon.

Afternoon became evening as we sat in the dining room and my mother ordered more food and rang her knife against her glass when it arrived. My father stood at the head of the table and smiled at Aaron, and talked like he had just weeks before about how proud they were of everything he'd done, and how excited they were for whatever came next. There were tears again as he said it all, and there were even a few in Aaron's eyes, too, as he hugged them both and turned to the rest of us.

"Thank you," he said simply, as a clap of thunder announced another storm. That's all you'd expect Aaron to say, so we didn't think he'd continue, and we certainly didn't expect what came next. "Thank you to everyone who helped me. Mom and Dad, and you guys," he said, pointing to the three of us. "And Bethany," he said, walking toward her as she sat in the chair next to Maggie. "You've been great to me, and I can't imagine doing this without you. So, don't make me." A second later he was kneeling, and I felt Maggie' hand clamp down on my leg. Apparently, she shared my shock. He took a black box from his pocket and looked into Bethany's eyes. "Will you marry me?"

If Bethany answered, I didn't hear it. Instead, all I heard was white noise and a clap of thunder, until after a second, a dining room of excited cheers hit me all at once. Bethany was in Aaron's arms, lifted off the ground, and my mother was already running into the kitchen for a bottle of champagne I didn't know we had.

"This is a whole different party now!" she yelled, and there were more cheers and applause, including my own. I'd stood up somewhere in all that commotion and was the first one to them, pulling them both into hugs broken only when Maggie and Ed jumped in, followed by all the aunts and uncles and cousins.

I watched as family member after family member embraced them both, and felt that shaking return to my body, the excitement running through me like the electricity flashing in the sky every few seconds, and I felt my heart swell with love for them both, like a balloon I thought might burst at any second. My father made another toast, this time with the champagne, and we stayed at that table for hours longer, the smiles never leaving our faces.

Eventually, though, as night fell, the crowd began to thin, until all that remained at that table were my parents, Ed and his wife, Maggie and her husband, and Aaron and his fiancée. And me.

And me.

And as I repeated those two words in my head, that balloon finally did burst, and a tsunami of freezing cold water exploded in every direction and took everything inside me with it. Suddenly, I was short of breath and I could feel my legs starting to move, maybe with one last rush of adrenaline trying to keep me from collapsing into the puddle I'd become, like when you flail your arms and legs in the final few seconds before sleep.

I found my feet while I could, suddenly aware that the walls were starting to close in on me.

"I have to go," I said, with regret and hatred for myself overtaking the terror for a brief second. I hated that I was leaving, but if I didn't get out just then, I wasn't sure I ever would. I could feel how heavy I was breathing as I hugged Aaron one more time. "I'm so proud of you," I said, my voice cracking as water welled in my eyes. "I love you. Congratulations. On everything." I shared the same moment with Bethany before bursting out the front door and into the rain, gasping for air as I sprinted to the car, wiping away tears as I ran.

I got back into my father's Cadillac and hit the gas, rolling down the windows as I left the neighborhood. I didn't know where I was going and I didn't care. I let the car drive itself as rain came in all four windows and lightning lit up the sky.

In my head, I could hear Mack and Z and Harry and Carl and I could see all that I'd wanted for myself, and all that I'd become. I saw myself as a young boy floating in the ocean, and as an old man trapped beneath it.

It was painted across the sky as I chased the lightning, each flash flickering across the horizon and lighting up different parts of my life hidden in the black, revealing something new each time.

I drove toward it all, desperate for the lightning to show me more, and terrified at the same time of what I might see. I saw the wave that washed me off the stage with Mike, and the one that swept me out of my graduation. I saw myself in college, running from the library, and a few years later, leaving the *Tribune*.

I saw Mack, and I saw Hailey, and I saw those lakeside mountains, and I saw myself running after them all, and never getting any closer to any of them.

And still I chased, driving on through the rain until it, too, had gotten away from me. And when I couldn't chase anymore, I parked my car and stumbled onto the beach, past the lifeguard stand with the hole worn into one its beams, where everything came pouring out. Tears fell quickly from my eyes as my whole body trembled and a crescendo built inside until I screamed out in anger and collapsed into the sand to watch the lightning dance across the ocean and out into eternity, and pray for some vision of myself other than the one I'd see in a mirror.

Chapter 61

When the sun rose the next morning, I was still sitting in the sand. I hadn't moved. I'd watched the lightning fade into the distance and saw the full, consuming black of night take hold. The sand grew cold and damp as the late-night wind whipped across the empty beach. Stars came and went above me, and all the while, my mind moved faster than all of it – even the lightning. I was still seeing my life in those far away flashes, and though the wind and stars and cold had all come, answers hadn't. And just as I started to think the sunrise wouldn't either, the black turned to blue and a splash of fluorescent color appeared on the horizon. Mocking me.

I'd made it through the long night, I was supposed to have come away with some kind of revelation. That's how these things are supposed to work. When the sunlight finally breaks through, so do you. But I didn't. So instead, the bright colors just became a reminder that time powers on, as cold as it is unfeeling.

I watched the sky grow lighter until the sun itself broke the horizon, and when nothing had stirred within me, I decided to stir myself. Slowly, I rose to my feet and trudged down the beach, not stopping, even as I hit the water's edge.

Without breaking stride, I walked into the surf until I tumbled over and into a crashing wave. Wearing the same button up and jeans I'd left the wedding in the day before, I flipped onto my back as I had so many times before in that same water. Arms out to the side, I let myself float in the waves, each one lifting me up and setting me down. I closed my eyes to that rising sun and thought back to when I was young and about how I wasn't anymore, and about the train fading into the distance, and that same spot on the tracks I'd always been on.

In and out and up and down I floated, the cold water stinging my skin until it had soaked through my shirt and filled the pockets of my pants and started to drag me under, so I turned my body toward the beach and let the sea throw me out onto my hands and knees. The sun was fully up as I pulled myself to my feet, feeling the weight of my clothes and so much more, and started slowly up the empty beach. Or nearly empty, I guess.

"Well hi," she said, looking up from her yoga pose, her back arched toward the sky with one leg pointed up. She had auburn hair tied back in a tight ponytail, with a wide, sly smile as she looked up at me, a messenger bag and a camera by her side. I stopped in my tracks and stared at her, dumbfounded. Saying nothing, I turned out toward the ocean before looking back at her, and then down at myself as water pooled beneath me.

"Hi," I managed, sighing as pleasantly as I could. I still can't imagine what I looked like to her as I emerged from the water still in my clothes, soaking wet as I climbed the hill toward her.

"How's your morning?" she asked smiling, unfazed and unmoving.

"Not as good as yours," I said, a small smile finding its way to my face. There was an ease about her you noticed instantly – an aura, like the very air around her was calmer.

"Well, I am the one walking away with the story," she said with the hint of a laugh, her other leg now reaching toward the sky.

"Speak well of me," I joked as I stepped away, and I heard her promise to as she moved into a new position.

I dragged myself back toward my father's car, which I'd parked haphazardly across two spaces. As I walked, I felt all that weight again, and as I made it to the door, I felt exhaustion overtake me. I grabbed a beach towel out of my suitcase in the trunk and drove up the coast to my parents' house.

It looked as pristine as ever as I parked the car. The white shell driveway shined in the sun, and the smell of the fully bloomed hydrangea bushes was almost overpowering. The streets and sidewalks were busy and bustling, but inside that house it was still and quiet, with just the ghosts of summers past stirring in its empty rooms.

Walking through the front door I felt the cold presence of one of those ghosts as I remembered walking through it with my friends, talking about our homework, my father hauling in a piece of wood from the neighbor's trash, muttering to himself about the molding.

I took another step and felt another as I pictured the family gathering around the kitchen island, hoping Aaron could breathe life back into the battery our nephew had helped drown.

In the living room there was another, where Maggie found out she'd passed her boards. Upstairs, there were more, one in each room – the first time Mack stayed with me there, the first time Bethany stayed with Aaron, the first time I gave Jack and Amy a bath. Each room brought a smile to my face, but with each room, the weight of my clothes seemed to get heavier, and I quickly realized how terribly I needed to be free of it.

I lumbered back downstairs and found the phone I didn't remember leaving on the kitchen island. I sent an email to work and a text to Mack telling them I was sick and wouldn't make it in, then saw a message from my father and a few missed calls.

'*Car?*' was all it read.

'*Sorry. I'm fine. I promise.*' I wrote back before leaving the phone there and walking out onto the beach and collapsing back into the sand.

Chapter 62

I spent three days alone in that house, until my father's voice startled me out of whatever corner of my mind I was exploring. I had taken up my spot on the patio after a long night with the ghosts, which came after an even longer day on the beach.

"Hey!" he yelled, calling to me from inside the house. When I turned to find him, his arms were stretched out as he walked toward me, his hands turned up as if to ask with his body language a question he promised my mother he wouldn't ask directly.

What the fuck?

"How'd you know I was here?" I asked, after climbing to my feet and meeting him at the door.

"I used the theft prevention to track the car."

"You tracked me?" I said as though that's not exactly what my parents were going to do.

"Yeah. You stole my car!" he yelled, a laugh bubbling up at the end of it.

"I'm sorry about that," I said, looking down to my bare feet. After all, I *had* stolen his car. "I don't know what happened."

"Later," he said, brushing it aside with his hand. "I've got lunch in the backseat and meat to grill for tonight," he said. "Go grab it while I call your mother and tell her you're alive."

"So, what did happen?" he asked a few hours later, wiping his mouth after finishing the last piece of chicken we'd grilled together.

"I don't know," I said, inspecting the meat I hadn't picked off my drumstick.

"Yeah you do," he said, elbows on the table. "And so do I." When I looked up, I was a kid again, sat down at the dinner table because my father knew I was the one who broke the lamp.

"Dad," I started, my heart beating faster as my eyes darted across the sand and the porch and the chicken on my plate, searching for something that wasn't anywhere to be found. "What am I doing? Why can't I figure this all out?"

"Connor," he said, looking me in the eye. "You've never had anything figured out." He laughed as he said it, drawing one from me, though I'm still not sure why. "It's what I love about you," he continued, and he took a long sip of his beer before going on. "When you guys were all young, you played doctor almost every day. And Maggie was never the patient. Never. She's been headed to private practice since she was five. Aaron's been an engineer since he fixed a problem with his mobile. Ed came to work with me when he was six and never thought about doing anything else. That's never been you. And it still isn't."

"But it's got to be at some point," I said, looking back on all those times Maggie had checked my heartbeat with her plastic stethoscope, and thinking about what she would say if she could have heard it on that porch.

"Why?" he countered quickly and waited for me to answer. A heavy silence hung there as I searched for an answer – opening my mouth to begin more than once, but never actually producing sound. "There aren't rules to all this, Connor. You don't 'got to be' anything. You just have to be you, and that's enough. Your mother and I love you, and so do a lot of other people. No one needs anything more or different." And with one more sip he finished his beer and stood up.

"But don't string along McKenzie's father. Now I'm going to bed. Goodnight son," and with that, he slipped inside the door and up the stairs, leaving me alone with the night sky and all the ghosts of the house, including the one that had just arrived – the one that heard me, I'm sure, as I thanked God for the gift that is my mother and father.

Chapter 63

I set an alarm for the first time since the wedding, hoping to wake up early and see my father, but he was already gone, leaving only a note and my beat up old Jeep – which he'd nursed across the Mass Pike.

'Life's too short,' was all it read, with a P.S. below it.

'And get out of the house a little. It smells terrible in here.'

I laughed out loud as I read it and realized only then that I hadn't showered or even cracked a window since I'd arrived. I spent the next few minutes opening them all, waiting to feel the breeze blow through each one before moving on to the next. After, I finally took that shower, and returned to the living room to stand in the middle of it, with those white, billowing curtains doing an eclectic dance in front of and around me, brushing past my face and chest until I let out a large sigh and took out the phone I'd only been using to keep telling Mack I was sick.

"Winter and Wall, how may I direct your call?"

"Mary, hi," I said, recognizing the voice on the other end of my phone. "It's Connor Hall. Can you connect me to Mr. Winter?"

"This is Wilson Winter," Mack's father said a second later.

"Mr. Winter. Hi. It's Connor," I started nervously.

"Connor!" he said, dropping the stern tone he'd started with. "What can I do for you?"

"Forgive me, sir," I said, my voice as low as his was when he'd first picked up. I took a deep breath to continue but stopped short when I heard Mr. Winter let out a quiet snort somewhere between a sigh and a laugh.

"Oh, Connor," he said. "Over the phone?" His voice was quiet, but heavy with an irritation he wasn't trying to hide. Looking back, it's clear he thought this would happen. It's why he came to see me when he did. But even if he expected me to leave, I'm sure he didn't expect that. I'm sure he expected me to respect what he'd given me, or, at the very least, respected my relationship with his daughter. I'm sure he expected me to be decent.

"I'm sorry, sir," I said, feeling what little air was in me rush out in all directions, my ribs collapsing in on themselves. "But I have to resign."

"Let's make something very clear, Connor," Mr. Winter said, his voice vibrating with tension the way an old piano can when it hasn't been tuned in too long. "You're not resigning, you're quitting. Resigning is coming into this office, looking me in the eye and giving me two weeks notice. Not calling me from wherever you are and pulling this."

"I know," I said, my own voice like a piano now, like a string pulled so tight it threatened to snap. "I can come back if you'd like," I said, knowing that I couldn't, but knowing that I had to offer.

"Come back from where?" he asked. "The Cape? No. I don't want you to come back. Ever."

"I'm sorry, sir," I said, though I don't know how. There was a bitterness and anger in his voice that startled me in the moment but seems so restrained as I think about it now.

"You know, part of me has been expecting you to leave," he said, quieter than he had been. "Part of me has been waiting for it since you took the job. And that wouldn't have disappointed me. But this does."

"I know," I sighed, seeing myself as he must have, and hating everything about what I saw. He started to say something more but stopped and exhaled into the phone. I heard that exhale again and again in my mind as we both considered what to say next.

"I'm sorry again," I said. "And thank you for the opportunity. I know I didn't deserve it, and I know you don't deserve this."

"I hope you figure this all out," he answered, and there was another pause before he spoke again. "Goodbye, Connor," he said, and he hung up the phone before I had a chance to reply, leaving me alone in silence with the billowing curtains.

On the phone, I hadn't noticed how quick and shallow my breathing had become, and as I focused on it in the echo of Mr. Winter's final words, I felt it quicken even more, with each inhale asking questions about all the nothing I'd earned, and each exhale confirming that I didn't have any of the answers.

I closed my eyes and tried to take a deep breath and fill my lungs as full as they'd ever been filled. I let it out all at once after I had, as a thought I didn't know I was thinking escaped my lips.

"I just quit my job," I said. With another exhale, I said it at again, and before I could say it a third time or a fourth, before the panic festering in my mind took control with new questions about what I would do next and how long I could get by without a paycheck, I decided to get out of the breeze, and made for that beat up old Jeep.

Chapter 64

A few minutes later, I was on the streets of Chatham, wanting little more than to walk up and down Main Street as I do with my family. I strolled into and out of the stores as easily as I could, as I might during any other summer, as I had that last fall following my mother and sister.

"Just looking around," I said politely as the sales woman in each store asked me the same questions. They couldn't help me find anything because I wasn't looking for anything they had – except in one shop, one I'd only been in only once before.

I ducked under a low hanging limb I didn't remember as I crossed the courtyard to Vivi Nell'amore. It was exactly as I remembered it, with big windows, and glass art hung throughout the front room, refracting the natural light and throwing color all across the crowded space.

"This is a long shot," I said to the young blonde who greeted me as I walked through the door. "There was a black and white photo of a lifeguard stand here a few months ago. The wood in the lifeguard stand has a big hole worn in it. Any idea if it's still here?" I asked.

"I haven't seen it," she said, "but I'm not in the photo room much. If you want to head back there I can send the owner back. She'll know."

I thanked her and started that way, stopping to admire a handmade bracelet the sign described as 'waxed and rolled hydrangea leaves with seashells and stones.' I considered buying it, but didn't know anyone who would wear it, so I put it back and continued into the photo room, which was even bigger and brighter than I remembered – with white walls and light hardwood floors soaked in sunlight, and beach scenes from across the Cape displayed at every turn. There was a fishing boat with the rising sun behind it, a sea of marsh with the sun setting into it, a breaking wave with the moon high above it. Each was more gorgeous than the next, and each reminded me why I love the Cape.

A few minutes later, I was leaning in to inspect a photo of the fish pier when I heard footsteps and turned to greet them. I could hear her talking as she came down the hall, before stopping abruptly as she made the door.

"Lifeguard stand with a hole in the wo-" she said.

I saw her auburn hair first and almost didn't need to see her face. Stepping back, I shook my head and smiled as she continued.

"It's you!" she said, and turned back to shout down the hallway. "Shelly!" she yelled. "This is the guy from the beach I told you about yesterday!"

"What?!" her assistant yelled back. "He doesn't look anything like how you described him!" The owner turned back to me with a smile, shrugging her shoulders.

"So, you've been speaking well of me?" I asked.

"In my defense," she said, stepping closer, "you had just walked out of the ocean fully clothed. There was only so much I could do."

"That's fair," I answered, and we both laughed. "So, this is your place?"

"Yip," she said smiling wide, throwing her arms out and taking a long twirl that sent her skirt flowing out around her. "This is my baby."

"Do you take all the pictures?"

"Take the pictures, make the jewelry, find the supplies. I do it all."

"Sounds like a lot of work."

"It's not work if you love it," she said quickly, bouncing up onto her toes. "It's a pretty good way to make a living."

"It sounds incredible," I said, stepping forward to extend my hand, thinking as I had once before about the kind of life she leads. "I'm Connor, by the way."

"Sonia," she said, taking it. "It is incredible, and that beach you found me on is my favorite. And I don't have the picture now, but I can get. I was thinking I'd go there tomorrow, but I was leaning toward an afternoon visit. For the morning shot, I can definitely have it for you if you come back in a week or so?" She smiled again and I got the sense she did it quite a bit. She wore it well, with full, red lips that almost matched the dark red of her hair, which hung past her shoulders with just a touch of curl.

"I could do that," I said, admiring those curls.

"Great. It was nice meeting you Connor, and seeing you dry." She winked as she extended her hand again and smiled once more as I shook it, before turning and leaving as quickly as a breeze might blow through the room.

Alone again, I turned to inspect a few more pictures before heading back to my Jeep and back to the house. I sat in quiet solitary there until just after night fell, when there was a pounding on the door and I opened it to find Mack on the front step.

Chapter 65

"You quit?" she said, pushing past me into the kitchen. "I'm starting home from Boston to see my sick boyfriend and I find out he's at his beach house and he just threw everything away?! I didn't think there was any way it could be true, but here you are!" She was standing by the island, having thrown down her keys and purse, staring straight at me. "Connor. What the hell," she finished pointedly, more of a statement than a question.

"I'm sorry," I said, shutting the door and stepping toward her. "I'm sorry I didn't call and tell you." I wasn't quite sure how to handle the big stuff, so I started small.

"What is going on?" she asked with a hint of fear and sadness behind the anger in her face.

"I don't know," I said, still unsure what to say next, still unsure what I was doing next.

"That's not an answer," she countered quickly and sharply, the fear and sadness disappearing entirely, but just for a flash.

"Well that's the answer I have, Mack," I said, my voice breaking a bit, something connected to it buckling within me. I waited for her to say something about me forgetting to use her full name, but she never did. "That's why I'm here," I said, stepping into the living room and collapsing into the couch, my head in my hands.

I don't know why I hadn't prepared for this. Of course Mack would find out and of course she would come. I should have been ready for it and I should have talked to her long before then, but I wasn't and I hadn't, and so there on that couch, everything Mack had

287

only seen in small waves came rushing out from behind the broken dam.

And there was Mack, waiting for me to explain it all, not knowing that I couldn't even explain it to myself.

"Aaron and Bethany got engaged," I said after Mack sat down next to me.

"I saw," she said, leaning into me. "But I want to hear about you."

"This is about me," I answered, turning to her.

"I still don't-" she started, but I cut her off.

"I'm miserable, McKenzie. At work. I'm miserable," I said, and we stared at each other silently for a moment as that sank in.

"You've only been there six months-" she started again.

"And I hate it," I said, cutting her off a second time, and startling myself a bit. I had still never said that. Not out loud. "I hate that I hate it, but I hate it. My cubicle feels like a prison I'm terrified I'll never escape, like I'm cursed to do the same work every day for all eternity. Like I'm the most boring Greek myth of all time. And I know you say it will get better with time, but what if it doesn't?"

"It will," she said, almost pleading with me, but the words landed on a hidden landmine that had been rigged to blow.

"And what if it doesn't, Mack?!" I practically yelled, the only time I remember raising my voice to her. "It may have gotten better for you, but what if it doesn't for me?" I was on my feet by the time I finished the sentence, crossing to the other side of the room before turning back to her, taking in the distance between us. "I don't want to work there." She flinched as she heard the words, but a second later she was standing, her high heels announcing her strong, determined walk toward me.

"Do you know how stupid you sound?" she barked, the anger overwhelming anything else in her, while I felt my shoulders slump.

"Yeah. I do," I said softly, soft enough that it was nearly lost beneath the sound of Mack walking away from me and into the kitchen to lean against the island.

"Dammit, Connor. Do you have any idea what you're throwing away?!"

"I do," I answered, but again it was all but lost as Mack continued on.

"And do you even know what you threw it all away for?"

"No," I said quietly one more time, but this time I know she heard me.

"Great," she said, throwing up her hands. "So, you just quit a great job with absolutely no prospects. You destroyed everything we've been waiting years for, for absolutely nothing."

"No, Mack," I said, no longer quiet. "I destroyed everything *you've* been waiting for. And I'm sorry about that, but I just can't do it. I can't live that life."

"Oh, grow up, Connor!" she yelled, both arms extending toward me, an expression on her face that I'd never seen before. "No one's asking you to storm a beachhead. I'm just asking you to be a fucking adult." There were years of anger pouring out of Mack in that kitchen, like her own dam had finally broken, and while I knew there was truth in each wave that hit me, I knew, also, the truth in what I said next.

"I can't be that adult, Mack. I just can't."

There was a long silence between us as she looked away from me and I away from her. Eventually she said something else and eventually I answered, and we went back and forth all night, bouncing at and away from one another like two fencers in a tragic, chaotic sparring match – Mack advancing at will while I did my best to parry away everything I could, the two of us stripped of our armor long before we'd ever picked up our swords. It was hours later when we both collapsed back into the couch, and back into the same things we'd been saying all night.

"Just give it a few more months," she begged.

"I can't."

"It will get better."

"I can't live like that."

But this time, there was no return thrust, just silence, as the sword fell from her hand. She wasn't looking at me when she finally spoke again.

"So, what now?" she asked.

"I don't know," I said. "But I'm going to figure it out."

"And what's this mean for us?" she asked, turning back to me with tears in her eyes.

"I don't know that either," I said, wiping away my own.

"Do you love me?" she asked quietly.

"Yes," I answered quickly. Because I did. And still do. And always will.

"Then can we at least have tonight?" she asked, standing and taking me by the hand, a whole world of unsaid truths hanging in the air, lingering like a dense, thick cloud. We went upstairs and laid down together, Mack resting her head on my shoulder like she had so many times before. For a while, neither of us slept. She listened to my heart beat beneath my chest and I rubbed the smooth skin of her back, leaning my cheek into her head, feeling as I had for years, the way they fit together like a puzzle piece. Eventually, I felt her drift away and then I did the same. In the morning, I rolled to my right and found an empty spot where Mack had been. Downstairs, there was another note.

Connor,

I don't understand. Or maybe I do and maybe I've known for a long time and been ignoring it. But either way, I won't wait around anymore. I've waited for a long time assuming you'd come back, but I won't do it again. I want you to know I don't regret anything. I love you. Goodbye.

McKenzie

A breeze blew through as I read the last lines, and I knew another ghost had just arrived.

Chapter 66

The construction noises hadn't registered yet, not until I stepped out onto the back porch. The wind and the waves were loud, but the screeching and beeping of the heavy machinery was louder.

Our neighbors had finally gotten sick of the pool house the previous owners had built in the backyard, and after a winter spent fighting the town on how to demolish it, they decided to just pay a crew to tear it down. I'd slept through the backhoe arriving, but as it raised its bucket high in the air and crashed it down through the pool house roof, it was all I could hear.

The carnage was spectacular – roofing tile and lumber splitting and shattering with each stroke of the backhoe's claw. It stabbed a dozen or so times into the heart of the pool house. I could feel the raucous noise in my chest, until all of a sudden it powered down, leaving an eerie quiet in its place. It was silent for a second before a loud groan replaced the scream of the diesel engine. The house started to lean toward the water, the remaining wood straining to keep its shape. For a moment, I was sure its momentum would take it down, but it held on, stopping just before that point where you knew it would all give way. I turned my head as I looked at it, waiting for it to fall while it stubbornly held on in silent desperation, clinging to itself until the engine scream came back, and with one final shove, sent it crashing down to the ground with a deafening boom that shook me as I stood next door.

The quiet came back as I inspected the wreckage and waited for the crew to pack up and head out. But one more time, that engine came back, and as they began sifting through the rubble and started what I guessed would be a long clean up, I gave a wistful look at our beach and decided that it wouldn't be where I spent my day.

I didn't realize it was Saturday until I parked at the beach and remembered why my father always avoided taking us there on weekends – choosing to stay at the hotel pool until the Mondays of our pre-beach-house summer vacations. Still, with nothing but a towel I'd managed to grab on my way out the door, I found a spot just to the left of that familiar lifeguard stand, just about where we always liked to settle when dad decided we could go.

I didn't bother laying out the towel, choosing, instead, to sit on the one small patch of bare earth left untouched by the families that surrounded me on all sides – families that had me feeling like I'd been taken back to the past to see it from a different angle.

To my right were four kids, one napping and tanning, and three others trying to find the best seashell, running into and back up from the water. In front, there were three more, all working together to build a massive sand castle. Behind me were two brothers; the older burying the younger in sand and then dumping a bucket of water on his head. And to the left was one final set of three, playing badminton in what little space they had.

They all played for hours, their laughter and shouting replacing the screeching and roaring as the music of my day. I remembered when we used to play like that on the beach – when Aaron would make his sandcastles and Maggie would bury Ed, and I would lie in the surf. I let their noises wash over me, enjoying them, letting them take me to the past. I reveled in them for hours, until the beach started to thin out and a sound I think I was hoping to hear pierced through it all.

"Three times this week, you must be stalking me," she said, popping down into the sand next to me – her deep, Auburn hair bouncing off her shoulders as she did.

"I was here first," I said, turning to her. "If anyone is stalking, it's you."

"You came into my store," she said, laughing.

"How do I know that's your store?" I answered, a smile breaking through my dead pan. "For all I know, you could have the real owner tied up in your basement."

She laughed again, louder this time, with her whole body, her head tossed back toward the sky. It was a full laugh that came from her toes and resonated like an opera singer's voice in the final notes of an aria.

When she finished, she thought for a moment, looking at me with a side-eye before jumping to her feet. She was wearing old, faded jeans and an even older t-shirt, which she started pulling up.

"You remember the name of the store?" she asked, pausing.

"Vivi Nell'amore," I said, slowly, questioningly. She pulled the shirt all the way up to the bikini top she had on underneath, revealing a large, colorful tattoo up her right side. It started somewhere near the front of her hip, below her waistline, and wound up her smooth, toned side and around to her shoulder blade. There were green vines and leaves with flowers spread throughout, and written in the middle, tucked into the curve of the vines was 'Vivi Nell'amore.'

"I don't know," I said, examining it without trying to stare. "This could be a set up," and she laughed another time.

"But if it is, you have to respect my commitment, right?" This time, I laughed as she plopped back down next to me and asked what I was doing there.

"I couldn't stay home," I said. "They're demolishing a pool house next to the house I'm staying in."

"The worst," she said, mocking me. "I'm only here because my neighbor's putting in a helipad."

"I guess I just needed some peace and quiet," I said.

"So, you chose a crowded public beach on a Saturday afternoon? Hell of a plan." And we laughed yet again.

"Well, maybe more the peace than the quiet," I answered as we turned toward each other.

"Then come with me," she said, standing back up and extending her hand. I took it and she pulled me to my feet. Sunset was coming and much of the crowd had left, though I'll never understand why. There's nothing like sunset on an emptying beach, with the flicker of fire in the distance and its drifting smell carried by a stiffening wind, as a bracing cold takes hold and color explodes across the sky.

We started down the beach but stopped after a few steps while Sonia raised the camera she'd been holding at her side. She snapped a few pictures of the lifeguard stand, the waves behind it brightly lit by the orange sun sinking toward the dunes.

"Those are for you," she said, starting back down the beach again. I jogged up beside her and she told me she was coming back one morning that week to get the sunrise picture I'd asked about the day before, and we made small talk about her assistant Shelly running the store while she goes out to search for shells or take pictures.

While we talked, the beach emptied of the last few tourists, but started filling back up again with locals who probably came each night to walk the sand like Sonia and I were – eager for the view and the feel I just described.

I always admired the couples that came then, especially the elderly ones who could maybe only barely get down the stairs to the beach, but who kept coming back – not wanting to miss even a single sunset. I stole a look back over my shoulder at them as Sonia and I kept walking, past the next two lifeguard stands and, as I realized then, onto a part of the beach I'd never been on. I'd walked for miles on that beach with my family, but we only ever walked north, and never south as I did with her, until she ducked under a rope and disappeared into the dunes.

I took a quick look around to see if anyone was watching, then followed her under the 'Keep Off' sign. We climbed to the top of a hill and back down its other side, following a narrow, winding path of sand through the grass until we stepped suddenly into a clearing with deep green marsh surrounding a large saltwater pond and the stream that fed it.

She kept walking but I stood still, looking over the marsh and the pond, taken aback. All those years, I'd never known they were there, hidden just out of view.

"Come on," she called through a smile, and I followed her further along the path across a small wooden bridge leading over the stream and around to the sand on the other side of the pond.

We turned back toward the ground we'd covered and surveyed the view – the pond and marsh giving way to the dunes, and beyond that, miles of beach and ocean stretching out to the horizon, distant enough that you could only just make out all the couples strolling the sand and taking in the sunset.

"How'd you find this place?" I asked, watching a seagull swoop low over the pond as it shimmered under the fluorescent sky.

"Accidently," she said. "My mom and I used to come here when I was in high school. I was taking pictures…on this camera, actually, when this gorgeous heron flew right over my head. I started to chase it, right up over the dunes and back here.

"Did you get the shot?" I asked, and she turned to me with a sly smile on her face.

"Of course I did." With that, she jumped up and pulled off her t-shirt and shimmied out of her jeans, then took off running toward the water and dove in headfirst, the ripples of her dive stretching out across the pond. "Are you coming?" she said after surfacing.

Until she asked the question, I hadn't been planning on it, but after she had, there was only one answer. I stood up and took off my shirt, but took my time walking down to the water, and slowly waded in as she laughed. It was warmer than I expected, and deeper than I imagined, too, forcing me to tread water as I drifted toward her while she floated on her back, her feet together like a mermaid, kicking gently to keep herself moving.

"So," she said, kicking herself upright. "What are you doing here?"

"I thought you asked that already?" I said. "The guy next door—" and she cut me off.

"No, not here today," she said. "Here in the Cape. You're not a local, and most people don't just jump up in the ocean fully clothed."

"How do you know I'm not local?"

"Well, you're not tan enough for one thing, and earlier you talked about 'the house where you're staying,'" she said. "And because locals don't come to this beach."

"But you're here," I pointed out, diving under water.

"I'm from Boston. I only moved here a few years ago," she said when I came back up. "Now quit stalling and spill," and there was that smile again.

"I don't know why I'm here," I said out of nowhere, like it just bubbled up from beneath the surface of the pond.

"Sounds confusing," she said, nodding, and floating toward me.

"I just quit my job," I said. "Shortly after realizing that I hated it."

"So, you came out here?"

"Yeah. I guess I thought I'd come crash at my parents' beach house, eat their food, and mope about everything that's gone wrong in my life," and there came that laugh yet again, her head thrown back once more, the deep, dark red hair whipping back as she did.

"What were you doing?" she asked, kicking away from me and toward the water's edge.

"I was a paralegal in a big law firm," I said, following her as she climbed onto the sand, her black bikini clinging to her body.

"That sounds awful," she said, drawing a loud, sharp, staccato laugh from me.

"It was," I said, still laughing.

"Do you know what you're going to do next?" she asked, both of us sitting down to watch the final few minutes of sunset.

"Nope. Any ideas?"

"Actually, yeah," she said, standing back up and turning toward me. "Read right there," and she pointed to her tattoo.

"Vivi Nell'amore."

"It's Italian. It means 'live in love,'" she said. "'My mother used to say it to me and her mother used to say it to her.'"

"Live in love," I repeated as she sat back down.

"You think about that while we watch the sunset," she said. "Then meet me back here on Monday, 4:30 AM."

"What?" I asked, confused and surprised.

"The sunrise picture. You have to actually be here for sunrise if you're going to help me take it." One more time I laughed, but I agreed to meet her, and then we both went silent as the sun dipped below the horizon and the stars led us back to the beach and back to our rides home.

Chapter 67

When I pulled back into the driveway, Brady's car was waiting for me, and stepping through the door, I found him on the porch with Mike. They'd let themselves in with the spare key they both knew was behind a false brick near the front door.

"You should bring your phone with you when you go out," Brady called to me, holding it up and waving it in the air. I hadn't even realized I'd left it at home.

"Shouldn't you be with your wife?" I asked, stepping out to join them on the porch. He and Kaitlyn had been too busy to take their honeymoon after the wedding, so they'd taken just a few days at the start of the week and planned a trip to Europe for the spring.

"She's on call this weekend," he said, "so we thought we'd swing out here for a night. What's up with you? Anything new? Any major life changes?" Apparently, word had filtered through the wives.

"Depends on what you call quitting your job and losing your girlfriend," I said, stepping to the edge of the patio and looking into the neighbors' yard. The construction crew had cleared out, with nothing but a patch of dirt left where the pool house had been. "Is that major?" The lot looked different. Empty. Like it was waiting for something new to be built. "I'm sorry I dragged you guys out here," I said to them, happy and grateful they had come, but with a pit of guilt in my stomach that I'd pulled them away from their lives. "You've got bigger things going on."

"What happened?" Mike asked, ignoring me. I had turned back toward them to apologize, but I looked back at that patch of dirt as I answered his question, starting back one week before with Z and the wedding. I told them about Aaron selling the battery and proposing to Bethany, and about the drive to the Cape and my dad coming to find me, and about Mack doing the same, and about everything after she'd shown up at the door through to when she walked out while I was asleep.

"So, what now?" Mike asked after they both offered their condolences and understanding.

"I guess that's what I'm here to figure out," I shrugged, and I thought back to what my father had said on that same porch just a few days before. "How's Mack?"

"She's Mack," Brady said. "She's pointing her chin toward the sky, adjusting her timelines and soldiering on."

"Sarah says she's pretty upset but isn't letting on," Mike said, chiming in with a real person's answer on top of Brady's sarcastic one. A rush of sadness ran through me as I mourned my years with Mack with a silent moment we all happened to observe.

"I'm going to miss her," I said, ending it.

"Are you?" Brady asked quickly. "I love Mack," he said when I didn't answer, "but you two weren't right for each other." I looked at him for a long moment before I turned to Mike, and noticed for the first time the sharp, cut jaw line that must have been under what he'd worked off.

"Don't look at me; I'm not the one who said it," Mike said, his hands in the air. "I just agree with it." I laughed at how he'd phrased it, and thought more about Mack, trying to reflect on our entire relationship in a few split seconds.

"She wasn't right for you," Brady said. I started to protest but he ran me over, maybe getting something off his chest. "Again, I love Mack, but she is way, *way* too uptight." There was a silence for a second as the three of us looked at each other, each with a smirk forming on our faces.

"I don't know how you could possibly think that," I said, and we all laughed, the first laugh of many that night, and the only one tinged with sadness and regret for me, as I mourned the loss one more time.

Over those next few hours, we hardly left the porch and we were hardly ever quiet, and it was everything I didn't know I needed – like we were back in the screen house saying whatever came into our minds. We played Questions for hours that night, and for the whole time they were there, I was one of three good friends not trying to figure out his life, but enjoying it instead – at least until Sunday night, when I stepped out onto the driveway to say goodbye.

"Thanks for coming out," I said for the fourth or fifth time that afternoon.

"You're welcome," Brady said. "Cause it was a real hassle to come hang out at a beach house and shoot the shit with my friends." Then he took a long look over my shoulder at the house behind me, his expression changing as he did. "I miss weekends like this."

"Good luck with everything," Mike said from the passenger seat of Brady's sedan. "When will we see you again?"

"I don't know," I answered, as I felt the cold water start to trickle out all the holes their visit had helped dam up. "Eventually."

"You'll figure it out," Brady said, shaking my hand and climbing behind the wheel, and I thought back to what he had said just seconds before, and the things we'd all said in the hours before, and about everything Sonia and I had said in that marsh the day before. And the more I thought, the more I was starting to form an idea in my head.

I rolled it around as the car started rolling over the driveway, the seashells crunching beneath the tires as a joke I hadn't heard produced a laugh from within the car.

I love that sound.

Both of them.

Chapter 68

I listened to the first of those sounds the next morning as I pulled out of the driveway. It was well before dawn, with no sign in the sky that it could be coming anytime soon. Mine was the only car on the road as I drove to meet Sonia – my headlights breaking through the black in front of me like the stars broke through the black above. I wound through the streets I know so well, seeing them as I hadn't before, and pulled into the beach's parking lot up next to what must have been Sonia's SUV.

Stepping into the cool, pre-dawn morning, I remember looking up to the sky and those stars. I'm always amazed by how many more there are outside the suburbs – away from all the houses crammed onto postage stamp lots between all the blinding lights of the fast food joints and big box supermarkets trying to blot out anything but the path inside.

That night, from that parking lot, you couldn't see any light but what nature had made, and those stars lit up a path toward the beach where Sonia was waiting. I stopped at the top of the stairs as I looked out onto the horizon where clouds were pushing out to sea and felt a shudder as it reminded me of the night I'd chased the lightning to that beach.

"You're in my spot," I called to her as I looked down to where I'd collapsed into the sand just a few days before and saw her sitting with her legs out in front of her.

"Oh, this is yours?" she asked, flipping her head toward me with a smile.

"Yeah," I said, stepping up beside her and sitting down. "The night we met, remember?" She tilted her head and squinted as I said it.

"We met in the morning and you were down there," she said, pointing toward the water, and I remembered that she hadn't been there all night.

"I forgot you weren't here for the sitting, just the swimming," I said with a snort.

"There was sitting? I'm sorry I missed it," she said, that smile still on her face.

"It was a night like this one, but with a thunderstorm out on the horizon," and I turned out to face the water.

"That must have been incredible," she said, turning to do the same. "I'll have to do that sometime." I didn't say anything; I just kept looking, maybe hoping for one final flash, or maybe for dawn, or maybe for neither.

"That's a story for a different day," I sighed eventually, still looking.

"I hope I get to hear it," she said, popping up with her camera. "Watch, the sky is going to brighten any minute now."

We stayed quiet for two or three, both looking out into the never-ending darkness, waiting for the light, which came just as she said it would. The stars faded away quickly as the black began to lighten. Sonia was already snapping pictures while I used the light to take the same look around I always do when I go there. I looked up and down the beach and out into the ocean and back behind us at the dunes, which is when I noticed the camera buried in the sand.

"What's that?" I asked, as she came back to sit next to me for a minute.

"A time-lapse," she said. "I thought it would be cool to get the whole sunrise." I nodded as we sat quietly and watched it take over the sky. A minute later she was up again, and a minute after that, the tip of the sun made its first appearance, its very top appearing as an arc of brilliant light breaking through the water out in the distance.

I watched it climb higher, but more than that, I watched her, stalking and skipping in her baggy sweatpants and sweatshirt, jumping from one spot to the next. I always thought of photographers as machines, like difference engines evaluating the possible options and selecting the best one. She wasn't like that. She danced around as erratically as she did gracefully, standing in some spots for long stretches, and others for just a moment.

"Where did you learn photography?" I asked her, still watching her dance.

"Nowhere!" she called, not stopping to look my way.

"You didn't go to school for it?"

"I didn't go to school for anything," she said, stepping up to the lifeguard stand and shooting something on it. Something I couldn't see.

"You didn't go to college?"

"No," she said, stopping only then and turning toward me. "I didn't really feel like it." She laughed before spinning back to the lifeguard stand. I didn't know how to respond after that, so I said nothing and eventually, she continued. "I looked at a few schools, but I wanted to do this, and I didn't want to spend four years taking some English Lit or Chemistry classes I'd already hated once, so I came out here."

"How'd you make money?" I asked, smiling both at the romance of it and at the cartoonish look I would have gotten if I'd told my parents I was skipping college.

"I worked as a freelancer," she said. "I sold photographs and jewelry to the shops in town – at least until I had enough money to sell it myself." Taking her camera off she turned back to me. "Ok, your turn." She put the camera down on the lifeguard stand and stepped toward me. Seeing the reluctance in my face, she grabbed me by the hand and pulled me to my feet, her hand lingering on mine while we stood face to face. "Come on, you're gonna shoot some," and she leaned in close as if to whisper in my ear. "Don't worry, I already got most of the good ones." I laughed when she said it, and took the camera from the lifeguard stand, noticing only then that it was an older one that shot on film rather than a memory card, forcing you to look through the viewfinder rather than at a digital display.

"It's been a while since I've seen one of these," I said, lifting it up to my eye and looking through it at the sun.

"Yeah," she said. "There's a long history to that baby. Don't break it." We both chuckled at that and I asked her what she wanted me to get. "Whatever," she said. "Just shoot what you like."

The sun had already climbed into the sky as I took a few wide-angle pictures with as much of the beach and ocean as I could fit in the frame, then remembered the picture I'd seen in her shop, and the dream I'd had on that beach, the one where I watched the sun set through the hole in the wood. I stepped back and sat down in the sand, then laid down onto my stomach when that wasn't low enough. I moved to my left to line it up perfectly, and clicked the shutter just once, then stood up and handed her the camera.

"I think I got it," I said, and she smiled.

"Good, let's go see. Follow me."

She grabbed her bag and the time-lapse camera, and jogged up the sand toward the parking lot, but not before stopping at the stairs to take one last look at the empty beach. Smiling, her eyes turned from the surf to me. I hadn't moved.

"Come on," she urged, and turned to go. I hurried to follow her and made it to my car just as she started hers.

We pulled out of the parking lot and I followed her toward parts unknown, weaving and winding our way through back roads I'd never been on. They were tight, narrow roads with dense brush between each of the houses. She was driving slowly, and slowing more every now and then as you might when searching for an address. I was following closely, so closely that I nearly hit her when she slammed on the brakes and pulled the car off to the shoulder.

I pulled in behind her as she jumped out.

"Sorry," she called to me. "We'll head into town in a minute, but I felt like stopping off quick." She disappeared into the woods and yelled for me to follow from behind the trees. I climbed out of the car and stepped toward a small path she must have been taking. I followed it as it twisted through the brush, still not seeing her until I turned one final corner and found her standing on the edge of a bluff overlooking a cove I recognized as one I'd seen countless times, just never quite like this.

"Wow," I gasped.

"I know," she said. "Sorry, I just felt like stopping."

"It's fine," I almost whispered back. "But you don't have your camera."

"I know."

Chapter 69

"This was my mom's favorite spot," she said. "She used to come here with her family. There was a campground here before the houses went in."

"This must have been a great place to camp," I said, imagining it.

"Right?" She asked. "Shame they developed it."

"My family used to come to that beach over there," I said, pointing over the cove back toward shore, to a small patch of sand just off the road, a few miles up from the beach we'd started our day on. "We'd get ice cream in town and eat it there before going back to our hotel."

"I thought you had a house out here?"

"My parents do now, but back then we stayed at a hotel in Chatham."

"Chatham!" she exclaimed as if remembering something. "We should go." She took a deep breath in and sighed a warm, satisfied sigh, and started back up the path. I followed her again, first on foot and then by car, on the winding path out of the woods and onto the winding roads back into town. We parked behind her store but walked past it and onto Main Street. This time, she had her camera.

"There's, like, 30 minutes each morning," she said, framing up a shot, "when the light is perfect and there are a few people in town, but not too many." I already knew that. I used to drive in for breakfast when I could, and always tried to time it for those 30 minutes, when only the coffee places were open, and the owners of the other stores were just getting in and just getting ready – before the tourists and shoppers. Sometimes I still go into town to get that breakfast and sit on the old stonewall out in front of the church.

Sonia skipped up and down Main Street taking pictures. From behind, I watched her as I had that morning, and watched the store hands sweeping their sidewalks and putting out the signs with the day's specials. Eventually, we made our way back to her shop, and as we stepped into the courtyard, she leaned into one of the gardens to smell a flower, then plucked it off the stem and slipped it into the bag she wore across her chest. I tilted my head, my expression asking her why.

"I don't know for what yet, but that'll end up in something. It's gorgeous," she said, just as her assistant Shelly stepped out the front door to open up for the day.

"You're back!" she said to me, her curly hair bouncing as she snapped her head back in surprise.

"He is, and he has work to do," Sonia jumped in, faking a stern look.

"You heard the boss," I said to Shelly, as Sonia handed her the time-lapse camera and we both stepped inside the store and through the main section of the shop, where beams of green and blue were already taking over.

We walked back toward the photo room but stopped short of it, and ducked into the shop's office area where a pair of desks sat across from each other – one with what looked like random books and papers, the other with a few cameras, some wire for jewelry, a couple dried out flower petals, and a dozen or so shells and stones. On the walls were old photographs, and on the far wall was a door with a photo of its own – a young Sonia and an older woman.

"Is this your mom?" I asked as she put her bag down on the more cluttered desk and grabbed the camera from inside it.

"Yeah, that's her," she said, stepping toward it with a softer, almost sad smile. She lingered on it for a second longer before stepping through the door behind it and pulling me with her into the dark room.

There were photographs scattered across it, and what looked like thousands of dollars of equipment.

"You know, I've never let a man into my dark space," Sonia said, shutting the door behind us and laughing hysterically at her innuendo. It was then I realized how much I loved the sound of her laugh.

"I'll be gentle," I joked and she laughed again. She moved quickly, taking film from her camera and bouncing across the room as she worked to develop it.

"How did you afford all this?" I asked.

"I inherited it," she said, still working, "from the woman on the door."

"Your mom was a photographer?"

"The best I've ever seen," she said, and I think for a second she stopped working, but it was hard to make her out from the other side of the room.

We made more small talk for a while after that, only it didn't seem like small talk. It wasn't forced or labored; it was the opposite. She asked me about my favorite bands and I asked her about hers. I asked her about movies and sports and she asked me about politics and books. She liked all kinds of music, but only goes to see jam bands in concert. She likes comedies and dramas and anything with a chainsaw on the cover. She reads a lot during the winter and always watches *Miracle on 34*ᵗʰ *Street* around Christmas. She's not in either

311

political party and her dad used to take her to Red Sox games so she's always had a thing for baseball. She didn't love that I'm a Yankee fan, but she promised to get over it.

"You seem to think you know a lot," she said to me at one point a while later, at the end of some long answer about nothing in particular. She was smiling and pointing at me with the tongs she was using to lift the photos from the wash.

"Lady, that could be the title of my autobiography," I said, and she laughed again with her head thrown back.

"Then come over here and do this," she said, and I slid up next to her and saw the picture I'd taken in the wash she was working in – the one with the sun bursting through the lifeguard stand, with the sand in the foreground and the waves behind it all. "You did get that shot," she said. "It's gorgeous."

"I'll take it," I said, my eyes scanning it with a wide smile on my face.

"Forty-nine ninety-nine," she said quietly.

"What!?" I laughed. "I shot it!"

"Fine. Thirty-nine ninety-nine." This time, it was my head that was thrown back as I laughed. "Let it dry," she said, "and when you come back, I'll have it framed." I agreed, and we left the other pictures there and stepped back out to the office and then into the store. We exchanged phone numbers as we walked back into the main room where Shelly was waiting.

"Look at this," she said, pointing to the computer in front of her. The screen was black and still, but only for a second. Soon, there was action. One shadow, then another, then the black turning navy blue and the shadows becoming bolder. One stood and moved while the other watched, as the sun appeared and brought new colors with it. Then they were both standing – together, then apart, then together

312

again until they were gone and only that sun remained. "I was able to grab this," Shelly said when it had finished, and clicked over to one single photograph. It was two silhouettes standing together, one hand clasping another, the sun high in the top corner, shining down on them both.

"Beautiful," Sonia said.

Chapter 70

The tires screeched when I slammed on the brakes and spun the wheel, deciding only at that second to pull off the road and into the parking lot on the shores of the cove. I hadn't thought about stopping, but passing that small patch of sand on my way home, I couldn't resist.

Climbing out of my car, I stepped onto that sand and thought about the times my family used to go there – like when Maggie smashed Ed's ice cream into his face then spent the next few minutes running away from him. I always liked the view there, but looking up toward the bluff where Sonia and I had been standing, I realized how much better it was up there.

When I got back to my parents' house, I opened all the windows, fell into the couch and enjoyed the breeze, as the sleep I'd forgone the night before finally caught up with me.

It was a restful, dreamless sleep that ended hours later when I finally stirred. Sitting up, I rubbed the sleep from my eyes and took stock. I scanned the room for all those ghosts of the past – new and old – until I settled on the porch where Brady, Mike and I had sat a day before. I thought about them for a moment, and about that night we'd just spent together – about the idea that had started to form as they drove away, and about all the nights before that one. I stood up to shake off the sleep, then walked into the kitchen where I'd dropped my computer bag however many days before.

I pulled the laptop from it, opened to the *Tribune's* website and started clicking through it at the kitchen island, surveying all the headlines I'd missed. I don't know how long I was there or how many articles I'd scanned, but sometime later I clicked to the opinion section to scroll back through the archives, stopping to reflect on the ones I recognized and remembered – the ones I'd written.

Eventually, I found the one that bore my name, about that controversial football coach. I clicked into it and read it again, and smiled as I remembered the emotion I'd written with, and the emotion I'd felt when I saw it published.

Still standing, I searched the coach's name for any updates on his story and found two new articles – one about a new pledge he was having his players sign, and a second by Wallace Williams commenting on the first. I read that too, and debated with an invisible Wallace standing on the opposite side of my parents' island. I countered all of his points with arguments of my own, and countered his imagined retorts, too.

And down the rabbit hole I dove.

Anyone who grew up in the suburbs – or anyone who grew up with an Internet connection, probably – knows how time can get away from you somewhere in all those tubes, how one page can lead to another can lead to another can lead to hours disappearing in what feels like an instant.

That night, it I lost more than just a few hours. From that Wallace Williams column, I clicked to a few others before branching out to other writers, too, lining each of them up in the kitchen and discussing their points as if they were there to answer. There was an article on gun control and another on action movies. There was one on vintage video games and another on immigration. One on women's rights and another on rap music. It didn't matter who'd written it or even what it was about. I just kept reading and debating out loud to no one in particular. More than once I started to sketch an outline in my head of the response that needed to be written, and one time, I actually put pen to paper, late in the night when I'd circled back to Wallace Williams, wishing more than anything that I could write back. When I'd finished the outline, I picked up my phone and found Sonia's number.

'*Are you shooting tomorrow?*'

'*Yeah Provincetown Pier Why?*'

'*Mind if I come?*'

'*Not at all. Just be there before dawn.*'

I looked at the clock and saw that it was just a few hours away.

'*I'll be there.*'

Chapter 71

There were even more stars that morning than the day before. There were billions, and each felt like it had been laid out for me to follow, pointing me the right direction out of the more crowded towns and into the dunes, which finally gave way to Provincetown and its pier near the end of the Cape, where Sonia's SUV was already waiting for me.

There were other cars, too, but I picked hers out immediately, and picked her out just as quickly. She was the one with long hair spilling out the front of her hoodie, perched on a railing at the end of a dock, waiting.

It was pitch black, but all those stars were bright, and they all seemed to shine on her, so as I stepped closer, I could see that the sweatshirt she wore was the same my mother used to buy us every year – the one every mother buys, that says 'Cape Cod' on the front in whatever color you want. Hers was green with white letters.

"How tourist of you," I said, pointing to the familiar logo emblazoned across her chest.

"I've had it since I was a tourist," she said. "My mom bought it for me the first time we came out here."

"How long ago was that?"

"Well, it was middle school, so…" and she trailed off, maybe stopping to try and do the math, turning to the water before giving up on it. "So, I don't know, whatever that works out to."

The pier was dark and quiet as we sat listening to the water lapping ever so gently against the dock, rocking the boats just enough to make them look like they were swaying along to the same bit of music I couldn't hear – but Sonia could. She was swaying too, from side to side, her eyes scanning the stars, a content smile on her face.

"Have you ever been here this early?" she asked me, those scanning eyes of hers finding mine.

"The list of places I've been at this hour is pretty short, and almost everything on it is a Denny's." Her hair flashed across my face as she laughed in that certain way, her hood falling off as she did. The noise of it cut through the bay air and surrounded us. I imagined it spreading out in concentric circles and wondered how far it could be heard, whether maybe it would be carried on the wind and heard as a whisper in some far-off land, and whether if we listened hard enough, we could hear whoever, from wherever, whispering back.

I could have spent the rest of the day hoping to hear the reply, but the pier was starting to fill up. It was still dark, with just the stars and the occasional lamppost providing any light, but fishermen were already showing up to start their days. They walked past us with purpose, all headed for their boats and setting off for sunrise and beyond on the sea.

There was a fog rolling in, too – a sign, Sonia said, that dawn was coming. She took her camera from the bag at her feet and started taking pictures, waiting for crews to pass us and step into the light of a distant lamppost just before they disappeared into the fog. We listened as the motors roared and saw the waves of their wake come up the dock. I thought about what they might see on the open ocean that day, and about a lifetime spent there – sunrise to sunset.

"Look at this guy," she said. "He's my favorite." He was a tall, thick man, with the beard of a mountaineer. He was older and he walked with a limp, and you could tell it hurt, even if it wouldn't show on his face. It was still dark, but even against the black, I could

318

make out a large scar running up his hand and disappearing beneath the flannel of his sleeve. It matched the one he had next to his eye on that same side.

"That is a grizzled son of a bitch," I whispered, watching him walk by while he paid us no mind at all, maybe not even noticing us.

"I know," she said, doing the same. "He has stabbed a sperm whale in the heart no less than twice." She paused while we both laughed before continuing. "I followed him to his boat last week, it's just him. He doesn't have a crew."

"You were here last week?" I asked while she took a few pictures of Captain Ahab.

"Yeah, I'm here a lot," she said. "Pictures from here go so quickly I have to keep coming back," and she put the camera down and looked at me. "Plus, I love it. Wait until the sun's up." Just then, I started to notice the sky starting to lighten.

"Don't you make copies?" I asked.

"No," she said, standing up and slinging her bag over her shoulder. "I don't sell the same picture twice. Each one is unique, same as each moment." She snapped a few pictures as color came to the sky, and started moving a few steps either direction, and then a few more steps beyond that, each one quick and graceful. "It's not just the pictures, either. I don't make the same jewelry twice, or the same chime twice. It's all unique." I followed her as she moved, charmed.

She was right; the harbor was gorgeous as the sun rose over it, the seagulls awake and ringing in the morning with loud squawks as they dove down into the water. Dockhands called to one another as more motors roared. I smiled as I watched her move, enchanted by the romance of it all – the docks and the boats and the sunrise and that moment, which would never come quite the same way again.

319

We walked down to the end of the pier, the sun reflecting off the white tops of the new, polished boats, casting light onto the other, older ones, warped after years in the elements. Behind us now was Ahab, in one of those boats the sun had bore into over decades, with cracks and small holes in its wood. His stare was straight ahead, but on something past the two of us, past everyone, I think. I thought about his life beyond the boat and considered that maybe he didn't have one. Maybe he'd gotten into it early as a greenhorn crewmember fresh out of high school. It had been in his family for years and he hadn't wanted to but he followed in their footsteps, and now it was just him, with a stool at a local diner and a beat up pick up. I felt a crashing wave of sadness for him as we reached the end of the pier and watched his boat join dozens of others heading beyond the breakwater and into the rising sun.

"Look at that," Sonia said, pulling the camera away from her face just for a second, just to see it through her own lens before going back to the camera.

"Yeah, look at that," I said.

Chapter 72

We spent that whole day up in Provincetown. After all the
fishing boats had left the pier, we walked slowly back toward our
cars, stopping every few feet for her to collect stray pieces of rope or
driftwood she'd use later. We got breakfast in a diner neither of us
had been to before, but one that looked like all the others on the Cape,
the type I'd imagined Ahab in. We walked further up the coast after
that, out onto the rock wall and to the very tip of the island where it
curls back in on itself – where the whole coast line is laid out to be
surveyed, everywhere you'd driven through on your way, some parts
as clear as when you were there, others faded and obscured in the
distance.

We watched the boats return from that point, sliding past us
back to the marina to exchange their haul and maybe, just maybe, get
home to whoever was waiting before the sun had fully set. Ahab's
was the last boat we saw, alone behind the others, slowly making its
way back in. When it finally docked, we turned back to the rock wall
and with Sonia's bag as full as her film, we headed back to our cars.

We never stopped talking as we walked back – as we hadn't
on our way out, or up and back on the pier, or at the diner, or at the
hole in the wall we hit up for lunch. I told her about seeing the Boss at
the Meadowlands and she told me about the time he sat in with her
favorite band at a festival in Rhode Island. I told her about home and
the *Tribune*, and she told me about Boston. I told her about Aaron and
the battery and the rest of my family, and about Mike and Brady and
the guys and how we used to waste our hours in the screen house at

my parents', and she told me about her friends and how for them, it was the rooftop garden of her apartment building. They used to go there after school and sit between the dahlias and talk about whatever they could until the sun set over the Charles and the lights of downtown took over.

Night was starting to fall when we made it back to our cars, and for a second, I caught her looking out across the bay, maybe wondering if she could see those lights in the distance.

"This was fun," she said, and we locked eyes as I agreed, and the whole world seemed to pause for a second, then melt away until it was just us, but came rushing back a second later when her smile got wider and she broke that silence. "You're good company; I'll let you know when I'm doing it again."

"Make sure you do," I said, as she climbed into her car to go home and let out her dog, Beau. Earlier that day, she'd recounted the story of rescuing him from a kill shelter as a puppy. I watched her taillights fade and turned back toward the bay and looked down the coastline, searching for any lights from all those towns I'd been through before.

When I sat down that night, the Wallace Williams op-ed was still open on my computer. I read through it again, thinking of that coach and his players, and of what I'd written a few months before, and how I'd change it if I could. And then, like the night before, I dove down that rabbit hole, clicking through the *Tribune's* site with no real destination, like all those teenage nights I spent letting my curiosity take me through the Internet.

I read through all the articles that peaked my interest, and then started in on the ones that didn't. I clicked through each section – even, as the night grew late, obituaries. I've always admired obit writers – the professional ones who make art out of a biography – and

I'd started checking in on them every now and then, ever since my dad began searching them regularly for friends he knew in high school. There wasn't anyone we knew that day, but scrolling to the bottom, I'd swear I saw Ahab staring back at me, but my phone buzzed before I could read the article. It was Sonia, just getting up to go meet the sunrise, I imagined. She was telling me to meet her at the store sometime the next day.

When I did, she presented me with a large, framed print of my photograph from the beach, with the sand and the sun and the lifeguard stand. She showed me more she'd already put up for sale, too, of Ahab's boat fading into the distance, and even the two of us silhouetted by the sun.

We walked out to the beach and collected supplies after that, before both heading home as night fell. I spent that night back at my computer, reading through and beyond the *Tribune*. I read all the articles I hadn't, and branched out after that to other websites, too, stopping after each column to imagine, and sometimes write out, a lede I'd author in response. Late that night, I texted Sonia about joining her the next day and we fell into a pattern that carried us out of June and into the middle of summer.

I spent my days with her, exploring the beaches and bays and dunes, and returned home at night to explore the web. We took long exposure photographs at a lighthouse one morning before dawn, and scavenged for parts at a boat repair shop. We blew glass at her studio and fought for foul balls at a Cape League baseball game. I became a regular at Vivi Nell'amore, getting to know Shelly and even picking up a few shifts behind the counter, covering for her as she started acting at a local theater. She had loved doing it all through college and was thinking about getting back into it. She was funny and smart, and was the first employee Sonia hired. As she tells it, she walked into the store while it was still being finished, just minutes after quitting her job at a bank a few blocks away, still carrying her name plaque, begging for anything that meant she wouldn't have to go back. She told me the job at the store was just something to pay her bills until she could figure out what she wanted to do next, which she'd wanted to have figured out a while ago. I taught her how to play Questions – to the extent that you have to *teach* someone to play Questions – and she told me how her friends had a similar game, and some nights, the three of us would stay at the shop long after closing, playing and laughing and sharing stories about similar nights we wished would come around more often.

It became the four of us when Sonia hired Jason to help out with Shelly's hours. He wasn't as loud as the three of us, but he loved listening to us argue. He said it reminded him of college, when he spent most of his time in his dorm's common area, with all these different conversations happening around him. He had graduated a few weeks before but didn't know if he wanted to use his accounting degree and hoped he could help Sonia take pictures for the shop. He came with Sonia and me once or twice when we went back to all those beaches and bays and dunes, taking Sonia's camera when she felt like doing yoga or walking into the surf with me to search for shells, while I remembered how much I loved to do the same when I was younger.

Other times, it was just Sonia and me and she told me more about her friends and that rooftop garden, and I told her more about the screen house and everyone I used to spend time with in there – who I was still talking to every day. I asked the guys all the questions we were debating in the shop and we debated them amongst ourselves via phone and text and email. Mike sent me pictures and videos of Lou, and Brady and I talked every day, mostly about married life and movies and sports, but occasionally about the meetings he and the executive team had started taking, as that idea continued forming in my mind.

I missed them, and my siblings and our parents, too. I asked them every week or so when they would be coming out to the house, but they were too busy helping Aaron set up his new business – or so they said. Sometimes, I'd get in my car after a day spent telling Sonia about some debate I'd had with my friends, and I'd think about driving home to Saratoga, but I'd always end up back at the beach house, reading through the *Tribune* and sometimes, writing a full column I'd end up deleting. Late in the night, I'd text Sonia about the next morning and some nights I'd go to sleep, but most, I'd stay up and read and write even more, until I wasn't reading or writing at all, just listening – to Mack and Carl and Harry and all those ghosts that had crept in quietly but grown louder and louder until they were shouting over each other. Their refrains were the same that had been stuck in my head for months, and as I listened to them again, I'd think about Mack and all she wanted of me, and Harry and all he wanted for me, and Carl and all that he wanted for himself, and my parents and my place in the world, and my family and friends and each of their places too, and I considered it all in all the ways I had before, and remembered why I didn't want to go home yet.

Chapter 73

At low tide, the thick wet sand of Cape Cod Bay stretches out for miles, and a thin layer of seawater shimmers on top of it. At sunset, the colors of the sky reflect off the water, and the whole world becomes one of color.

"So, he left to open a surf shop?" Sonia asked as we walked on the bay, Beau running ahead of us, chasing the tennis ball I'd thrown a second before.

"Yep," I said. "Just left it all and went west."

"That's great," she said, smiling and looking out toward that setting sun, toward California – the same way we were walking, I couldn't help but think.

"Yeah, it is," I said quietly. We weren't taking pictures or gathering supplies. Not that night. That night we were just walking. And it was a perfect night for it, too. The kind you get in towns and places like that. The kind you remember forever. The kind that keeps you coming back. As I was telling her about Carl, Sonia had interrupted me to say that nights like those were the reason she'd moved to the Cape, and it was easy to see why.

I'd already told her the story of how Harry hired me at the *Tribune*, which had come just after telling her about Mack for the first time. Those stories followed ones she'd told about her first boyfriend and her favorite teacher and the photo album her mother left her. She listened eagerly, asking all kinds of questions and laughing when I thought she would, as I had when she talked. Again, it was easy conversation, even as personal as it was at times, and as we stopped to turn back toward the shore – and saw just how far out we'd walked, and how faded the houses looked in the distance – she asked the question she hadn't yet.

"So, what about you? Are you going west?" I took a long look up the coast before I answered.

"I don't know," I finally said, thinking about all the times I'd already said that.

"Where are you leaning?" We were facing each other as we stood in the wet sand, Beau dancing and jumping around us. She was standing close, looking up at me as I noticed for the first time how short she is.

"I don't know," I said again, chuckling to myself, wondering whether I'd said that hundreds or thousands of times. "How did you know?"

She smiled at the question and lifted up her shirt, revealing the colorful tattoo on her side.

"I just did what I liked," she laughed, pointing to her ribs, never breaking eye contact. Her eyes are full and emerald green, and in that moment, I was lost inside them, considering her words as they fluttered on the wind somewhere above the tide and beneath the sky, until Beau made it clear that he, like Sonia, knows what he likes.

We hadn't noticed it, but while we were talking, the thick, black lab had dropped the tennis ball between us, and when his jumping and nudging didn't help us see it, he took a more direct route. Backing up, he took a running jump into the back of my knees, buckling them instantly and knocking me forward into Sonia's legs, and then down into the sand when she jumped back laughing, her head thrown toward the sky and her whole body shaking.

"Beau!' she yelled through the laughing and the mane of hair that had been flung across her face. "That is so much funnier when it happens to someone else."

"Yeah, it's a riot," I moaned, rolling onto my back and digging the tennis ball out from under me. I threw it back toward shore and felt myself sink a little into the wet sand. Feeling the cool water spread across my back and legs, I pressed my body into it a little more to enjoy the sensation.

"Can you stand?" Sonia asked, still laughing a little, looking down at me.

"Yeah," I said. "But in a minute, it's nice down here." I sunk deeper into the sand before hearing a small splash as Sonia fell back and laid down next to me.

"It *is* nice," she said, looking up and then gasping. "Look at that, it's like the sunset and the stars are meeting."

I looked up for the first real time and saw what she did. Directly above us – between us, really – was a split in the sky I'd never seen before. On one side were the bright, vivid colors of the sunset, and on the other were the darkening night sky and the stars that came with it. We laid there quietly for a moment, thinking – at least I was – about the connection between the two, and how much it looked like the night sky was turning lighter rather than darker, lit up by its opposite.

"Sonia," I said, still looking up. "Would you want to go to dinner with me?"

"To a restaurant?" she asked, eyes still to the sky. "Or do we just want to have a few of the clams lodged in the small of my back right now?"

"I was thinking a restaurant. Maybe tomorrow night?" Finally, she turned to look at me and smiled as I turned to her.

"Yeah, that sounds like fun."

We looked at each other a second longer until Beau ran back to us and dropped the tennis ball on my chest. We both laughed as I threw it one more time and stood up to watch him run after it. I pulled Sonia to her feet and we stood close for a second until she stepped back and started spinning in a slow circle.

"Look at all this," she said. We were still well-off shore and you could see miles of coastline up and down the Cape, all of it laid out in this new way to see it more fully than before – more fully, even, than in Provincetown – the massive expanse of the bay stretching out beyond view.

You could go anywhere from that spot, I thought. The possibilities were endless. Out toward the bay in whatever direction you'd like, or in toward shore and any of those hundreds of homes and everything that laid beyond them. All you had to do was choose. And as I stood there, I swear I felt the tide start to change, thinking that the bay looked good, if I could just find the strength to put the houses behind me.

Chapter 74

"Let me say this again, they would never find me," Sonia said, leaning over the table between us to stress her point. "Ever."

"Ever?" I asked.

"Ever. I'd blend in; I'd live off-book. Make my way out of the country and settle some place random – a field in the Austrian Alps or a town on the Mediterranean. They'd never find me." She said it with such confidence I thought that maybe she could pull it off.

We were hours into our date at a small restaurant off Main Street. We were sitting on the patio with a view of the town to one side and the ocean to the other. It's a quiet restaurant I'd stumbled on years before but had never found time to visit.

We'd told dozens of stories through four courses and two bottles of wine at that point, when she interrupted my recounting of Brady's bachelor party to tell me we were all wrong – that the law would never track her down. I was telling her about the Bridge Troll, shocked that it had only been about a year since that night, when she brought it back to the fugitive question and then told me a story of her own as we ordered a second dessert.

"It was Christmas and my friends were on break and we'd all ended up back in Boston and decided to go out to the bars, but while we were getting ready, we were watching *It's a Wonderful Life* and someone asked if we would want the 'George Bailey treatment.'"

"Forced into taking over your father's business for the sake of 1940's American values?" I joked.

"No," she said when she'd stopped laughing. "If you could see what the world would be like without you, would you want to?"

A million thoughts ran through my mind when she said it, like how good a question it was and why'd we'd never thought to ask it back at home and what all the guys would say if we did, and last of all, what I would say if it was asked to me. I didn't need to hear Sonia's answer, but as I answered each of the other questions in my mind, I listened as she gave it anyway.

"Everyone else was saying how much they'd love to – *love to!* – and they all looked at me and I remember it so clearly. 'Fuck no,' I said. You should have seen them, the looks on their faces!" She laughed again. "We didn't stop talking about it all night."

"*We* might not stop talking about it *this* night," I said as the waitress came with our second helping of cheesecake.

"You want to go with me on this?" she said slyly, licking her fork clean.

"Please understand," I said, putting up my hand. "It's not that I *want* to. It's that I *need* to. I live for inane debates."

"Well then," she said, leaning forward. "Please," and she floated her hand across the table, gesturing for me to proceed.

"Thank you," I said, nodding and leaning back. "My objection comes in two parts," I started, "the second, admittedly, a subpart of the first." I was channeling a different, never realized version of myself, one arguing an important point in front of a skeptical judge. "I can't reject your conclusion outright, but I'm afraid I take issue with the forceful nature of it. Would you stipulate that this is a difficult, nuanced question?" I asked playfully.

"No," she countered quickly and simply, but just as playfully.

"No?!" I exclaimed. "Permission to treat the witness as hostile?" I asked the waitress who'd just stepped over to our table.

"Sure," she said, confused. "But you'll have to do it somewhere else. We're closing." I looked past her and saw the restaurant empty for the first time, the chairs of the other tables flipped up off the floor while a busboy swept beneath them. The surprise in my face was in Sonia's, too; she must have just been noticing then, same as me.

Quickly, I paid the bill and taking her arm, we walked out into the empty street, laughing as we went. We strolled onto and through Main Street where it was as dark and quiet as it is bright and busy in the daytime. We passed all the stores I'd come to know and love – including hers – each of them empty, like the streets of that whole town had been set up just for us.

"Aren't you curious what things would look like without you?" I asked as we stepped off Main Street toward her apartment. "Don't you want to know what kind of impact you're having?"

"I'd be curious," she said.

"Then how can you be so certain?" I asked, and she unhooked her arm from mine and stepped toward a streetlight.

"Because I don't actually *care*," she said, reaching out with one arm and using it to swing around that post as if she was singing in the rain.

"It's that simple?" I asked, stepping toward her.

"It's that simple," she said, taking my hand and pulling me up a flight of stairs to her apartment door.

"Of course I'd be curious about my impact, and I hope it's a positive one," she said. We were standing toe-to-toe outside her door, her green eyes shining in the moonlight, our bodies close. "But I swear, Connor, I don't care how I fit into it. At all. Because I just want to live-" and I cut her off.

"In love," I said, a wave of something strong swelling inside me.

"Yeah," she said, and I leaned my body against hers as she stepped up onto her toes. We kissed gently but passionately, and I put my hand on the small of her back to pull her even closer.

She found the lock without pulling away and we stumbled into her apartment still clasped in our embrace, our lips and tongues exploring each other's until they weren't anymore – until they found our necks and chests, and until we fell together into her bed, where we stayed for hours. Where we stayed until morning.

Chapter 75

If I had to pick one moment to relive for eternity, it would be the one just after I woke up that next morning, lying in that bed with Sonia. We were still together, her body folded into mine, her back to my chest with that auburn hair pressed against my neck and chin. My arms were wrapped tight around her and her legs were tangled up in mine. We were facing the windows, where the morning sun was shining and where the wind was blowing in from the ocean, billowing the curtains that hung at their sides. The breeze was cool and fresh in that way it only seems to be in the morning, in those first few seconds after waking up from a peaceful sleep.

Sonia must have woken up at that second, too, because as I enjoyed the moment, I felt her shift. She pressed her body against mine, then rolled onto her back. She put her hand on my face and smiled, haloed by the sun behind her. It was perfect, that moment, the split second before I leaned forward and kissed her – a soft, simple kiss at first, but then the same passionate one we'd shared the night before.

"Good morning," she said, turning her head back toward the windows and out to the rising sun."

"Yeah, it is," I said, pulling my own gaze back inside the room. I kissed her again and she rolled onto her side to face me, her hands tucked under her pillow to support her head.

"These last few weeks have been fun," she said.

"Not bad for someone you picked up in the ocean?" I asked.

"You know, you've never told me why you were in there," she said, leaning up, her elbow digging deep into her pillow. I thought back over those weeks and realized she was right. We had never talked about it.

The beach where we'd met was just a few miles from her apartment, and I looked through her out to the sea as I thought about it, and suddenly, it was like I was back there.

"I was running away," I said, still looking past her. "I was panicking. I was scared and I was angry. And I guess I still am," I said, staring that million-mile stare. "There's a certain way things are supposed to work – it's like a road map you get handed when you're younger. You get good grades; you go to college; you get a good, respectable job; you meet a girl; you start a family. That's how it works, and you just know it. And Aaron had just gotten engaged and he'd just sold the battery and Brady had just gotten married and Mike had his son, and I was looking at all of them following the map while I was still nowhere, because I hated the only thing that would help me go with them. And it scared the shit out of me. And I was so angry at myself. So, I ran, and ended up on the beach where our parents used to take us when we were young." I closed my eyes and thought back to those years. "I used to lay in the water all day back then. I'd just float right out where the waves broke and let them toss me wherever they liked. And that's what I was doing when you found me. Just floating. And all I really want to do is find the ground and put my goddamn feet in it." I opened my eyes and was almost surprised to find Sonia still there, still laying on her side with her elbow in her pillow, still looking at me with those big, green eyes. "How'd you find it?" I asked.

"Easy," she said. "I just put my feet where I wanted to."

"It's not that simple," I started, but stopped before continuing.

"It is," she said, sitting up. "It is exactly that simple." She took a deep breath and squared her look, a resolve I'd never seen before washing over her. "You know my mother was a professional photographer. She was good. Great. But she only did it for a few years. My father was a doctor and making more money, and she gave it up to raise me." She paused for a moment as her voice waivered. "And it killed her," she said, closing her eyes. "It drove this wedge between them and they split up, and she was a single mom and needed something more stable so she took a job doing HR and I swear, bit-by-bit, it broke her down to this different person." She opened her eyes before continuing. "That's the other side of it. At least the one I've seen. And it's awful." I nodded as my heart sank, thinking of a younger version of Sonia watching her mother wilt, and in my mind, I flashed forward to a different version of myself – one that never left the firm, one with disappointment and a desperate resentment buried somewhere deep inside. "Which leaves just one question," she said. "What have you always wanted to do?"

The question hung with me the rest of the morning Sonia and I spent together in her bed, and it stayed with me throughout the afternoon I spent alone after she was called down to the store. My car was parked out front of her apartment and after I watched her walk down the street toward her dream, I set off in search of my own – hoping to pull it from the periphery and into clearer focus. I drove up the coast to Provincetown and followed the rocks out to the tip of the Cape, where you can look across the whole shore and survey it all. I don't know how long I stayed there, but I know the sun was high in the sky when I left and went to the bluff Sonia took me to, the one that overlooks the cove. And I know it was heading toward sunset when I climbed into the dunes and sat on the shores of that pond, and I know

336

the light was starting to fade when I stepped onto the beach at the bay beneath the split in the sky, and I know it was fully dark when I pulled back into my parents' driveway – dark enough that I didn't notice the smoke when I first stepped through the door.

Chapter 76

It was the noise I noticed first – a loud hiss with an occasional metallic clanging. But then I saw it, a haze hanging over the living room – like a dozen ghosts were standing shoulder-to-shoulder, slowly approaching, reaching out as if they needed to pull me close, as if they had something I needed to hear. I flipped on the lights and they blended into the smoke behind them, which was pouring out from under the basement door.

I threw it open and started down the stairs. I already knew what had happened; it had happened years before, too. I hit the bottom step and saw the water heater shrouded in smoke, the repairs Aaron had done those years before having finally given way. I stepped toward it but stopped when I felt a splash, and noticed the steady stream of water leaking across the basement. I sloshed through it toward the breaker and threw the switch. The hiss stopped immediately but the smoke was still coming, dimming the lights I'd managed to turn on and reaching out to me like those ghosts upstairs. The water was still coming too, flowing toward stacks of cardboard boxes in the corner. I ran to them next, hoping to pull away as many as I could before they were destroyed. I worked quickly, but even as I did I could see what was in each one. They were packed with clothes and trinkets from our rooms, time capsules of our past selves cleaned out on cardboard crusade days when our father got tired of looking at the clutter.

Maggie's box had old magazines and pictures of her and her friends, all young and tan and happy, and what looked like a love letter from an old boyfriend. Aaron's had a stack of LEGOs and some old comics, and the lineup cards from baseball games I remember Ed and I taking him to.

Mine came next. It heavier than the others, and the smoke surrounded me as I picked it up, as somewhere above my head a fire alarm began blaring. I had to strain to see inside, but beneath the fog, a mosaic was taking shape. The box was packed with old CD's and cassette tapes and DVD's, and my own set of those lineup cards. There were a few playbills and some seashells, too, and poker chips we used out on the porch, and some pictures I'd taken with my dad's old Polaroid. There were entire stacks of ticket stubs from concerts and movies, and an old notebook with pages and pages of ideas for Questions – some we'd answered and some we hadn't. It said 'Earth Science' on the front. There was a security pass from a presidential debate Will and I had somehow attended during college. It was held in Boston and we blew off school the next day and came to the beach for the weekend.

Smoke was still pouring out of the water heater but I hadn't moved in minutes. Instead, I kept leaning over my box, picking through those past versions of myself and mourning each one as a family member that had been taken too soon. With each trinket came a memory – a potent and stirring one, full of nostalgia and joy. I tried to let each one envelop me and let it transport me back, but each time I caught only a glimpse before another memorial pushed it away. I remembered all of the poker games and the hours spent with each of those CDs. I remembered the night of that debate and the discussion Will and I had in the car. I remembered writing with Z the screenplay I found behind the notebook, and all those baseball games with Aaron and Ed. And I remembered coming home from class one Friday night with that Earth Science notebook stacked full of questions and asking as many as I could that night in the screen house. And with it all, I thought about how I missed it all, and how badly I wanted to be back with it all, and as I wiped away a tear, a few of the DVD's shifted and revealed a paper I hadn't seen. It was getting even harder to see as the smoke took hold of the basement, but I snatched the paper out of my box, grabbed Ed's and set them both out of the way before tracing the water back to the shut off valve, the sound of sirens building behind the fire alarm.

The neighbors had heard its warning cry and called the fire department when they saw the smoke, and as I made it to the front door they were on their way in. I wasn't sure if I was desperate to be out of the smoke or if I wanted only to stay in it forever, but as I stepped out into the cool, clear air, I leaned my back against the fire engine and slumped to the ground. I put my head in my hands and only then remembered the sheet of paper I'd taken from the box.

Slowly, I took a deep breath and unfolded it, and while the firefighters worked their way through the house, I uncovered a secret it had kept for a decade – a long lost school assignment I must have written there and forgot when my father packed my friends and me into his car and took us back home to Saratoga.

I took another deep breath and by the lights of the fire truck, with a small crowd of neighbors gathering at the end of the driveway, read about where my high school self wanted to be by then.

WHERE I SEE MYSLEF IN 10 YEARS

In ten years, I see myself in many different places. First, the version I think you want, I see myself arguing my case as a fully certified lawyer. I am already looking at colleges and law schools and hope I will be through law school and practicing at a firm. Maybe at my own.

But I also see myself in a new house built somewhere with a nice view and a screen house like the one my parents have.

And most of all, I see myself with my friends. Doing everything we've always loved to do.

I hope one of those is what you're looking for.

I exhaled at the end of it and thought about my box and thought again about everything I'd seen and done and been over the years, and about Brady and Mike and Mom and Dad and Aaron and *The Tribune* and Winter and Wall and Mack and Sonia and the screen house and the waves, and I saw it all like I would have when I was young. One final flash of lightning.

Chapter 77

The fire trucks were only there a few minutes before clearing out. The crowd that had gathered went home, too, and all that remained was the smoke. It was still there, hanging in the living room when I walked back in.

Immediately I went back down in the basement, where the smoke was still thick and all-consuming. I could hear the sump pump working and could see my box waiting for me where I'd left it. I grabbed it and ran back upstairs and turned it out onto the coffee table, the CDs and ticket stubs and playbills all spilling out.

I ran around the living room and opened all the windows, then sat down on the couch and felt the breeze blow through, and watched as the ghosts danced in the haze above the sprawled-out version of me built with the spare parts you find in the bedroom your parents haven't touched since you moved out.

I sat for hours in that fog, turning over each and every item, replaying and reliving each and every memory that came with them, scouring them for something I could use to build what would come next. I started with the larger items, but over the hours, I picked my way down, and as the night started turning to morning, I found myself flipping through the pages of that Earth Science notebook, asking and answering each question I'd written, and editing a column I'd hand-written back then on the school censoring its student-run newspaper, and reviewing a list I'd made with Brady before a familiar feeling overtook me.

I looked up and saw in that haze everything I'd seen for years – the house and the kids and the job, and a cold flood ran through me. My legs moved from under me and a second later I was outside on the sand, staring into the sun. I started up the beach, ready to run as I had so many times before, my body taking control. But this time, I stopped myself after just a few steps and turned back. I didn't want to run anymore. I wouldn't.

I sat down on the chair across from the coffee table and stared a hole through it, then grabbed the computer in front of me and opened it to the *Tribune* – my mind on that idea I wanted to pull into focus. I clicked through it all again, one eye on the table and those ghosts, the other on *The Tribune*, until I ended up on obituaries and saw a familiar face looking back at mine.

Jacob Lerman entered eternal life on Monday at his home. He was 59-years-old. A loving son, brother, and father, Jacob is survived by his three children, who will celebrate his life on Friday at the Parker Lane Funeral Home in Saratoga Springs.

Chapter 78

I had been leaning forward as I read the short paragraph, but slumped into its back when I finished, locking eyes with the picture just to the left of the text. I recognized the man framed within it, but the picture was nothing I'd seen before. He had a wide smile with laughing eyes – an expression he never wore around the apartment complex.

I leapt to my feet and ran out of the haze. I stopped only once, grabbing the Earth Science notebook on my way out the door. A second later I was in my car, peeling out the driveway, the sound of the shells beneath my tires nearly drowned out by the roar of the engine.

It was still early morning and the Cape was only just coming to life. Around each turn were joggers and shopkeepers just starting their days beneath the sun. I texted Sonia and told her where I was going and promised to be back soon, then pointed the car due west and pushed on for hours. As the miles clicked by I saw that picture in my mind, and thought about my neighbor Doug, whose real name was Jacob – who I'd lived above for years, but who I'd just learned more about in a few sentences than I had in all those times I'd seen him walking in and out of the building we shared.

I drove as fast as my Jeep could handle, racing back to my hometown for the first time in months, not bothering to think about stopping home or about what I'd tell my mother or friends if I saw them. I knew where I was going.

I pulled into the parking lot at the Parker Lane Funeral Home at the same speed I'd done on the Mass Pike, remembering the last time I'd been there. Mike's father's wake was held there in the large Victorian home the owners had converted to a funeral parlor in the 60's. It blended in with the neighborhood and the parking lot was hidden, but I knew where to turn.

For Mr. Anderson's wake, parking spilled out onto the street and the line circled around the block. For Doug – or Jacob – there was no crowd. There were no police cars directing traffic. Instead, there were just a few sedans dotting the parking lot, and one Parker Lane worker crushing out a cigarette by the front door. He was in a dark suit with a white shirt and dark tie, and as I climbed from my Jeep and walked toward him, I was suddenly aware that I was still in the jeans and button up I'd worn on my date with Sonia almost two days earlier. Still, I needed to see inside, so I nodded as he opened the door and I stepped past him into another world.

There were hundreds of pictures spread across the main foyer that led to the viewing area. I looked past them for a brief second and could see Doug lying in his coffin, his eyes closed, with that familiar hint of sadness in his face. Beside him were Jacob's three children – the children I didn't know he had. They hadn't noticed me, and my eyes darted away before they did, bouncing back to all the photographs.

I scanned them all, all from years and years before. There were dozens from when he was young and hundreds of him with his kids and a woman I'd never seen. They were at Disney and at the beach and in the backyard of a big, beautiful house – all together and all smiling. My eyes followed the pictures around the room, inspecting photos of school concerts and plays, and one image I recognized. It was Jacob with a paintbrush in his hand, painting the set from one of those plays. He was smiling wide, with his eyes as much as his lips. It was the smile I'd seen in the *Tribune*, but the picture's full version this time, not just the headshot.

I kept turning to see more photos and saw more and more of him with a brush in his hand, and more and more with that smile on his face, until I turned one more time and was frozen solid by what was in front of me.

There were three paintings standing on easels. The first two were beautiful landscapes, breathtaking, really, but not in the same way as the third – because the third I recognized as one I'd seen through Doug's basement window, one I'd wondered about for months.

There were swirls of pink and purple on the edges, and at its center was what I'd always thought was a man in a dress shirt – because I'd never seen it clearly before.

It was Jacob in a smock, not a dress shirt, with a brush in his hand – a self-portrait bordered by faded splashes of color, the same 'JL' in the bottom corner as was in the two paintings beside it.

I stepped back and this whole vision of Jacob and Doug flashed in my mind. I saw Jacob as a young man, and the life as a painter he never pursued, and I saw the way it broke him down and ended his marriage and forced Doug into that basement apartment to wonder about what could have been through a haze of pastorals.

I took one more step back and gave one more look to my neighbor in his coffin before turning and exploding out the door. I was at a full sprint through the parking lot and I practically leapt into my Jeep. I reached for my phone as I pulled out of my space faster than I'd left the driveway a few hours earlier, and called Brady, who picked up on the 2nd ring.

"Brady!" I shouted over the engine. "I figured it out!"

"Figured what out?" he asked, clearly confused.

"I'm coming to your office," I said, ignoring the question. "I need to meet with your bosses."

"My bosses?" he said, and I could hear the skepticism in his voice.

"Trust me," I said. "I know what I'm doing."

Chapter 79

Back at the beach house, there on the coffee table, was still sitting the overturned contents of my box, dumped and thumbed through. I dumped them out again in my mind, and went through each piece on my way to Brady's office. I thought about Sonia, too, and about her mother. And I thought about Doug and Jacob, and Shelly and Jason – Sonia's drifting staff – and the acting Shelly had started and the photography Jason wanted to do. And again, I thought about Brady and Mike and Will and Noah and Z, and I thought about the essay I never turned in, and all the nights with them and all the nights in Vivi Nell'amore. And I thought about the words in my Earth Science notebook – a notebook that was only a few pages of Earth Science. A notebook that became so much more than that. A notebook that always was so much more than that.

And finally, it all came together.

I told Brady about everything when I got to his office – about the previous few days and about why I needed to see his bosses. He listened quietly as I talked, and at the end of it all I handed him the notebook, open to a list of names we'd made together, the list I'd seen while standing in my parents' basement. I was pointing to one name in particular.

"Jack of All Trades," he read aloud.

"That's us," I said. "And it doesn't matter how we do it if that's how we do it."

"That doesn't make sense," he said, looking up at me.

"I know," I said, still talking fast. "But trust me. It will. If I can pitch this, it will," and I gave him a long, hard look. "I won't make a fool of you, I promise." Brady gave his own long look back and then finally nodded.

"Then let's go," he said, standing up. "Everyone's still in the conference room talking about today's pitches." I followed him out of his office and down a hallway, flattening my shirt and brushing back my hair as I went.

"Wait here," he said as he stepped up to the door and disappeared inside. "Excuse me, everyone," I heard him say. "I'd like you to hear one more pitch today, if you can. My friend Connor is here and he has an idea I really think will work. He's got writing experience; he used to write for the *Tribune,* and if you're up to it, I'd like you to hear him out." I waited for someone to object but no one did, and a second later Brady was back in the hall, leading me into the conference room. "Good luck," he whispered to me, and he took his seat around the table.

There were a dozen people in that room, and I felt my heart quicken as I stood before them. My legs never so much as twitched.

"Well, to start," I said, noticing the ties and blouses before me, and the skeptical expressions that came with them. "I apologize for how I'm dressed, but I've been up for two straight days and this was all I brought with me when I drove in – which I know isn't the best way to start, but it will get better, trust me," and there was a chuckle across the room as I said it.

"Brady said you wrote for the *Tribune,*" said an older bald man at the head of the table. "What did you do there?"

"I wrote opinion," I said. "I don't know how much you read that section, but if you've ever read Pablo Garcia or Esther Weeblehowzer, that's me."

"Pablo Garcia isn't Pablo Garcia?" someone else asked, incredulous.

"Afraid not," I said, shrugging my shoulders in apology. "I was hired to boost the opinion section, so I created characters to write from. Pablo was one of my creations."

"It's true," Brady said to his colleagues, chuckling. "I've helped him invent characters." And there were smiles of surprise mixed in around the table with more than a few angry grumbles at the con I'd helped run.

"I remember Pablo," the bald man said through a mix of both. "I liked him. This new guy they have is terrible," and I felt a smile form as he continued. "Well, what do you want to do here?"

I took a deep breath and realized in that moment that I hadn't thought about how to articulate it yet, but as I emptied the box out one final time, I knew I had the words.

"I'm 28-years-old," I said, looking through the board room and out onto the horizon, onto the images lit up there by the lightning. "For probably 20 of those years, I was sure I was going to be a lawyer when I grew up. And I was ready to be one." I pulled myself back into the room for a second to look everyone in the eye before bouncing back to the horizon. "But I hate it. I went to work at a law firm because I was supposed to – or I thought I was – and I hated it. As I probably knew I would. As I'd probably hate most jobs – except this one, of course," I said quickly, laughing along with everyone else. "My parents' basement just flooded and while I was trying to rescue these boxes of old stuff, I found one my dad had made of everything I'd collected over the last 20 years, and it's this perfectly preserved record of my life. And there's all this random stuff in there that doesn't really go together. They're puzzle pieces that don't really fit, but somehow, they make up who I am. And that's why I'd hate any other job, because it's only one piece of the puzzle, and I'm not one piece. I'm all of them. And I think there are a lot of people like me – people built of and passionate about so much more than just what they can make a career of. People who grew up with this whole box and don't want to give any of it up."

"There's one at this table," Brady said, raising his hand and nodding.

"So, here's what I want to do here," I said, smiling at Brady. "I want to be Pablo. I want to write about whatever interests me, and I want to give others the same chance. I want to give a voice to everyone out there like me. I want to hire good, young writers who don't know what they want to be when they grow up and tell them they don't have to. Each writer will have a specialty page they curate – one in charge of music, another in charge of movies, another on politics, fashion, sports, whatever – but everyone would be allowed to write on whatever page they want. We'd be a home to passionate writers allowed to write about whatever those passions are – whatever they have in their own box. No restrictions."

"How would you set it apart?" the bald man asked, leaning in over the table.

"I wouldn't," I said, locking eyes again with everyone in the room. "Not what you expected me to say, right?" and I joined in as they chuckled again. "I don't think you need a gimmick if you've got good writers doing good writing they're passionate about. That's enough." There were nods around the table and a few more questions from others about the logistics, before the bald man asked another of his own.

"What would you call it?" he asked, and Brady answered before I did.

"Jack of All Trades" he said.

351

"What does that mean?"

"That's what Brady used to call us in high school," I said, jumping back in. "When we'd spend hours bouncing between topics in my parents' screen house. We were jacks-of-all-trades and masters of none."

"And you think people would read it?" he asked.

"I do." I said. "Because we're all jacks of all trades. Or almost all of us are, especially people our age. We all have a screen house where we would go with our families and friends to get away from our school and our work – where we were our fullest, truest selves. And I think a lot of us just want to be back there." I looked around the table as each person seemed to leave the boardroom and go somewhere else in their minds. "So, what if I told you that you never had to leave, or that a visit was just a click away?" And I watched them all smile and felt myself do the same.

Chapter 80

If you're reading this, you probably think you know what happened next – I'm assuming you've noticed the title.

You're wrong.

I stepped out of the boardroom to let them talk it over and a few minutes later Brady stepped back into the hallway with an expression that told the story. The answer was no.

He apologized and threw his arm around my shoulder as we walked back down the hallway. He said the vote was close, but there was a hot new TV show they wanted to jump on instead.

"Do you want to go get a drink?" he asked when we got back to his office, offering me a seat at his desk.

"Soon, but not yet," I said, choosing to stay on my feet. "Thank you for this, Brady," I said, extending my arm. "I can't tell you how much it means to me."

"I'm sorry it didn't work out," he said, shaking my hand while shaking his head.

"Don't worry about it," I said. "It will," and I turned to leave.

"It's a good idea," he said, stopping me.

"I know," I answered, and slipped out the door.

I set out all across the northeast after that, pitching my idea to anyone who would listen, bouncing between Saratoga and New York and Boston and the Cape. I worked in Sonia's shop to get by and got my own apartment in Chatham, choosing not to bum off my parents anymore. I wrote every chance I could about whatever I felt like, and it was the best summer I'd had since high school.

Most developers were as skeptical as I was certain, so I set on without them, publishing my own writing under my own name and searching for other writers who would do the same – so sure that there were others out there like me. And that's why we wrote this long, rambling story, so you could read how it came to be – so you know who we are and who we always want to be.

Brady was my first hire, brought in to help with design and write about art and comics. We found others from there, and in the year since that first pitch meeting at GNS, two years since Brady's bachelor party, we've built this budding network some of those doubting developers are starting to ask about, and we're excited about what's to come – knowing only that we'll never leave the screen house.

But before all the trips and pitch meetings, I made a drive every bit as important as the rest. Leaving Brady's office, I ran to my Jeep and drove back out to the Cape, to catch the last few minutes of sunset.

I told Sonia to meet me where we'd first met, and drove straight there, where I found her sitting in the sand next to that lifeguard stand, with her camera at her side.

"I love you," I said, sitting down next to her.

"I love you too," she said, her smile widening. She leaned slowly into me, but instead of kissing her, I jumped to my feet and took off running down the beach, tearing off my shirt as I went.

I dove head first into the water and waited for a wave to overtake me. It came a second later, lifting me up toward the sky and hurling me toward the beach as it had so many times before. But this time, I twisted my body and reached for the sand, and my feet hit hard and dug in deep, and I snapped up as they did, and stood strong against the thrashing surf.

Made in the USA
Middletown, DE
24 January 2019